PAX BRITANNIA

ANNO FRANKENSTEIN

"MY EYE," ULYSSES mumbled, painfully aware of the throbbing coming from the middle of his face. "What's happened to my eye?"

"This eye, you mean?" Folter said casually, holding up a pair of forceps. Gripped within its metal teeth was a glistening ball of white jelly, shreds of fine muscle still attached.

Ulysses stared into the small, dead pupil of his own right eye and was unable to stifle the scream of horror that burst from him then. It felt as if his eye-socket was on fire.

As terror seized him he tried to form a question between his howls of horror.

"You want to know why?" Folter asked.

Ulysses nodded furiously, unable to stop looking from the monstrous surgeon to his grisly prize and back again.

"I would have thought that was obvious. But here, let me show you. Seziermesser?" the surgeon called to his assistant, the two of them turning Ulysses' gurney about.

"There," Folter said proudly.

Ulysses could see the arcing capacitors now, bursts of chained lightning coursing between them, filling the air with the tinny stink of ozone and static electricity.

But it was the contraption standing in front of it that seized his attention a

It was a huge rus rust, and other things bes ra of leather restraining st des. Chained to it now w must have on nster.

Ulysses Quicksilver adventures
Unnatural History
Leviathan Rising
Human Nature
Evolution Expects
Blood Royal
Dark Side
Anno Frankenstein

Other novels from the world of *Pax Britannia*
El Sombra
Gods of Manhattan

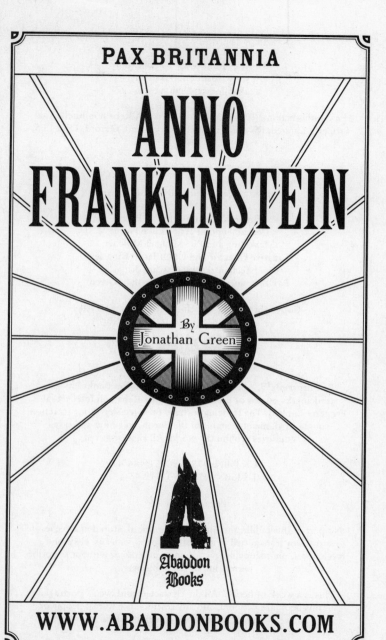

PAX BRITANNIA

ANNO FRANKENSTEIN

By
Jonathan Green

Abaddon
Books

WWW.ABADDONBOOKS.COM

An Abaddon Books™ Publication
www.abaddonbooks.com
abaddon@rebellion.co.uk

First published in 2011 by Abaddon Books™, Rebellion Intellectual
Property Limited, Riverside House, Osney Mead, Oxford, OX2 0ES,
UK.

10 9 8 7 6 5 4 3 2 1

Editors: Jenni Hill & David Moore
Cover Art: Mark Harrison
Internal Illustration: Pye Parr
Design: Simon Parr & Luke Preece
Marketing and PR: Michael Molcher
Creative Director and CEO: Jason Kingsley
Chief Technical Officer: Chris Kingsley
Pax Britannia™ created by Jonathan Green

UK ISBN: 978-1-907519-44-4
US ISBN: 978-1-907519-45-1

Printed in the US

For Adam -

Congratulations!

And for the Durston Dads -

Didn't wipe out on this one, but only just.

*"So God created man in His own image...
And God saw every thing that He had made, and,
behold, it was very good. And the evening and the
morning were the sixth day."*

(Genesis 1:27,31)

PROLOGUE

All Quiet on the Western Front

What luck for the rulers that men do not think.
– Adolf Hitler

YPRES, BELGIUM, 1941

THIS PLACE HAD been a forest once, or so he'd been told. Eric Baer certainly wouldn't have known otherwise. The occasional blackened stump remained, but on the whole the battlefield was now just a grey expanse of mud, a morass of crater holes flooded by the incessant rain. He could see right across the quagmire to the French lines, where soldiers could be glimpsed in uniforms reminiscent of the Napoleonic era. The French looked as miserable as Eric was feeling.

The rain was a relentless barrage on the heads of the weary soldiers, whether German or French. It drummed against their helmets, blew into their eyes, blinding them, ran down the back of their necks and soaked into everything. Eric couldn't remember the last time he had been dry.

But it was nothing compared to the cold.

Eric couldn't remember the last time he had felt warm either. The occasional cup of milky coffee or tin of unidentifiable boiled meat did little to warm his cockles and snatched moments beside an oil drum brazier only brought life to his fingertips for fleeting moments.

Days of inaction didn't help. Days of sitting in freezing bunkers burrowed out of the earth, soldiers living as if they were some species of rodent. Days listening to the juddering crump and boom of the distant barrages while the walls of the dugout shook around you until you were either numb to the noise or your nerves were shot to shreds and you were never able to sleep again. Sleeping, grabbing what meagre warmth you could from a threadbare blanket, keeping your boots on in bed so as to keep the rats from your gangrenous toes.

And the cold and the damp together were as bad as any form of torture the Gestapo could come up with for the Third Reich's enemies to endure in the long run.

It was the First Great European War all over again. They had said it would be different this time, but it wasn't. Not as far as Eric Baer could tell, anyway. They might be fighting for the Führer now rather than the Kaïser, but the result was the same; hunkered down in trenches as the war ground down to a stalemate.

There was talk of the automaton armies of Magna Britannia joining the battle on the side of Queen Victoria's European cousins if Hitler threatened Russia's borders. Eric Baer didn't know if the rumours were true or mere campfire conjecture spread by war-weary men, like him, who had joined up to fight for the honour of the Fatherland and their families.

They said that war was hell and Eric Baer was starting to believe them. He had seen enough of war to last him a lifetime. But there was never any consideration of desertion. That thought never entered his head, no matter how miserable the drudgery of the campaign became.

And now here he was, two years after signing up – motivated by idealism, by an intention to avenge the Fatherland for the wrongs that had been committed by the imperialistic powers in the aftermath of Kaïser Wilhelm's war. Cold and wet and miserable, and facing what was likely to be his last day on Earth.

Today was the day of the big push, the day the German army unleashed its newest and most terrifying weapon on the enemy; but the grunts had little enthusiasm for it. The thrill of joining up and fighting for the Führer had long since withered to resignation after months of stalemate, living – if it could be called that – in the cold and damp of the trenches of the Besson Line.

The stalemate had to be broken. The orders had come from the top. Perhaps the Führer was worried that the British might soon join the war; just as Magna Britannia had stepped in to stop the Kaïser's bid at empire-building more than twenty years before. The Third Reich had to act now and act fast, to secure the rest of Europe and make any attempt by Magna Britannia's automaton forces to halt its advance futile.

Two years after Herr Hitler had occupied Czechoslovakia, the Nazis were advancing across the no man's land of Belgium only to be halted here at Ypres, the site of another stalemate almost thirty years before. Much of Europe had already fallen to the inexorable march of the armies of the Third Reich, but a few pockets of resistance still remained. To date the Magna Britannian government had yet to get involved.

To the east, the Nazis' advance was currently contained by Russia. However, once the whole of Europe was under Nazi rule, it could only be a matter of time before the power-mad Führer set his sights on Russia or mounted an invasion of the British Isles. And if Magna Britannia should fall to the might of the Third Reich's armies, then Hitler would become *de facto* ruler of the world. They were on the verge of a glorious dawn for Germany and the Third Reich, and it unsettled Eric Baer to the very core of his being. He wasn't the only one.

But here they were, following orders handed down from distant generals – warm in their procured castle strongholds, sitting before roaring fires, with hot spirit in their bellies – preparing to break the stalemate and, from there, march for Paris.

If the Allies won today, the beleaguered French and Belgian forces might be able to hold out until their masters could persuade Magna Britannia to wade in at last. That knowledge lent them a ferocity and a determination that even the perpetual drizzle and sodden grey clouds couldn't dampen.

The Germans were fighting to conquer their enemies, but their enemies were fighting for survival, with a strength of will that few of the grunts among the German army possessed in the same measure.

But then it wasn't the average German soldier that was going to win this war for the Führer and the Third Reich.

Eric Baer shivered, and this time it wasn't solely down to the bone-numbing cold. The mere thought of them made his flesh crawl. The official line was that they would be the Fatherland's salvation but to Eric Baer's mind they were the unholy spawn of a science that was little better than necromancy. When a man died he should stay dead, that was the natural order of things; not be brought back as part of some horrific amalgam.

Eric Baer gripped his rifle closely to him. It was the only thing that made him feel safe; and it wasn't the enemy he was afraid of.

An unnatural stillness had fallen over no man's land. It was as if the combined French and Belgian forces had some inkling of what the German soldiers already knew; as if Mother Nature herself was holding her breath, aware that something contrary to the natural order of things was about to be unleashed upon the world.

The dead should stay dead, it was as simple as that, and yet here was Man – in the form of the Frankenstein Corps, carrying on the work of the legendary scientist himself – about to commit the ultimate hubris without even giving it a second thought. Even God Himself had brought a scant handful of people back from the dead.

Supposedly only the top brass were party to the top secret documentation; it hadn't been passed on to the rank and file. All they had been told officially by their commanders was that today they would lead the offensive and that they would be supported by members of the mysterious Frankenstein Corps.

But news like that couldn't stay secret for long, threat of execution by firing squad or no. Eric Baer, like many others, had heard the rumours – the stories of the horrific, ungodly things that went on in the bowels of the castle overlooking the town of Darmstadt.

A gust of chill wind blew across the grey, muddied wastes of no man's land, carrying with it an eddy of dancing black leaves – remnants of the dead forest – and the anxious murmurings and disbelieving gasps of the French forces, half a mile away across the pot-holed field, ready to repel the German advance one last time. But then they could see what Eric Baer and his fellow German soldiers could not.

Eric felt the tremor of their lumbering steps and fought to resist the urge to turn around and see for himself what the flesh-smiths of Castle Frankenstein had created.

It was like an itch at the base of his skull, an unbearable need to know, no matter what the cost, but married to a fear that penetrated right to the very core of his being, a fear of that which should not be. There was a reason why the dead should stay dead after all. What the Führer and his supporters did for the good of the war effort seemed too high a price to pay. After all, if they were fighting for humanity in the face of oppression, following the First Great European War, what was the point if they only threw away what humanity they had left?

Wasn't there a saying along those lines? Just because you could, didn't mean you should?

Science was capable of many amazing and wonderful life-changing things, but could ensure Mankind's destruction by its own hand.

The ground shook under the *thud, thud, thud* of their advance, almost as if they were following Lovelacian algorithms like the automaton armies of Magna Britannia.

Another gust of wind and the enemy lines were murmuring no longer, but shouting in shock and fear. The new battle company were already having an effect on the enemy and they hadn't even engaged them in combat yet. Eric pitied them; but not as much as he pitied the things now bolstering the German lines, the monsters that were about to be unleashed on the enemy on this auspicious day.

The top brass's strategy was working. It looked to Eric like the French line was faltering, and the signal to attack still hadn't been given.

He could almost smell their fear – or was it, in fact, the Corps' creations he could smell?

That was it. The battlefield scents of wet mud and cordite had merged with another aroma; a mixture of formaldehyde, sickly sweet putrefaction and axle grease. But more than anything, it was the smell of death defeated, of overreaching ambition, of the hubris of Man.

In the face of the terrified reaction of the French troops and the shuddering tremors of their massed lumbering steps, as they marched ever closer, Eric Baer could hold out no longer. He turned.

His own gasp of horror caught in his throat as he laid eyes on the Corps' creations for the first time.

They were even worse in the flesh than they had been in the darkest corners of his imagination. In his dark dreams, they had been giants all, manufactured from stolen flesh.

Now, he saw that they were in fact an amalgamation of man and machine. No two were completely alike in shape or form, but all were united by the scars they bore; marks that were testament to the nature of their unnatural creation.

The Frankenstein Corps; dead soldiers re-united piecemeal, their lifeless flesh reanimated that they might fight again. A terror weapon, cannon fodder, soldiers who could never truly die, as long as there was someone to put them back together again once the battle was over.

Eric Baer turned from his observations of the resurrected cyber-organic soldiers and caught the look in the eye of the trembling soldier standing next to him.

"Hans," he said, addressing the nervous wretch with the familiarity of men who have fought together, side by side, and seen their fellows fall in the same fashion.

"I know," the other replied. "They scare the hell out of me too."

"No, it's not that," Eric said.

"What then?"

"If I should fall today, will you promise me something? If I should die today, or, even if I'm only maimed, if I look like I'm going to lose my legs or something..."

He broke off, watching the dead leaves pirouette across the churned grey sludge in front of him. As the wind carried the dancing debris away he turned back to face his friend.

"Blow my brains out, would you? Shoot me in the head, my friend. I don't want to end up like that." He nodded towards the advancing monsters behind them. "If it's my time to die, I want to stay dead. Do you understand?"

Hans Richter smiled at him grimly. "Only if you do the same for me."

A shrill whistle pierced the air, sending a shiver down Eric's spine. The signal had been given.

"This is it," he said. "Good luck, my friend."

Hans Richter threw him a sharp salute. "For Germany and the Third Reich!"

"For the Fatherland! *Charge!*"

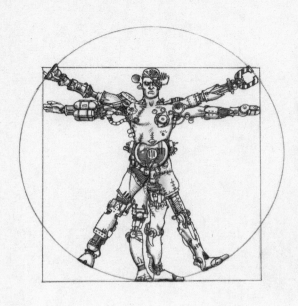

ACT ONE

The Labours of Hercules

"Through clever and constant application of propaganda, people can be made to see paradise as Hell, and also the other way around, to consider the most wretched sort of life as paradise."

– Adolf Hitler

CHAPTER ONE

An Unexpected Arrival

DARMSTADT, GERMANY, 1943

THE SOLDIER CAME to attention. The sharp click of his heels echoed the ticking of the ancient clock on the mantelpiece above the grand fireplace.

Colonel Wolf Kahler took a moment to finish scanning the page of production statistics in front of him. Leaning back in his chair, he glanced up from the business of the day, and stared at the messenger with hawkish attention, eyes unblinking.

"Yes?" he snapped curtly.

"Herr Colonel," the young man began, "a spy has been captured in the hills outside Darmstadt."

Kahler's eyes and expression didn't falter once as he addressed the messenger in return. "Fascinating. A spy, you say?"

"A British spy," the young man went on, "although his German is very good."

"Then how can you be so sure he's British?" Kahler asked.

"He told the commander of the squad that captured him."

Kahler blinked at last. "What else did he tell his captors?"

"That he wanted to see you, Herr Colonel. In person."

At this Kahler frowned. He didn't like the sound of that. "His information must be very good; too good." The facility, and all personnel operating within it, were classified top secret. "Where is he now?"

"In a holding cell in D block."

Colonel Kahler got to his feet. "And you say he simply volunteered all of this information when he was captured?"

"Actually, he wasn't really captured, Herr Colonel." To his credit, the messenger continued to meet Kahler's stare, although his cheeks flushed.

"What do you mean? You said he had been captured."

"I know, Colonel, but according to Captain Engelbrecht who brought him in, he more or less gave himself up. It was as if he wanted to be found."

"I have to admit I am intrigued," Kahler said, taking his jacket from the back of the chair and pulling it over his starched shirt and blood-red braces.

"Then you'll come, sir?" the messenger asked, surprised.

"I am intrigued," Kahler repeated as he smoothly buttoned up the jacket. "I don't suppose this 'prisoner' happened to tell anyone his name, did he?" He moved towards the door of the palatial study. His office was where the family must have once taken their meals, still adorned with the paintings and faded tapestries of another, nobler age.

The messenger scampered to keep up with him as they left the office and moved into the stone corridor beyond, cold after the warmth of the office with its fire crackling in the hearth.

They passed beneath red banners bearing the swastika symbol of the Nazi party and the eagle and wreath of the Third Reich, along with other pennants emblazoned with the warped Vitruvian Man emblem of the Frankenstein Corps. The flags flapped in the bitter breeze that howled along the chilly corridor.

"There's something else you should know about the prisoner, sir."

"And what's that?" Kahler asked, striding away along the passage, tugging at his jacket to straighten it, making sure he looked as smart as possible. The heels of his gleaming jackboots clicked on the stone flagged floor.

"Well..." The messenger hesitated.

"What is it man? Spit it out."

"He is... disfigured."

"Disfigured?" Kahler turned his hawkish gaze on the young man once more and gave him a withering look. "I have been commandant here at Castle Frankenstein for the past two years, corporal. I have seen all the horrors that war has to offer. It would take a very great deal to disturb me now, I can assure you."

"Nonetheless," the messenger pressed, "his appearance is... unsettling."

Kahler smiled, a cold, unsettling thing. It was the smile of a man inured to the horrors of war and who now found the prospect of being horrified properly for the first time in years almost appealing.

"Have you seen him then, corporal?"

The youth hesitated before giving his carefully considered response. "No, Colonel. But I have heard the others –"

"Enough then; your concerns only serve to make me more curious," he said. "So come, let us give this prisoner that which he wants and see for ourselves the horror of his appearance."

COLONEL KAHLER AND the corporal made their way at speed through the warren of corridors and laboratories that made up the fortress-factory.

D Block was the name now given to the dungeons located under the central keep of Castle Frankenstein, although most of those stationed at the facility referred to it by another name: Hades.

Once the seat of a powerful noble family, the castle was the place where one man had broken the bounds of human constraint and created life, usurping the power of God. But since Hitler had started on his plans for the domination of Europe, the castle had been re-built, modified and extended to house the burgeoning Frankenstein Corps.

Since the offspring of Project Prometheus had first set foot on the battlefield and proved their worth at the Battle of Ypres, the castle had gone into full-scale production. The former medieval border fortress had turned into a factory production line, turning out half-human, half-mechanical monsters.

Colonel Kahler's office had once been the private apartments of the family that had owned the castle in more peaceful times. From his office, he led the way through the operations centre, which took up the rest of the eastern wing, and out into the courtyard. Kahler passed the parked up half-tracks and steam-driven trucks of the car pool while the thunderous ringing of the production line presses in the western range opposite echoed from the age-weathered walls.

What had started out as a field trial of twenty units – twenty units that single-handedly took down an army more than a hundred times that number – had become a full-scale operation. But it had taken more than ten years to produce those initial twenty. In the two years since, Castle Frankenstein's technicians and surgeons had constructed at least two hundred more.

And they had never been as busy as they were now. Word was that the Führer was preparing for another big push, that Magna Britannia was ready to wade in at last with its mighty automata armies and put an end to his dreams of Aryan supremacy.

Black against the purpling dusk, the pylons connecting the fortress-factory to the Darmstadt Dam, sixteen miles away to the west, loomed like giant steel sentinels. The esoteric energy generated by the force of the River Rhine powered the unsleeping production line, while the scientists and their lackeys worked in shifts to maintain the steady manufacture of 'remades' to bolster the troops at the front line.

The products of Project Prometheus were the perfect resource, the ideal soldier, able to shrug off egregious wounds that would finish a mortal man and brutally powerful in and of themselves. And of course, if they did fall in battle, as long as their bodies could be recovered, they could be rebuilt, or their parts cannibalised in the creation of more of their kind, ready to be sent back to the front to fight for the Fatherland once more.

Behind them, the main gates were opening as the checkpoint guards admitted another truck carrying body parts from the front, more than three hundred miles away. The smell of old blood and carrion wafted across the courtyard, catching in the messenger's nostrils and making him wince. Kahler, if he even registered the smell at all, didn't even blink. The young man was glad once they had crossed the courtyard and entered the keep. It was here, in the lower levels, that the flesh-crafters blended technology and anatomy and made their final improvements to the bodies that had first been stitched together on the body looms, applying thousands of volts of electricity, generated by the Darmstadt Dam turbines, to give them some semblance of life again.

From the lightning labs the infantile remades were sent for imprinting by the Enigma Engine, after which stage they possessed all the knowledge they needed to go back to the front and bludgeon the enemy to death all over again – no more and no less – before they too were beaten down, crushed by tanks or blown up by landmines, their bodies recovered once more, to be brought back to Castle Frankenstein for the process to begin all over again.

The technology required to reawaken the dead had been around for some time, but it had only been in the years since the last war that Doktor Folter – a leading figure in the field of necro-reanimation – had perfected what had previously been an unreliable, hit and miss procedure, with more misses than hits.

The greatest obstacle faced by researchers attempting to create new bodies from old was not the process of having to piece them back together, for in practice that was no more difficult than assembling a particularly tricky jigsaw puzzle. Nor was it the process of passing enough voltage through the corpse to reactivate its heart and get synapses in the brain firing again. No, it was the brain itself that presented the biggest problem.

It wasn't that irreversible decomposition set in inside the brain within moments of death, for the remade Prometheans did not need to be particularly smart and only fifty per cent of the grey matter was required for a body to be able to function again. No, the problem lay in the fact that the freshly reanimated Prometheans were like newborn babies, in that their minds were blank slates, wiped clean of their memories, like the *tabula rasa* spoken of by Aristotle.

Incidents in which the childish monsters had run amok, trashing whole laboratories in their tantrums, had set the project back time and again and almost resulted in the plug being pulled on Project Prometheus altogether.

But in the end, as was always the case, war accelerated the search for a solution – necessity truly being the mother of invention – and the process now known as imprinting had been developed.

Twenty-four hours was all it took. One day in a chemically-induced coma, inside an imprinting helm connected to an Enigma engine. After that time you had another malleable, obedient super soldier, ready to send back to the front.

Kahler nodded in acknowledgement at a scientist-surgeon – the man's lab coat brown with blood stains – before trotting through another archway and down a flight of stone steps into the bowels of the building.

The ever-present thunder of the machinery was muffled by the stones of the keep down here, but it was still there, more felt in the bones than an audible sound. As they went deeper and deeper into the dungeons of C block, however, even that began to fade.

The messenger took over then, leading the way, eventually stopping before a heavy iron door. The single guard on duty stood to attention on seeing Colonel Kahler, his rifle gripped tightly in his hands.

"I take it the prisoner is in here?"

At a nod of the messenger's head, the guard sprang to open the door. Kahler paused to check the load in his Mauser; it was always best to be prepared.

The door opened with a steel groan and the guard stepped aside, admitting Kahler to the cell beyond.

"Colonel," the guard suddenly piped up, "I should warn you that –"

"It's alright private, I've already heard," Kahler said dismissively. "Don't worry, I'm not about to lose my dinner over a few war wounds."

The guard looked as though he had been about to say something else, but thought better of it. But Kahler had caught the look of remembered horror in the man's eyes.

As Kahler entered the musty cell beyond, the figure seated in the middle of the chamber remained facing the opposite wall, his back to the Colonel.

The light levels in the cell were low. The sky showed purple beyond a tiny barred square high in the wall.

By the light spilling into the cell from the passageway behind him, Kahler could see the man was wearing a tatty suit that had seen better days. It was scorched at the elbows and the breast pocket had been torn off. His head and shoulders, however, remained in shadow.

"Ah," the prisoner said in meticulous German, although his precise diction did not entirely mask his British accent, "would that be Colonel Wolf Kahler deigning to meet with me" – adding – "out of curiosity, no doubt."

"I am Colonel Kahler, commandant of this facility," Kahler confirmed.

The prisoner was toying with something in his right hand; something small, metallic and locket-shaped.

"Excellent. Excellent."

Unfolding his legs, the man turned around, although he didn't stand up, and his face remained hidden in shadow.

"And who might you be?" Kahler asked, adjusting his grip on the pistol in his hand.

At that the man rose to his feet – clearly taking care not to make any sudden movements – and took a step forward into the light.

Kahler looked into a face that was more bone than flesh.

Behind him the messenger gasped, and he heard the splatter of vomit on the stone-flagged floor.

Colonel Kahler swallowed hard as he felt his own gorge rise. But he was unable to tear his gaze from the face – the debrided nose, the blood-shot, lidless eyes, the lipless mouth, the cauterised flesh of the hairless scalp.

"You won't have heard of me, Colonel Kahler, but I've heard of you. My name is Daniel Dashwood, and I'm here to win your war for you."

CHAPTER TWO

Spymaster

LONDON, ENGLAND, 1943

THE GENTLEMAN CUT a dash as he strode purposely along Whitehall, cane in hand and opera cape tight around his neck, with top hat firmly in place. The skies above the capital were thick with clouds, great grey sponges that had soaked up half the world's oceans, which they were now emptying onto the city streets.

The click of his heels on the paving slabs was deadened by the splash of puddles. Water ran in torrents along the gutters, carrying with it the last of autumn's leaves and sodden shreds of yesterday's news.

The man glimpsed the headline on a scrap of disintegrating newsprint. It read:

WAR

One simple word that spoke volumes.

He knew the date without having to check it: 1 September 1943. It had been all over the papers and street-corner broadcast

27

screens, not to mention every radio station, only the day before. It had been brewing for months, of course, if not years. Ever since the Nazi menace had first reared its ugly fascist head a quarter of a century earlier. Its leader, Adolf Hitler, had capitalised on the German people's dissatisfaction with how they felt their nation had been treated in the aftermath of the First Great European War to achieve his own aims for power and dominance. But Britain had been watching, and none more closely than the spymasters of Department Q, hence the reason for the gentleman's jaunt through the deluged streets of London, from Mayfair to Whitehall, at the behest of Mr. Churchill himself.

He had always suspected it would come to this. Once he had a taste for power, there was no way the Führer was going to give it up again so easily, or even just stop with Germany. He already had both Russia and Magna Britannia within his sights, and with those mighty powers out of the way, there would be nothing to stop him conquering the whole world should he desire it. And the Führer was the kind of man who would.

The gentleman suddenly halted beside a pillared doorway where an old man, filthy under his matted beard and sodden rags despite the downpour, sat cross-legged in the rain. The battered collecting tin in his lap was empty other than for a broken button and what looked like a dead beetle. Putting a hand into his pocket, the gentleman jangled the change within for a moment before pulling out a coin, tossing it deftly into the beggar's tin.

"Thank you kindly, sir," the old tramp said, touching the brim of his hat.

"You'll catch your death out here in this," the gentleman replied, regarding the filthy beggar for a moment.

"This?" the old man said, looking up at the sky as if he hadn't noticed the rain until it had been pointed out to him. "This is nothing. If you'd tried sleeping rough in the depths of winter then you'd know what hardship was."

"Still, could be worse," the smartly-dressed gentleman said.

"Aye, that it could," the old man replied, sounding surprisingly cheery. "There's always some poor bugger worse off than yourself."

The tramp lent forward, shooting a couple of wary glances left and right along the rain-slicked street, before pulling on one of the iron railings that ringed the white stone Palladian building. The railing gave in his hand and, with a noise like a turning grindstone, the alcove wall behind him slid open.

"Go right in," the tramp said. "He's expecting you."

"I know," the other replied.

Glancing slyly left and right himself, he stepped through the secret portal and into the passageway beyond.

THE DANK PASSAGEWAY smelled of wet stone. The gentleman didn't linger, but made his way along it to an elevator that was little more than a grilled metal bucket. The safety gate folded back at a sharp tug, the rusted hinges and rivets squealing in protest. The cage wobbled unsteadily as he stepped into it. Pulling the gate shut again after him, he pulled a lever at the back of the carriage and, with a jerk and a clank, the lift descended at speed down a crumbling brick shaft, black with mould and slick with running water.

At the bottom of the shaft the elevator came to an abrupt halt. The man pulled back the rusted gate awaiting him there and stepped out into a circular tunnel. Flickering yellowed bulbs suffused the underground passageway with a dusty amber glow. The walls of the tunnel were tiled, although many of the tiles were cracked and everything was covered in an oily sheen.

The gentleman's rapid footsteps rang from the tiles as he made his way along the passageway deeper under Whitehall. A pattern had been picked out in the tiles: a red circle crossed with a name in white and blue.

Department Q.

From the tunnel, the man turned suddenly into a narrower, brick-lined passageway. The lamps were fewer and further between, here, but the man could still make out the monster standing beside the rusted, wheel-locked door at the far end.

His heart skipped a beat and, just for a moment, his stride faltered. No matter how many times he encountered the gate's guardian it still made him feel uncomfortable. He couldn't explain why, there was just something about automatons that he didn't trust.

A small angular head sat atop a narrow body, little more than a chassis to support the monstrous pile-driver pistons of its arms and legs.

The air here smelt of damp rust and burnt coke.

Slowly, with careful steps, he resumed his approach.

The atmosphere around him was suddenly thick with steam, the hiss of hydraulics and the clanking of metal joints. A baleful fire sparked into life behind the droid's visor-plate as it rose up on powerful legs to its full height.

"PASSWORD!" the droid boomed, with the voice of a pressurised steam-engine.

The man glanced at the yellow slip of paper now in his hand. It was the telegram he had received earlier that morning from the Department. He read the one word printed upon it again, just to be sure.

Taking a deep breath, he said, in as strong a voice as he could muster, "Angel storm!"

For a moment nothing happened, the automaton remaining motionless. The only movement was the to and fro motion of the glaring light visible through the slit in the visor-plate.

The droid could crush him to paste in a second if it so chose, or, to put it another way, if he had got the password wrong, somehow, or the droid had misheard him. It had been known to happen.

His pulse began to quicken.

"PASSWORD ACCEPTED!" the droid growled at last and promptly deactivated, folding in on itself again.

Letting out a relieved sigh, the gentleman crumpled the telegram in his hand and let it fall to the floor before approaching the door. Seizing the locking wheel with both hands, he strained to turn it clockwise. It was reluctant to move at first but then it gave with a screech of rarely-oiled pivots and the snap of metal bolts, the man stumbling backwards as the door abruptly opened towards him.

Stepping through the portal, he blinked against the glare of the lights and entered the brightly lit sub-basement. Large iron pipes ran the length of the roof above his head. Between the red bricks, parts of the walls of the basement were formed of older building foundations – large blocks of rough-cut stone and what could well have been sections of the old Roman walls of London. Sturdy doors led off from the broad chamber and the whole place was teeming with bustling figures in white lab-coats and men and women in uniform. The gentleman exchanged curt nods with a few of them as he made his way through the Department's base of operations, only stopping when he came before a grand-looking walnut-panelled door.

He raised a hand to knock.

"Enter!" came a gruff, gravelly voice from the other side, before his kuckle touched the door.

The gentleman shook his head in disbelief. How did the old man do that?

Opening the door, he entered a large office that was suffused by a cloud of blue tobacco smoke. From the shape of the room, it looked as though it had been built beneath a railway arch.

The gentleman put a hand to his mouth to smother a cough, and blinked excessively as his eyes began to water.

Sitting behind a large mahogany desk, positioned strategically in the middle of the room, was a portly old man, all wobbling jowls with only a few wisps of silvery hair on his otherwise bald pate. He was wearing a black waistcoat and a spotted bow-tie. His jacket and bowker hat hung from a stand in the near corner.

The man took the cigar he was smoking from between his teeth with fat white fingers and said, "Ah, Quicksilver. There you are. And about time too."

"You wanted to see me, WC?"

"Yes. About two bloody hours ago! What kept you? Some fine filly over in Soho, was it? Or stayed too late at the blackjack table, did you? Game of poker you couldn't get away from?"

"Breakfast, WC," the other replied curtly.

"Breakfast?" Churchill blustered.

The gentleman looked at the head of the mysterious Department Q, eyebrows raised. "You know; the meal you break your fast with after sleep."

"Sleep?"

"Don't tell me you never sleep, WC."

"No time for sleep! You can sleep all you want when you're dead. Haven't you heard there's a war on?"

Quicksilver said nothing, merely fixing the older man with a piercing stare from beneath the brim of his top hat.

Winston Churchill, in return, regarded the young man standing in front of him.

Somewhere in his mid-twenties, he was tall, classically handsome, with a chiselled jaw and patrician nose, and he moved with the grace of a natural athlete.

He removed his hat, wiping the drips of rain from it with a gloved hand, releasing a thick mane of brown hair, the same colour as his well-developed moustache.

Churchill knew he was from a long line of loyalist agents of the Crown of Magna Britannia. Indeed, his great-great-uncle Erasmus Quicksilver was the man who first proposed the life-support throne for her ailing Majesty back in 1901, when it was feared that her death might result in the collapse of the British Empire. The man was as patriotic as they came. He had no other ties to hold him – no wife, no family – and would do anything for Queen and country. He was just the man for the job.

"So, what did you want to see me about?" Quicksilver said, bringing Churchill back to the reason for the agent's summons to the bowels of Whitehall.

"Ah, yes, that," Churchill blustered, taking another drag on his smouldering cigar. "Got a job for you."

"I rather thought you might," the other replied.

"I want you to go to Edinburgh and pick up a package from the Medical School there."

"Right," Quicksilver said, warily. "And what do you want me to do with this 'package' after I've collected it?"

"Deliver it, of course," the old man grunted, and then added, "behind enemy lines."

"Ah, I see," Quicksilver said, sucking in air noisily through his teeth and leaning back in his seat.

"Rum do and no mistake," Churchill went on, pushing a file across the desk. Quicksilver looked at it, but assiduously avoided picking it up.

"I can imagine."

The old man looked at him, the concern in his eyes evident to the younger man. "We've received intelligence that the Nazis are developing a secret weapon – one that could change the course of the war and ensure their victory."

"I see," Quicksilver said, sliding the folder towards himself with a tentative finger, his curiosity piqued.

"And I want you to destroy it before it can be used against our great nation," Churchill added casually, as if asking Quicksilver to pop out and pick up some more brandy.

"Just like that?" Quicksilver picked up the slim file and flicked it open, casting a weather eye over its contents.

"You'll have help," Churchill added. "That's what the 'package' is for."

Quicksilver turned a page and read on. "I see."

"So you'll do it? You'll take the job?" the old man pressed, jowls wobbling as he lent forward across the desk, inadvertently blowing smoke into the younger man's face, causing him to cough again.

Quicksilver closed the file and put it back down on the desk. Stroking his moustache with one hand, he said, "When do we start?"

Churchill took another puff on the cigar clamped between his teeth. "We already have."

CHAPTER THREE

Frozen Assets

Rags of clouds scudded across the coke-choked sky over Edinburgh, chased across the heavens by the approaching storm like lambs running before a wolf.

By the time the horse-drawn hansom deposited him before the imposing gothic façade of the Medical School, the sky had turned the colour of a bad bruise as the sun began to set.

Hercules pulled his cape tighter about his shoulders as the wind tugged at it hungrily. Seizing hold of one of the heavy verdigris-coated doorknockers, he hesitated, glancing left and right along the empty cobbled street. It was devoid of life, other than for the departing carriage, the gig's iron-shod wheels clattering over the cobbles in counterpoint to the *tink, tink, tink* of the horse's hooves.

Happy that his arrival at the Medical School had gone unobserved, he slammed the knocker against the cracked wood of the door three times.

The sound echoed ominously along the empty street, like the

tolling of a funerary bell, or the hollow knocking of the Grim Reaper himself at the home of one not long for this world.

It was only a matter of moments before he heard the rattle of a latch and the door groaned open. A hunched porter stood in the shadows – looking like a carrion crow in his black porter's garb – and ushered him inside.

Before he could even announce himself the porter said, "Professor Knox is waiting for you in his study."

Hercules Quicksilver raised his eyebrows, but he was not wholly surprised. His masters at the Department moved in mysterious ways at the best of times. Since Magna Britannia's declaration of war against Nazi Germany, even more so.

"Then lead on, Macduff."

"This way," the porter rasped, turning and shuffling away into the dusty gloom of the arching hallway beyond.

THE PLACE SEEMED to be deserted. All the while as the porter led him through its echoing, marble galleries and down wood-panelled corridors, the air redolent with beeswax and camphor, they didn't see another soul.

Finally, after walking for what felt like miles through the halls and passageways of the Medical School they came at last to a musty office that smelt of mildew and preserving fluid. A thin, bespectacled man sporting a straggly beard sat behind a desk overloaded with books and teetering piles of paperwork.

"Professor Knox," the porter said, "Mr Quicksilver is here."

Knox looked up from what appeared to be a book on anatomy, judging by the printed plates Hercules could just make out over piles of unmarked essays and yellowing professional journals. A pair of heavy purple drapes were half-drawn across the office's one window, but by the sliver of grey daylight that made it into the stuffy room, he could see the Professor's face was unnaturally pale, his cheeks gaunt, the tiny eyes behind his glasses sunken and red-rimmed. Considering that he was a Professor of Medicine, he wasn't a very good advert for the accomplishments of the medical profession.

"Ah, yes, Mr Quicksilver," Knox said, sounding out every syllable in the name with clinical precision. He looked at the porter waiting at the door. "That will be all, thank you, Muir." The porter departed.

Neither of the two men that remained said anything for a good few seconds as they listened to the aging porter's receding footsteps, making his way back along the hallway outside the office.

"So," Professor Knox said at last, "you're here for the…" He broke off, looking away from Hercules and peering at a spot just beyond the edge of his desk.

"The package," Hercules finished for him.

"Ah, yes. The 'package,' as you put it."

The professor smiled at him enigmatically, which made Hercules feel even more uneasy.

"You do have it, I take it?" he challenged, casting an unimpressed eye around the cluttered room.

"But of course."

"Then what are we waiting for?" Hercules asked. Now wasn't the time for pleasantries. Didn't the man know there was a war on?

"What indeed?"

The Professor rose to his feet. Opening a drawer in his desk he took out a set of heavy iron keys.

"If you'd like to follow me," he said, making for the door.

And so Hercules Quicksilver set off again through the echoing, empty corridors of the Medical School, easily keeping pace with the professor, who seemed to be dragging his heels. Thankfully, this time, the journey was a much shorter one.

He followed Knox to the university's Anatomy Museum. Every chamber and gallery was suffused in shadow. Above their heads, in the streaked gloom, the skeletons of whales and dolphins creaked on their suspending wires.

They passed skulls entombed within smeared glass cabinets, displayed alongside death-mask casts and a full human skeleton. The bones dated from the last century and before, when only the bodies of executed criminals were allowed to be used for the purposes of anatomical dissection and study. There were other dusty glass cases filled with unborn babies' bones. Grotesques, stuffed and mounted in frozen poses by the taxidermist's art so that they might horrify generation after generation of morbidly-fascinated museum visitors. Alien things pickled in huge jars of yellow liquid that surely couldn't be human; things that made Hercules' skin crawl.

And as they made their way through the museum, deeper into the depths of the university, Professor Knox raised his objections.

"You should understand that I and my colleagues are not, ah – how shall I put it? – happy about this."

"About me being here?" Hercules asked, as they walked past rows of glittering cabinets crammed with bottled embryos with malformed crania.

"No, not that so much – although it has implications for the other. No, we are not happy that you are taking the…"

"Package."

"Of course. The package," Knox laughed. It was an unpleasantly mirthless sound. "Yes. We are not happy that you are taking it away."

Hercules arched an eyebrow at the professor's back.

"I have my orders," he said, plainly. "Besides, this is a matter of national security. For Queen and country."

"So I've been told," Knox replied.

Having reached the furthest limits of the eerie Anatomy Museum, leaving the mummified freaks and foetuses behind, Knox took his bundle of keys from his pocket again.

"It's this way," he said, fumbling an old iron key into the lock of a sturdy oak-panelled door, set back into a porticoed alcove.

The door opened onto a marble spiral staircase that corkscrewed its way down into the depths of the Medical School.

The two of them began to descend.

"My colleagues and I have tried to continue the doctor's ground-breaking work, in our own small way," he said as the staircase wound deeper and deeper into the basements of the museum. Knox passed one landing after another, along with the doors leading off from them. As far as Hercules could tell, peering over the rail into the persistent gloom below, they were heading for the very bottom.

"Really?" Hercules said, not really sure what Knox was talking about now.

"However, as unpalatable as it may be, we were unable to replicate its effects."

Reaching the bottom of the stairs at last, Hercules saw a single door.

He glanced back up the staircase. It was a long way back up to the top. Hercules guessed that they must be some way below the cobbles of the Royal Mile, deep within the core of granite on which the Auld Reekie had risen up over the centuries.

"And so, he remains unique."

It felt cold down here; cold and damp. Hercules pulled his cape tighter about him.

Cold, like a tomb.

Knox rammed another large iron key into the black door's lock and gave it a turn. There was a click and with a firm push from the professor the great portal creaked open.

The temperature instantly dropped by a few degrees. Nitrogen mist coiled about their feet.

Clutching himself against the chill, Professor Knox stepped through the evaporating cloud into the eerie blue glow beyond it. Hercules followed.

His breath misting in front of his face, feeling that his lips must already be blue with cold, he looked about him in wonder.

They were in some kind of cryogenic vault. Pipes, encrusted with hoarfrost, covered the walls and ceiling.

As the two men advanced further into the cryo-crypt, the soles of their shoes crunched on the brittle sheen of ice covering the floor.

Arrayed in front of them were a number of large, coffin-like, steel pods, from which the blue glow was emanating. Each pod reclined at forty-five degrees and was connected to a whirring, half-frozen Babbage engine via a network of cables and flexible hoses. In the front of each was an ice-crusted glass panel.

Knox approached one of the pods, Hercules close at his shoulder, his indefatigable curiosity well and truly piqued.

He peered at the glass panel. There was something in there and, while he couldn't see clearly through the frosted pane, it appeared to be a body.

"And so he remains unique," Knox said, concluding his little speech, "and on ice."

There was an etched plate at the foot of the cryogenic coffin. Hercules lent forward and brushed the needles of frost away with a hand, reading what was etched into the metal beneath.

It was a name.

Doctor Henry Jekyll

CHAPTER FOUR

The Return of the Bloody Red Baron

<small>HESSEN, GERMANY, 1943</small>

GERMANY WAS A land at war with the rest of the world. Every ancient family estate and crag-perched castle had been commandeered by the army to become barracks, or prisoner of war camps, or weapons caches. Listening posts and early warning stations pointed their scopes at the sky whilst the giant clanking walkers of the swastika-daubed Landsknecht legions stalked the landscape, keeping the native populace in order as much as looking for enemy escapees or Allied spies.

But the sky over the town of Darmstadt was empty, but than for one lone zeppelin. The first fingers of dawn stretched over the eastern horizon, caressing the dirigible's sails, bathing the red, white and black of the airship's swastika markings in vibrant sunlight as the new day chased away the last scraps of the previous night's storm clouds.

Below, Darmstadt was little more than a huddle of dun-coloured buildings, many dating back two centuries or more in their construction. The more recent additions included minefields and barbed-wire-topped fences, along with a checkpoint on every road leading into and away from the small Hessen town. If it hadn't been for the castle and its former master's legacy, it would have remained an insignificant speck on the map. As it was, Darmstadt was the location of the jewel in the Führer's crown, Germany's great hope, home to the Frankenstein Corps and their near-indestructible, undying super-soldiers.

And that was, after all, why the zeppelin was there.

Over seventy miles from the castle, the town and the dam named after it, Lieutenant Eichmann of early warning lookout post Valkyrie 7 set down his coffee, turned to the radar operator and said, "A zeppelin, you say?"

"Yes, sir."

The two men stared at the return on the scope, a green, fish-like shape that was closing on the town.

Eichmann picked up a clipboard and flicked through the ruffle of curling papers attached to it.

"There are no flights scheduled for this time today." He flicked his gaze back to the scope. "Speed?" he asked.

"Approximately thirty knots," the operator replied after a moment's hasty calculation.

"And it's heading for Darmstadt."

The lieutenant frowned. He picked up a telephone handset and quickly wound the call handle.

"Kahler?" he said as the line connected. "Are you tracking the zeppelin approaching from the north-west?"

"Yes, sir," a voice came back in a crackle of static. "Tracking it now."

"Can you see any registration markings or identifier tags?"

"Yes, sir," came Kahler's voice again after a moment's empty static. "NCC-1701. Repeat, NCC-1701."

Lieutenant Eichmann stared into the middle distance, the lines of his frown etched more deeply into his face.

"NCC-1701, you say?" he echoed, scouring another sheet clipped to the board.

"Yes, sir. That's right, sir."

Five minutes later, Lieutenant Eichmann was at the top of the watchtower himself, out of breath, with a pair of binoculars held up to his eyes, the cold wind biting at his face. With the coming dawn the zeppelin was clearly visible now, as was the designation stencilled on its tail fin.

"NCC-1701," he repeated once more. "So, coming in at dawn, eh? Hoping the half-light would hide your approach, eh?"

"Sir?" the look-out beside him asked, his face crumpled in consternation.

"NCC-1701,"Eichmann said again, as if that should explain everything.

The corporal continued to stare at him in confusion.

"You don't read the High Command communiqués regarding airship losses, do you corporal?" Eichmann went on. The attention of everyone on duty at the top of the tower was now focused on the drifting dirigible.

"NCC-1701, also known as the *Baron von Richthofen*, went missing during a routine patrol of the Channel a month ago," Eichmann said, with a distinct tone of self-satisfaction in his voice. "Along with all of her crew."

Eichmann picked up the telephone receiver from its warped wooden box, against the wall of the tower-top, and wound the handle.

"Eichmann here... See that zeppelin? Well, I want a cyber-eagle escort sent out to bring it in."

"So they're back," the young telescope operator said, eyes fixed on the approaching airship.

"Someone is," Eichmann replied.

"How far now?" Hercules Quicksilver asked the pilot as he stared out of the glass cockpit at the front of the dirigible's gondola.

"Eight miles, sir," the young woman at the flight controls replied, peering resolutely ahead through her tinted goggles at the lightening landscape below.

"Dawn's here. Damn!" Hercules cursed.

The plan had been to come in over the drop site just before dawn, using the twilight to mask their arrival. Travelling on board a purloined Nazi airship would only get them so far. Up close, chances were that they would soon be found out.

Hercules adjusted the officer's jacket he was wearing. It felt strange to be got up like one of the enemy. As an agent of the Crown, he didn't often find himself in uniform. The stiff jacket, the iron eagle pin and the swastika-emblazoned armband lent him an unmistakeable feeling of efficiency and authority. He wondered if it had the same effect on the German military personnel, and supposed it did.

The problem was that the wind had been against them as they crossed the Eifel range. Then they had run into a squall that had forced them off course and robbed them of precious minutes.

He turned his attention from his jackboots and the stiff, grey-coloured cap in his hands to the steadily brightening view beyond the cockpit once more.

"What's that?" he asked, leaning forward to get a better look at the jagged shadow looming ahead of them on the horizon.

"Er, we have incoming, sir," the pilot suddenly announced, raising her voice over the drone of the aero-engines.

Hercules peered out of the glass bubble of the cockpit. A flock of black shapes, eight in all, were rising from the still-dark turrets of a crumbling castle, anonymous silhouettes against the salmon pink sky.

"But they're only birds," Hercules said.

The flapping forms immediately began to move towards them. As the gondola and the flock closed on one another, however, he could see that they were very large birds and even caught the glint of sunlight on their machined parts.

"With all due respect, sir, they're not just birds. They're weaponised cyber-eagles. We've been found out."

"Damn!" Hercules cursed.

"Your orders, sir?" the pilot said desperately, hands on the zeppelin's control levers, body tensed, ready for action.

Hercules watched as the cyber-eagles continued to close on

the airship with a ruthless, unnatural determination. "Evasive action – now!"

The pilot pulled back on a control lever. The pitch of the port-side engine dropped perceptibly and the airship rolled sideways.

The approaching birds wheeled and turned in response, matching the manoeuvre.

The pilot pushed forward on another lever and the nose of the airship dipped sharply towards the indiscernible trees, hills and structures that were just shadows in the gloom below. Hercules grabbed hold of a railing and hung on, bracing his legs.

With a screeching cry that could be heard even over the scream of the engines, as they were pushed to their utmost limit, the eagles turned again – and struck.

Folding back their wings, the cyber-eagles dived at the dirigible. And then, as they came within reach of the reinforced aluminium and canvas outer skin, they spread wide their wings again and swung their talons forward. Brass-tipped points as sharp as surgical instruments tore at the thinly-armoured surface of the zeppelin. Steel beaks punctured the sheet metal as the birds' dreadful claws ripped their way through, like the savage Stymphalian birds of myth.

Impotent inside the gondola slung beneath the massive gas balloon, there was nothing Hercules could do but hang on for dear life as the cabin began to tilt along its horizontal axis. They were going down.

There was only one thing for it now.

Clinging onto whatever handholds he could find, Hercules dragged himself back up through the cabin. Secure in its cradle at the rear of the gondola, the large, coffin-like cryogenic pod rattled and jolted as the pilot jinked the craft left and right to try and control the falling craft.

The pod hummed, drawing power from a coupling with the airship's own steam-furnace to ensure its occupant remained on ice. Beneath the ice-frosted glass panel in the front of the capsule Dr Henry Jekyll slept, while all about him was chaos and confusion.

The pod's thermostatic controls were sunk into a recess on its hinged edge. As Hercules threw switches, cryogenic gas began to vent through an outlet in the side of the pod, filling the cabin with ethereal vapour.

"Sir, what do you think you're doing?" the pilot called back, a look of horror on her porcelain features.

"You just worry about getting us down in one piece!" Hercules shouted back.

The airship lurched again, Hercules losing his grip on the slippery, frost-rimed capsule. The angry screeching of their avian attackers rang through the gondola again as the pilot fought to keep control of the zeppelin.

Exerting himself, Hercules grabbed hold of a frozen length of piping, wincing as the cold burned his palm, and set to work on the pod's control panel again regardless.

A regular chime sounded from somewhere inside the pod, and the needles on the ice-rimed dials at the side of the device began to rise.

"Sir!" the pilot shouted. "Our orders were to deliver the package to the target before defrosting."

"And if I don't defrost the good doctor now, and we crash, he may well die!" Hercules bellowed back over the protestations of the airship's engines.

With a *pop*, the container's seal was broken and the lid levered upwards, automatic systems opening the front of the steel sarcophagus. There lay the slight form of Dr Henry Jekyll, his naked skin prickled with ice crystals.

He looked dead. Hercules studied the body critically for a moment. Had he indeed been too hasty? Rather than revive the doctor, had he in fact killed him?

A wisp of icy-mist suddenly escaped the man's motionless lips and Hercules saw his chest rise and fall, almost imperceptibly.

He let out his own pent-up breath in a relieved sigh. Doctor Jekyll was alive! Now Hercules just had to keep him that way.

The cabin rocked again and this time, for a split second, Hercules' stomach leapt into his mouth, as if he had gone into free-fall. The portside engine spluttered and suddenly died.

"We're going down, sir!" the pilot cried.

"Tell me something I don't know," Hercules muttered.

The zeppelin had gone into an uncontrollable spin, the centrifugal force created by the one remaining engine whirling the dirigible around with frightening force.

Jekyll still lay motionless in the cryogenic pod.

"We have to bail out while we still can, sir!"

Abandoning the controls, she ran for the exit hatch, only hesitating to pull on one of the two parachutes that hung beside the cabin door.

Clipping the pack tight across her chest, the pilot opened the door. Wind howled into the gondola, louder than the scream of the starboard engine.

Hercules looked from the pilot and the crashing cabin door to Jekyll's still half-frozen form. He didn't have time to wait for the thaw to finish.

Reaching into the pod, he tried to move the ice-stiff body but it wouldn't budge. The doctor's limbs were locked and there was nothing Hercules could do to manoeuvre the man out of the restraints in which he was secured, other than to break all four of his limbs.

"Come on, sir! There isn't time, and the parachute won't take the weight of two!"

It might, Hercules thought, but there was no way he could manhandle Jekyll as things stood. It had all been for naught. The zeppelin was going down and all he could do was try to save himself and then, if he managed that, try to come up with an alternative strategy once he was safely on the ground.

No! That was unacceptable. There had to be another way.

"Stop!" he shouted after the pilot. "There must be a way we can land this thing!" But it was no good.

His curses carried away by the wind howling through the cockpit, whipping the nitrogen mist away with it, Hercules scrambled for the door as the pilot disappeared through the hatch, arms and legs splayed, ready to be caught by the wind and pulled clear of the whirling vessel, the parachute ripcord clenched tightly in one hand.

The airship continued to spin, the note of the whirling engine rising in pitch with every dizzying rotation. Hercules had no idea how high up they were, or how close to the ground; only that every second counted.

Pulling on the parachute pack, his cold-numbed hands struggling to buckle the harness across his chest, he struggled against the tilting, dizzying flight of the zeppelin, trying to make his way back to the pilot's position. Surely he could do something to land this thing.

The craft lurched violently, and suddenly Hercules was no longer in contact with the floor. He tumbled backwards, unable to stop himself, and suddenly there was the exit hatch behind him. As he fell through it, he eyes fell on the cryo-pod in time to see the doctor's ice-flecked eyelashes flicker open.

And then he was sailing out of the cabin, screaming in rage as he was forced to leave Jekyll to his fate.

CHAPTER FIVE

Behind Enemy Lines

HERCULES SPUN AWAY from the airship, caught by the whirling wind and swept clear of the engine's propeller. Ground became sky and the sky became the ground again as he somersaulted through the air. The memory of the doctor's eyes flicking open haunted him, and for a moment he forgot where he was or what was going on. Below, the dark land rushed up to meet him.

Seizing hold of the dancing ripcord, Hercules gave it a sharp tug.

The parachute unfurled in a torrent of khaki silk. The wind caught it, and Hercules lost his breath as the harness pulled tight under his arms. He felt as if he were suddenly being yanked upwards.

Recovering his breath, Hercules grabbed the trailing cords of the chute above him, pulling on them first one way, then the other, directing his descent as best he could.

He watched as the zeppelin continued to spin away from him towards the ground. Pulling on the lines of the parachute again, he tried his damnedest to steer himself as far away from the falling airship as possible.

On the horizon he could see the silhouette of the castle ramparts quite clearly now. He was also keen to make landfall as far from the look-out post as possible.

As soon as the zeppelin was down, the Germans would be all over it and no doubt coming from the direction of the tower. They had obviously been spotted, and the raptors had been launched from there.

That one thought suddenly had Hercules scouring the sky above him again.

The eagles were still there. A few had gone down with the zeppelin, clinging on to the last to ensure that their prey didn't escape them, but the rest of the flock – four huge avians – were occupied with something else entirely.

They had the young pilot in their claws, and were tossing her ravaged corpse about as if it were nothing more than a piece of meat – which of course it was, now. The shreds of her parachute were knotted around her bloodied carcass and caught in the savage talons of the bird-machines.

Hercules gasped involuntarily. He couldn't even remember the poor woman's name. And now, here she was, sacrificed in the skies over Germany for the war effort, to bring him and his precious cargo behind enemy lines. And all for what?

If she wasn't already dead, she very soon would be. Doctor Jekyll was, even now, plummeting to his death aboard the doomed airship. Any minute Hercules would be lost behind enemy lines as well, and without the means to complete his secret mission.

The zeppelin hit the ground with a scream of twisting metal and the pop of erupting gas-cells. A second later there was a loud *crump* and the pre-dawn landscape was lit up by an explosion, as sparks from the failing starboard engine ignited the balloon.

The *Baron von Richthofen* had come down in a field. Hercules could see a herd of cattle fleeing from the flames, bathed in the flickering light of the conflagration.

Hercules' whole body sagged as he continued to drift towards the ground, the wind carrying him further and further south to a point roughly halfway between the crash-site and the look-out post. He felt sick to the pit of his stomach.

His mind was a-whirl. What was the point in going on? Without the means to complete his mission, what good was he to anyone? All he could hope to do now was somehow find a way back to Blighty, or at least one of her allied territories, and take the punishment meted out for his failure like a man.

Thankfully, distracted by their prize, the cyber-eagles had failed to spot him and he came down at the edge of a furrowed field. He hastily bundled up his parachute and stuffed it back into its pack, his heart racing as he did so, shooting anxious glances in every direction.

With the expanse of parachute silk out of sight, he ran for the edge of the field and the welcoming gloom of the small wood that lay beyond its bounds.

Early morning mist was rising off the clay-clumped ruts of the forgotten corn-stubbled field. Hercules ducked under a low branch and threw himself into cover amidst the dense undergrowth that had been left to grow wild between the coppiced stands of ash and elm.

The distant crackle of flames carried on the wind from where the requisitioned zeppelin had come down.

Happy that he hadn't been seen, Hercules took a moment to consider his options. He was wearing the full dress uniform of a Nazi officer, the insignia marking him out as a colonel, but he had lost his cap during his forced evacuation from the plummeting zeppelin. His German was good, but under intense interrogation areas of weakness would reveal themselves, like as not.

Doctor Jekyll was lost, as was the pilot; he might as well just forget about them now.

He was armed with a German Luger and had a knife tucked into his right boot, but other than that he had nothing. Nothing beyond the emergency survival kit – a compass, a garrotte and a tinderbox – provided by the boffins of Department Q and hidden inside the heels of his boots.

The parachute wasn't going to be much good to him, he reasoned, so he might as well leave it behind. But he didn't want to leave any suspicious signs that might lead a Nazi patrol to suspect that anyone had survived the zeppelin crash.

The knotty root of an oak made the perfect hiding place. He rammed the pack as far as he could into an animal burrow that had been excavated between its roots, and pulled up a few handfuls of nettles and spread them over the hole.

The only thing he could do now was make his way to the nearest road and from there, work out how he was going to get back to Magna Britannia from behind enemy lines.

FINDING THE NEAREST road wasn't a problem, not once he began to hear the steady thrum of engines from a whole convoy of vehicles heading for the crash-site.

Cautiously, keeping low, Hercules made his way towards the road. As it turned out, it was little more than a dirt track. Nonetheless, vehicles were pouring along it in a steady stream. Hercules ducked down behind the trunk of a fallen beech tree and peered out from beneath its mossy black branches.

As he watched, a truck rumbled past, heavy tyres bouncing in the water-logged ruts made by the vehicles that had gone ahead of it. German troopers were sat uncomfortably in the back, one or two even hanging onto the sides of the truck, machine guns slung across their chests. It was followed by a squad car, and bringing up the rear, a good hundred yards behind, an open half-track carrying a ranked officer – judging by his uniform at this distance – and his personal driver.

Back along the road, Hercules could see the dark shape of the look-out post, details beginning to appear in the brickwork around its turrets in the first light of dawn.

To the east lay the look-out post and a full Nazi platoon, no doubt. To the west lay the wreck of the *Richthofen* and another platoon's worth of soldiers, or so Hercules suspected.

And here, coming up the road towards him, was a way out of all of it.

Maintaining his crouched position, and following a rainwater ditch on the other side of the fence enclosing the field, Hercules moved from the shelter of the wood – his approach still obscured by the gloom. As the half-track containing the officer and his man drew closer he broke into a hunched run.

As the vehicle rumbled past, he scrambled out of the ditch and ducked under the fence in time to grab hold of a roll-bar and swing himself up onto the back of the half-track without either of the men noticing.

Pausing for a moment, he shot a glance further up the road at the retreating truck and jeep, as the two vehicles turned a corner in the road and disappeared beyond the edge of a spur of jutting, mist-clung woodland. Beyond the treetops, thick black smoke climbed high into the misty sky, pouring from the wreckage of the burning zeppelin.

Glancing behind him he saw nothing but the empty, rutted road. This was the perfect opportunity to get himself out of here with a minimum of fuss.

Eyes on the two men in the front of the half-track the whole time, Hercules stepped carefully over the uneven tarpaulin covering whatever was in the back of the vehicle. As he closed the distance between him and the two Germans his pulse quickened. One of them could look back at any moment and then it would all be over for him, the element of surprise gone.

And then, incredibly, he was there, right behind the driver's seat, the officer and his chauffeur completely oblivious to his presence, the half-track's chugging engine filling the air with sound. In that split second he made his move.

Lashing out with both fists clasped together, he struck the officer in the side of the head. The man grunted as he tumbled out of his seat and under the moving vehicle.

In the same moment, the driver jerked his head around in shock and surprise. With both hands on the wheel, he was defenceless against the punch that Hercules delivered. But the moment he landed the blow was the same moment the vehicle's tracks ground over the body of the helpless officer.

Hercules stumbled. The punch failed to connect fully, knocking the driver's head into the steering wheel, rather than knocking him out of the half-track altogether.

Recovering his balance, Hercules tried to grab the man by the collar, ready to slam his head into the steering column again, only harder this time. But now the driver was ready for him.

Letting go of the steering wheel with his right hand, he made a grab for Hercules himself. The British agent knocked the flailing arm aside but the driver still remained out of reach.

The half-track's engine suddenly roared as the German put his foot to the floor and the vehicle lurched forwards. Hercules fell backwards, unbalanced once again.

The vehicle tore along the track towards the jutting spur of woodland. If they rounded that and caught up with the convoy, Hercules would be as good as dead.

As he struggled to push himself up into a sitting position, his hand touched on something hard and solid under the tarpaulin. Yanking back the cover, his eyes fell upon the heavy-duty wrench lying there.

On his knees now, swinging the wrench with both hands, he brought it down on the driver's head and stove in his skull.

The man died instantly as the heavy tool splintered his skull, pulping the grey matter beneath. But his foot remained heavy on the peddle, as the weight of his body against the wheel steered the half-track sharply off the road.

The vehicle ploughed through a fence and into a ditch on the far side, throwing Hercules unceremoniously into the passenger's seat as it slewed to a halt, the pitch of the engine rising as it tried to push the half-track further into the unyielding mud bank of the gully.

Acting quickly, Hercules pushed the dead driver out of his seat and manoeuvred the half-track back onto the road before killing the engine.

Jumping down from the vehicle, shooting anxious glances up and down the road, uncomfortably aware of the presence of the watchtower, Hercules pulled the driver into the ditch. Jogging fifty yards back up the track he recovered the pulverised corpse of the officer, dragging that into the ditch as well, making sure that both bodies were hidden by the clumps of grass growing thickly over the lip of the gully. A close inspection would soon find them, but from the road they wouldn't be seen. Besides, they didn't need to remain undiscovered for long – just long enough for Hercules to put several leagues between him and the crash-site.

However, there was one last job he had to do before he could leave this spot. Running back down the road, Hercules collected the officer's cap from where it had fallen in the road, clear of the doomed man. Wiping it clean of dirt as best he could, Hercules rammed it down securely on his head, and his disguise was complete.

Climbing back into the driver's seat of the half-track – taking a moment to wipe a smear of blood and grey, soupy gruel from the steering column with his handkerchief – he turned the key in the ignition and felt the tension in his body ease as the engine started at the first attempt.

But he could hear something else over the purr of the rumbling half-track. He could hear the rattle of gunfire. He could hear desperate, shouted orders and agonised screams; the revving of engines and the dull boom of explosions. Worst of all, he could hear a monstrous roaring over the rattling report of machine-gun fire.

It sounded like an all-out battle, and it was coming from beyond the spur of trees ahead of him. It was coming from the crash-site.

If he turned the half-track around and headed east, he would be heading back towards the watch-post and into the jaws of the enemy. If he were to continue towards the direction of the crash-site, towards the sounds of battle, under cover of the conflict he might be able to find another route to take him away from here.

He found himself trying to recall the layout of roads he had seen as he parachuted to the ground, but he had been able to make out very little and certainly not enough to create a map of roadways in the vicinity.

Something else made him turn the half-track back towards the crash-site and the sounds of battle as well. It was a persistent, nagging doubt. What could the Nazis have run into at the heart of their own territory that had them embroiled in such a violent battle for their lives?

But as he drove on along the dirt track the sounds of battle faded, and the cries of the wounded were cut off, until only the crackle of flames remained.

Rounding the spur of woodland, Hercules came upon the crash-site. Clouds of grey smoke drifted past him, revealing a scene of utter devastation.

The twisted metal skeleton of the *Baron von Richthofen* lay in the middle of a field and half across the road itself, thick black smoke still billowing from the burning wreckage. But that was not the worst of it.

The truck that had passed Hercules on the road lay on its side, its front axle broken, its cab torn in two. The bodies of dead German soldiers lay underneath it as well as on top.

More bodies lay in the churned mud of the field, broken limbs lying at weird angles. The squad car had been flipped onto its roof. Another vehicle lay against a tree, its side panels buckled, something like the imprint of a giant fist at the centre of the dented metal.

Not a single body stirred. All appeared dead.

What could have done something like this?

The longer his gaze lingered, the more he could see that this scene of devastation was focused upon one spot. Crumpled cars, dead soldiers, a thousand shell casings, and at the centre of it all, half buried in the mud of the field, was Doctor Jekyll's cryogenic capsule. And it was empty.

Another body lay amidst the broken Nazi Stormtroopers, one that appeared bizarrely out of place.

Bringing the half-track to a halt and killing the engine, Hercules jumped down from the driver's seat and hurried over to where the doctor lay face down in the mud.

His body was warm to the touch and slicked with sweat rather than wet with thawing ice-water. Startled, Hercules put two fingers to the hollow of the man's neck.

He was unconscious, his body streaked with blood, but more importantly, he was alive!

CHAPTER SIX

Keep Calm and Carry On

WITH THE SUN steadily climbing above the woodland canopy now, Hercules Quicksilver turned the half-track off the road and onto the overgrown green pathway that led to the outbuildings of what appeared to be an abandoned farm. Jumping down to heave open the doors of a large, dilapidated barn, he returned to the half-track and parked it inside before returning to close the doors again.

The cloying mist had cleared from between the trees and the field ditches. The sky was clear of clouds, the sun a pale disc traversing the firmament. Hercules' forecast was that it was going to be a clear, crisp October day; not the sort of day to be trekking cross-country behind enemy lines, although he doubted they'd have much choice.

With the great creaking doors shut, the interior of the barn was shrouded in reassuring gloom. The air was damp with the musty smells of mildew and old straw.

Doctor Jekyll was still where Hercules had laid him, in the back of the half-track. As Hercules lifted the unconscious man across his shoulders, he found his thoughts straying again to the nature of the beast that could have taken on an entire platoon of German soldiers, wiping them out to a man, before vanishing like the mist.

He had heard the thing – that bullish bellow. And he had seen evidence of it at the crash-site – great footprints, like those said to belong to the Abominable Snowman that stalked the snowy peaks of the Himalayas.

He hadn't dared make a full examination of the scene. There was always the fear in the back of his mind that another patrol would turn up and discover them, or that the tenacious cyber-eagles would be back. And so, having recovered alive the 'package' it was his mission to deliver, he had gone on his way as quickly as possible.

He had come across the farm a few miles north of the crash-site, at the end of a twisting, rutted trackway through the woods, and had decided that it was probably the best he would find in the foreseeable future. Jekyll needed medical attention, of that Hercules was sure – the poor man having miraculously survived the zeppelin crash without a parachute and having just been defrosted. He felt cold again now and Hercules was worried that hypothermia would set in if he didn't get the doctor warm again.

Hercules laid the unconscious man down in a pile of straw, stripped him of his wet jumpsuit, and wrapped him in an old horse blanket he found draped over one of the stalls in the barn.

The presence of fresh straw and the blanket – along with a horse harness and feed that was still dry – made Hercules wonder if perhaps the farm wasn't as deserted as he had first supposed. If so, then there was all the more reason for them not to tarry here any longer than was necessary.

With the doctor warm, cocooned in the blanket and the straw, Hercules left the security of the barn, pulling back a broken plank to remain unseen from the road as he crept out.

Jekyll needed something to eat and drink. Hercules had his hip flask with him, with a full eight fluid ounces of whisky contained within, but Jekyll needed water and, ideally, something warm inside him.

Unholstering his Luger, Hercules made his way through an overgrown vegetable garden to the whitewashed, clapboard farmhouse, keeping low until he reached a cobwebbed window and was able to peer inside. He could see nothing in the room beyond; no light, and no signs of life.

He moved to the back door and tried the handle. The latch lifted and the door gave. Pistol raised, he let it swing open. A waft of cold air escaped the scullery beyond. Warily, his senses straining, he stepped inside.

The bone-numbing cold began to leech the warmth from his body and he shivered. Clearly no one had been here for some time. The kitchen hadn't seen a fire lit in its grate for a while.

Moving to the door on the other side of the dark kitchen, he found the room beyond just as lightless and just as cold. Returning to the scullery he found another narrow door that led to the pantry. Amazingly, there on a cold shelf, was a hard rind of cheese, an earthenware jug – containing what smelt strongly of cider – and two wizened apples; a veritable feast, at that moment.

Putting his pistol away and bundling up his finds in his arms, he hurried back across the garden and returned to the barn. As he pushed the loose planks aside, something shifted in the gloom. He dropped his treasures immediately, and a moment later his gun was in his hand again and pointed at the pile of hay in the corner stall.

"Who's there?" came a weak voice from the darkness, a slight Scottish burr colouring the words. Doctor Jekyll was awake.

Hercules slowly holstered his gun, before bending down to recover the food.

"My name's Hercules Quicksilver," he said, approaching the nervous-looking wisp of a man huddled in the blanket. He seemed even smaller than the slight form Hercules had rescued from the midst of the battlefield. "I'm with Department Q."

"Department Q?"

Jekyll looked around him at the criss-crossed dusty shadows of the barn.

"Where am I?"

"Germany. Behind enemy lines," Hercules replied, kneeling down beside the shivering man and pulling the blanket closer over his nakedness.

Jekyll continued to fix him with a glassy stare, his brows knotted in bewilderment.

"What year is this?"

"What year?" Hercules said, rather too quickly. Then he thought for a moment.

He knew that Jekyll had been in cryogenic suspension, but he had no idea how long. He could have been put on ice before Germany had even started her war.

"Nineteen-forty-three," Hercules replied.

But something else was niggling him now, a thought he had been harbouring for some time, but which had slipped his mind during the unfolding drama that had accompanied their arrival behind enemy lines. And that was, why had the doctor been frozen in the first place?

In his own brief inspection of Jekyll after recovering him from the crash-site, he was amazed not to find a mark on him, not one bone broken. Which, disturbingly, meant that none of the blood streaking his clothes and hands could be his own.

But then perhaps there was something else wrong with him, that had warranted his body being frozen until something could be done to cure him, something that you couldn't see just from an external examination. Cryogenic freezing, with the hope of future cures for one's affliction, was a common enough last resort for those in Magna Britannia rich enough to afford it.

"Nineteen-forty-three?" the doctor whispered. "It doesn't seem possible." He stared at Hercules, blinking as if trying to bring his eyes into focus. "And we're in Germany, you say?"

"Yes." Hercules unstoppered the jug and held it to the doctor's blue-tinged lips. "Here, try a little of this."

Jekyll winced as the heady alcoholic vapours assailed his senses, but did as he was bidden.

"What are we doing here?" he asked, after he had taken a mouthful and Hercules lowered the earthenware jug again.

"We've been sent behind enemy lines to stop the Nazis from

building a new super-weapon that could change the course of the war," Hercules explained. "Delivering you to a rendezvous point near the town of Darmstadt was a vital part of the mission I was given by WC himself."

Jekyll just stared at him, incomprehension writ large in his eyes. "The Nazis? WC?" he said. "Who are they? And who are we at war with?"

Hercules stared back, stunned. He found himself wondering again how long Jekyll had been locked away.

"Alright," he said, taking a deep breath, realising that time was of the essence, but also understanding that Jekyll needed to be brought up to speed, "let's take it from the top."

And so he told Jekyll the whole sorry tale: how the aftermath of the First Great European War had enabled the rise to power of the Nazi party in Germany; how Hitler had set his sights on not only Europe but Magna Britannia too; how Britain had at last been forced to make good its promises to France and Belgium, the greatest nation on Earth joining the fray on 1 September 1943; and again, how Hercules Quicksilver had been instructed to deliver the frozen Doctor Jekyll to a classified location deep behind enemy lines.

Five minutes later and his explanation had done nothing to dispel the look of confusion on Henry Jekyll's face, but to deepen it.

"But why have I been included in this mission?"

Now it was Hercules turn to look confused. "I was hoping you would be able to tell me that."

"Well, I'm sorry, but I honestly have no idea."

The two of them looked at one another, united in mutual bewilderment.

"No, wait a minute." A dark expression suddenly seized the man's face, as if a cloud had passed across it. "I suppose it must be part of my penance," he said, as if voicing his own private thoughts aloud.

What penance could he mean? Hercules was about to ask, but then thought better of it. It wasn't important right now. All that mattered at that moment was the mission, and if they were to still make the rendezvous with their contact outside Darmstadt, there was no time to waste.

"Here, eat this," he said, passing the shivering man an apple. Compliantly, Jekyll took a bite.

He grimaced. "It's rotten," he complained.

"It's not rotten, it's just a bit old. Besides, it's better than nothing," Hercules countered, taking a bite of the other one. The two of them ate in silence, sharing gulps of cider from the jug to rid their mouths of the acidic taste of the apple.

"Have you any idea what happened back there?" Hercules said at last.

"Back where?" Jekyll asked, blinking at Hercules, as if his eyes were having trouble focusing.

"At the crash-site."

"There was a crash? What sort of crash? A collision on the road?"

"So I suppose you won't be able to tell me how you survived it, then. You really don't remember anything?" It was a rhetorical question; the doctor clearly had no memory of anything before waking up in the barn.

"Clearly not."

Was memory-loss, Hercules wondered, some side-effect of the freezing process?

"You do know who you are, don't you?"

"Yes, of course," the man said distantly. "I am Doctor Henry Jekyll, medical practitioner and research scientist."

"Thank God for that," Hercules said, unable to help himself. He had been beginning to wonder how their mission could ever succeed if the good doctor's memory was as riddled with holes as a piece of Swiss cheese.

The two of them fell silent again as Hercules considered the enormity of the task ahead of them and Jekyll doubtless tried to piece together the scrambled jigsaw that was his memory, as well as trying to take on board all that Hercules had told him.

"So," Jekyll said at last, his voice croaky after so long asleep in the ice, "where do we go from here?"

"Time is running out," Hercules stated bluntly. "It won't be long before more soldiers are sent to find out what happened to the others, and we don't want to run into them."

Or whatever it was that did for the rest of them, he thought to himself.

"Besides, we're still miles from the rendezvous point. Our priority has to be to make our way to Darmstadt as quickly as possible."

He looked at the slight man under the blanket, his lips set in a tight-lipped frown.

"But before we do any of that, first we have to find you some clothes. Then, as WC would put it, KBO."

"And what does KBO stand for?" the doctor asked, weakly.

"Keep buggering on!"

CHAPTER SEVEN

Hell to Pay

HERCULES CURSED HIMSELF for not stripping one of the dead soldiers of his uniform, to clothe the freezing doctor, but he didn't dare to go back there now. Who knew how long it would be before a team of investigators turned up? It was going to be enough of a challenge making their way across country to Darmstadt and the rendezvous point without arousing suspicion, and Hercules didn't fancy their chances against a whole platoon of SS Stormtroopers when the Nazi High Command found out what had happened not ten miles from the farm.

Pistol in hand once more, just to be sure, Hercules returned to the empty farmhouse and made a more thorough examination of the property.

Upstairs, in the damp, abandoned bedrooms, he found signs of the family that must have once lived there. He had no idea where they had gone now, or why they had left in such a hurry, leaving so many of their possessions behind, but he was glad that they had.

In one bedroom he found a worn suit of black cloth. It smelt of mildew and the moths had had a go at it, but it was better than nothing. Thankfully there was a rough linen shirt to go with it, and under the steel-framed bed he found a pair of old boots. They had no laces and were almost worn through at the soles, but they were better than he might have hoped for and, he reasoned, beggars couldn't be choosers.

Back in the barn once more, he helped the still-unsteady Jekyll into his new suit of not so new clothes. The trousers were loose about his waist, but they would have to do.

He placed everything else he had collected from the house into the back of the half-track, and opened the barn doors. With the doctor sat in the cab beside him, the horse blanket around his shoulders, Hercules started the engine and steered the half-track out of the outbuilding, following the track away from the farm.

It was close on two hours after dawn. On reaching the main road – if the dirt track that had first brought them to the farm could be called that – ensuring that his cap was pulled down tight over his head, Hercules turned west, away from the watchtower.

It wasn't until another hour later that he took a turning cross-country, following a road beside a river that led them north through the apple orchards and pig-farms of a number of run-down hamlets.

Taking out the painted silk map that was hidden inside one boot heel, Hercules consulted the contour lines and road routes there revealed. He wasn't sure how long the fuel in the half-track's tank would last, or what other obstacles they might run into on the way to Darmstadt, but by giving the watchtower a wide berth he guessed that they would be on the road for a day at least. He only hoped that their contact would wait for them, otherwise their mission could still all-too-easily end in failure.

IT WAS ONLY a matter of hours before Lieutenant Eichmann and his senior staff reached the site of the wreck of the *Baron von Richthofen* themselves. Their initial reaction was one of utter shock, which soon changed into disbelief, and then anger and recrimination.

But questions of how such a total rout could have occurred in the middle of German-held territory soon gave way to a desire to know what had happened and what could possibly have done such a thing.

There was no evidence that the zeppelin had been carrying a crack commando squad that could have survived the crash and wiped out the force sent to secure the crash-site. Even if it had, given the amount of firepower unleashed at the scene, Eichmann would have quite rightly expected a number of casualties on the other side too, and yet there was no evidence of any.

Closer inspection found only shell-casings from German guns, so again, unless this mysterious commando squad – who seemed to have vanished like mist with the coming dawn – had captured German weaponry, there was no explanation for what had happened here. The devastation certainly didn't look like a fire-fight between opposing forces. It looked more like somebody had set about the platoon with a wrecking ball.

And so Eichmann and his men had started to try to unpick the pieces of the puzzle. The dead and wounded were stretchered away. There weren't many of the latter, and none of them were in any state to be interrogated.

He had been obligated to report the incident to High Command, of course, although he knew what the consequences for him would be.

He was proved right at dawn the next day, when the rumble of more vehicles on the road interrupted his own ongoing examination of the crash-site and the wreckage of the *Baron von Richthofen*. The fires had been doused, the twisted metal struts of the airship's superstructure *plinking* as they cooled in the chill of morning and looking like the bones of some great iron whale.

"Sir," a young corporal called to him, the blond-haired boy running over the muddied field towards the crumpled carriage where Eichmann was busy examining the instruments on board.

"What is it?" he snapped.

"Lieutenant-Colonel Teufel is here."

Eichmann felt a shiver course down the length of his spine and swallowed hard. "Gods, that's all we need."

He had feared that the SS would send one of their own to find out what had happened, but he had prayed that it wouldn't be Teufel. Teufel was the very Devil himself.

"Is the bitch with him?"

"If you mean Major Haupstein, sir," the boy said, suddenly looking uncomfortable, "then yes."

"Then there'll be hell to pay."

Lieutenant Eichmann straightened his back and his jacket, took a deep breath, and turned towards the crumpled door.

This was it. This would be the end of his career, he was sure of it. He was in command of look-out post Valkyrie 7, and this disaster had befallen on his watch. There was no escaping that fact. Good German soldiers had died and others had been brutally injured. Someone would have to pay the price for that loss, and Eichmann knew it would be him.

Taking off his cap, Eichmann swept the fingers of one hand through his hair before replacing the hat. If he was going to go down for this, at least he would do it with pride, facing his future proudly.

Ducking his head under the buckled lintel of the doorframe, he stepped out into the cold morning to face Teufel's icy wrath.

"Ah, Lieutenant – Eichmann, isn't it?" the lean-faced, black-suited Lieutenant-Colonel said, one eyebrow raised archly and a cruel smile playing about his lips. He slowly, and pointedly, removed his black leather gloves. "There you are."

Teufel was in his mid-fifties, his hair thin and grey, his face as sharp and cruel as a blade, his grey skin showing signs of liver spots. But he possessed a lean, wiry physique that Eichmann had already heard, from others, you underestimated at your cost. It was said he had the ear of Himmler himself and that even members of Hitler's High Command back in Berlin shuddered at the mere mention of his name. Not for nothing was he known as the Devil in Black.

But as if his own intimidating reputation wasn't enough, Teufel was always accompanied by his personal enforcer, Major

Isla von Haupstein. Some said that she was more than just his adjutant, that she was his own private assassin – loyal to him above all others, including the Führer – and some even went so far as to suggest that the Devil and the Bitch were lovers. But Eichmann didn't know of anyone who had ever suggested such a thing within earshot of either of them; at least, no one still living.

The major filled her tight-fitting uniform perfectly. Her body was taut and muscled, like a coiled spring that – he had heard – could be unleashed in a display of deadly savagery at the merest word from Teufel.

Lieutenant Eichmann saluted smartly, his body rigid as he extended his right arm out in front of him. "*Seig Heil!*"

"Quite," Teufel said, dismissing Eichmann's salute with a wave of the hand in which he was now holding his gloves.

He waved next at the churned and bloody mud, and the burnt and upended vehicles all around them, as he strode towards the taller Eichmann. "And this," he said, still smiling, "this is your responsibility?"

"Lieutenant-Colonel, the incident occurred during my –"

The slap with the gloves was more of a shock than it was painful, but it stopped Eichmann mid-sentence nonetheless. It was embarrassing more than anything else, to be treated in such a manner in front of the men under his command.

But the silence that followed was most painful of all; a collective holding of breath. He could feel the heat of shame and embarrassment spreading across his face.

"Now," Teufel said, in the same disturbingly calm manner. "Tell me some good news."

"Some good news?" Eichmann repeated hesitantly, fearing more humiliation.

"Yes, Lieutenant," Teufel said, still smiling. "Something that will demonstrate to me that you are not a complete incompetent."

"Well…" Eichmann hesitated, his nerves suddenly getting the better of him. As his cheeks burned, he desperately tried to think of anything that he could tell the Devil that wouldn't see him receive another shaming slap. "We found the body of Lieutenant Kunze and his driver."

Teufel let his gaze drift across the churned-up expanse of the crash-site. "It would appear, Lieutenant, that you have discovered a great many bodies. Too many."

"But Kunze and his driver, Private Lang, were found hidden in a ditch back along the road."

"I see."

An awkward silence fell as Teufel waited expectantly for Eichmann to continue. Haupstein stared at him, wearing a hungry, wolfish expression. The Major was beautiful, there was no denying that, but hers was the savage beauty of a tiger, scimitar claws outstretched.

Unable to endure the discomforting silence any longer, Eichmann felt compelled to speak.

"Kunze was travelling by half-track. But the lieutenant never made it this far."

"I see," Teufel mused, chewing at his bottom lip. "And is there any sign of the Lieutenant Kunze's transport here?"

"No, sir."

Teufel continued to chew his lip as he chewed over the evidence in his mind. "So we have a spy operating behind enemy lines, possibly masquerading as one of our own. And you consider this *good* news, Lieutenant?"

Eichmann swallowed hard, feeling his gorge rising in his throat.

"Is there anything else you can tell me that will sweeten the pill?"

"There's this," Eichmann said, pointing at the open casket, still stuck in the mud where it must have landed during the crash.

"And what is *this*?" Teufel asked quietly, shaking his gloves at the gleaming steel pod.

"It would appear to be a cryogenic containment unit," Eichmann explained.

"A cryogenic containment unit," Teufel repeated. "How wonderful. And was it occupied?"

"It was, but not anymore."

"I can see that, Lieutenant. With my own two eyes."

"I mean, Lieutenant-Colonel," Eichmann gabbled, "it had already been evacuated by the time we got here."

"I see."

Teufel paced across the field towards the pod. The tension in Eichmann's body eased a little.

He watched as Teufel ran a finger across the wet metal as a fastidious housewife might run her finger along a shelf looking for dust after the maid had finished cleaning.

"So we have a spy running around Germany in a half-track with – shall we assume – another passenger in tow. And all this happened – as you put it – on your watch?" Teufel added quietly, his expression suddenly stern, the masking smile suddenly gone.

"Yes, Lieutenant-Colonel."

Teufel turned his back on the pod, on the wreck of the downed zeppelin and, pointedly, on Lieutenant Eichmann.

"I want road blocks set up on every road between here and Berlin and I want the cyber-eagles made airborne again so that we might find these spies before they cause any more trouble," he commanded the assembled military personnel, his men running to obey his orders without hesitation, else they be found lacking in his eyes.

Eichmann moved to do the same.

"Not you, Lieutenant," Teufel snapped, without even looking back over his shoulder.

Eichmann froze.

"Major?" the Devil said, continuing to stride away from the crash-site towards the staff car that had carried him there, without looking back once. "Show the Lieutenant how we deal with those who fail the Führer."

Smiling like a hungry tiger, Haupstein sidled up to Eichmann, her hips swaying provocatively. Eichmann swallowed hard and knew then that this was it. This was his punishment. His time was up. And the end, when it came, would be neither quick, nor merciful.

CHAPTER EIGHT

Hunted

"Do you see that?" Doctor Jekyll asked, peering at the road ahead.

"I see it," Hercules said, his eyes fixed on the road ahead, hands tightly gripping the steering wheel of the half-track.

Two hundred yards ahead, at the end of a steady gradient where the road sloped down towards the outskirts of a clinker-built clapboard village, stood the road block. It had been constructed from what appeared to be oil drums, wooden railway sleepers and a hay cart.

Behind this hastily-formed barricade had been parked a rusting oil tanker and a dun-coloured jeep displaying Nazi insignia. Three troopers and a uniformed officer stood at the side of the thin strip of road beside the barricade. The troopers' hands rested on the rifles slung over their shoulders.

"Do you think they've seen us yet?" Jekyll asked.

Hercules laughed mirthlessly. "Oh, I'd bet my life on it."

As if on cue, the guards at the checkpoint started pointing. After all, they were pretty hard to miss; what appeared to be a Nazi officer at the wheel with a farmhand sitting next to him, as they drove their half-track down the country road. It wasn't the most effective disguise ever conceived.

"So what do we do now?" Jekyll asked, a tone of rising panic in his voice. Hercules caught a glimpse of the man's whitening knuckles as he clenched the sides of his seat.

Hercules dropped down a gear, slowing the half-track to a crawl, giving himself time to think and, at the same time, hoping to allay the suspicions of the guards at the checkpoint by giving the impression that they were obediently slowing to allow themselves to be searched.

Hercules hurriedly considered his options.

If he turned off the road, he would arouse the guards' suspicions even further. The half-track wouldn't have too many problems with the terrain, ploughing its way across a furrowed field, but its open cab wouldn't afford its passengers much protection either. They were outnumbered, and Hercules didn't fancy trying to fire back at the better-armed soldiers while driving cross-country. And he couldn't exactly turn around and head back the way they had come. He would soon find the soldiers in pursuit, himself and Jekyll heading into a steadily closing vice of armour and infantry.

Of course all of these considerations might already be academic, he thought. After all, how long would it take for the rest of the troops stationed at the watchtower to find the bodies of the officer and his driver and realise that one of their half-tracks was missing?

And then there was Jekyll's abandoned cryogenic capsule. If the Germans were already looking for them, what they knew about the fugitives would have been radioed half-way across Germany by now. The lethal cyber-eagles were probably already out looking for them, tasked with finishing what they had started with the airship.

Several of the guards had their rifles raised now. Hercules rather suspected that his worst fears had been realised.

The soldiers' commanding officer began to flag down the half-track.

It was now or never. If they were going to get away from the road block alive and in a fit state to be able to continue their mission, Hercules was going to have to do something, and fast.

There were no other vehicles on the road ahead of them to create a distraction, which meant that Hercules was going to have to create one of his own.

He glanced back over his shoulder.

"I need something heavy," he hissed at Jekyll, nodding at the tarpaulin spread out in the back of the half-track.

Jekyll shot him a terrified look before leaning over the back of his seat to rummage under the tarpaulin.

Hercules dropped down another gear, the half-track's engine coughing in response. The grey-suited soldiers were taking cautious steps up the road towards them.

"Quickly!"

"Will this do?" Jekyll asked, passing Hercules a wheel-jack.

"Perfect," he replied, taking the heavy object from the doctor and bracing it between the accelerator pedal and the underside of his own seat.

The half-track began to accelerate at once.

Hercules changed up a gear and the squealing of the revving engine became a steady purr as the half-track picked up speed once more.

The accelerator was taken care of, but he would just have to hope that the steering stayed straight.

The Germans started shouting urgently as they heard the changing note of the furiously working engine and saw the half-track powered towards the checkpoint once more.

Hercules checked the speedometer.

Twenty miles an hour.

Twenty-five.

He turned to Jekyll, a look of grim determination upon his face. "Get out!"

Jekyll returned his expression with one of weak-willed doubt. "What?"

The speedometer was still creeping upwards.

"Get out now or the fall will kill you. Try to keep yourself curled in a ball and as soon as you're on the ground, keep low and make for cover in those trees." Hercules nodded towards the coppiced woodland to their left.

Thirty miles an hour.

"Now!"

Echoing strangely from tree-trunks over the ploughed field, the sound of rifle-fire reached them as the bullets themselves spanged off the front of the cab.

Jekyll gave a yelp of surprise.

Another salvo, and this time the cab's flimsy windshield shattered, causing Hercules to duck on instinct.

The good doctor didn't need any more encouragement after that. Whimpering like a toddler, he rolled himself sideways out of the cab, arms flailing, and Hercules heard the swish of grass as the panicking man rolled down the grassy bank at the side of the road.

Still keeping his head down, Hercules fought to keep the half-track on target as he shifted himself across the cab to exit on the same side of the road as Jekyll.

More bullets skidded from the bonnet, one gouging a groove in the top of the steering wheel between Hercules' hands and ricocheting off.

But the half-track was picking up speed all the time.

Thirty-five.

Forty.

There was nothing the soldiers could do to stop it.

Forty-five.

When there were fewer than thirty yards between him and the road block, Hercules launched himself out of the cab with an almighty kick.

Wind whipped through his hair as he sailed through the air, and then the wind was knocked from him as he landed in the ditch, jarring his shoulder. Biting his lip against the pain, Hercules rolled over and threw himself flat amidst the tussocks of knotty grass in the bottom of the leaf-clogged hollow.

Over the roar of the half-track's engine he could hear the incredulous cries of the soldiers as they ran from the vehicle's hurtling approach.

Hands over his head to shield himself from falling debris, Hercules listened, panting, as the half-track collided with the barricade at over fifty miles an hour. He heard the tearing of metal, the splintering explosion of wood being pulverised and an ear-rending scream.

For a moment, compared to the initial collision at least, near-silence descended. The only sounds he could hear now were the screams of the Germans and the tractionless revving of the half-track as it left the ground. And then the hurtling half-track hit the road again in a cacophony of crashing white noise.

Hercules felt the impact of its crash-landing on the other side of the barricade through the earth under him and felt the heat-wash of flames as the half-track's fuel tank went up.

The cries of the Germans became banshee shrieks and Hercules dared raise his head for the first time since coming to ground.

The road block was a mess. The half-track had ploughed right through the middle of it, tearing the barricade apart and smashing the hay cart to smithereens before taking to the air for a few seconds and crashing down to the ground, landing on top of the jeep. The two machines were now burning merrily, as was one of the bodies lying face-down on the road. The burning man twitched every now and again but eerily made no sound whatsoever.

Another of the soldiers was crawling across the road towards his fallen rifle, leaving a trail of blood on the tarmac behind him.

Picking himself up out of the mud, Hercules made for the line of trees not thirty yards away, making it into the green gloom beneath the trees before anyone spotted him.

Once he was sheltered by the bracken that grew between the trees, he cast his eyes along the road. Of the four men who had been manning the make-shift checkpoint, one was clearly dead, his skull crushed to a pulp by a railway sleeper, one appeared to be mortally wounded, his intestines spread out across the road, and then there was the burning man, of course. But of the fourth, the officer, he could see no sign.

Gun in hand once more, he turned, hearing what sounded like

a wild boar crashing through the undergrowth towards him. It wasn't a boar; it was Henry Jekyll. The man was as white as a sheet, apart from the strange flecks of green Hercules could see in the corners of his anxious eyes.

Hercules shushed him with a finger on his own silent lips, and blazing anger in his own eyes. Jekyll took the hint, a grimace on his face. Moving more carefully now, he caught up with Hercules at last.

"Follow me," Hercules hissed, setting off east through the forest as stealthily as he could but always with one eye on the road beyond the treeline to their right.

He stopped abruptly and turned back to face Jekyll, the same thunderous look of annoyance on his face. "And try not to make any more noise," he glowered.

CHAPTER NINE

Call of Duty

THANKFULLY, THE GRIMLY resolute Hercules and the agitated Doctor Jekyll didn't run into any more trouble after the checkpoint. If any of the soldiers on duty had survived their run-in with the runaway half-track, they had obviously decided that discretion was the better part of valour and decided not to pursue the fugitives themselves. Chances were, however, that they would have alerted others of their encounter, and so it could only be a matter of time before they did eventually run into trouble again.

They took a break to clean themselves up a bit, so that they might maintain the illusion just a little longer, at a distance at least. Thirty minutes after evading the roadblock, they emerged from the wood, negotiated a barbed wire fence running the length of a turnip field, and crossed a low bridge into what a peeling signboard claimed was the small town of Alsenz.

Alsenz was all whitewash and timber buildings and pleasant paved squares, spread out along the length of a river in spate.

It was a pretty place, Hercules thought, but its beauty was besmirched by the proliferation of barbed wire, concrete road blocks and Nazi banners that adorned the Rathaus and other public buildings in the town.

It wasn't a big place and the streets were eerily quiet, but the abundance of eagle-emblazoned staff cars and troop transports attested to there being a large Nazi presence in the town. Hercules' only question was, where were they?

"What are we doing?" Jekyll hissed in agitation, whilst trotting to keep up with the striding Hercules.

"We're seeing our mission through to the bitter end."

"Your mission maybe," Jekyll retorted, "but not mine!"

"You're as mixed up in this now as I am, doctor," Hercules bit back, suddenly turning on him. "Forget your 'penance'; just do your duty to the Crown, man, that's all that's being asked of you."

Jekyll's own expression darkened, and was it just his imagination, or did Hercules see a ripple of green light in the man's eyes?

"Now do you think you can start behaving as if you're meant to be here rather than shuffling around the place like some skittish pony?"

"But we're *not* meant to be here," Jekyll insisted, shooting anxious, darting glances at the silent buildings all around them. Who knew who might be watching from behind their shuttered windows? "I mean, what are we doing walking right into the middle of an occupied town when you've just gone and crashed a half-track into a road block? That's hardly operating undercover now, is it?"

"If you do anything confidently enough, it's my experience that you can practically get away with murder, and," Hercules added, "on more than one occasion I have."

"But come on! As soon as we open our mouths we'll be rumbled straight away."

Hercules sighed. "Then *you'd* better keep your mouth shut."

Jekyll opened his mouth to protest again. The sound of music and merry-making wafted towards them across the platz from a large timber-and-daub building taking up one whole side of the square.

"Have you never heard the expression 'hide in plain sight,' doctor?"

Jekyll raised an eyebrow, but before he could reply, Hercules turned sharply on his heel and made for the entrance to the building. Above the door hung a painted tavern sign bearing the peeling paint image of a foamy stein of beer.

Tugging at his jacket, trying to dislodge a few more creases, Hercules brushed the drying mud from his knees once again, shined the toecaps of his jackboots against the back of his trousers, and boldly pushed open the door.

It was only around eleven in the morning, but noise and tobacco smoke wafted out of the undercroft of the *bierkeller* over him like the warm embrace of a chain-smoking uncle.

Hercules sensed Jekyll tense behind him. He half expected some sort of startled reaction from the military personnel – regular troopers and ranking officers – congregated at the bar and crowding the tables spread throughout the cellar, but the few who turned to see who had just arrived, turned away again in disinterest a moment later. As far as they were concerned, another officer looking for a drink and somewhere to unwind for a couple of hours was nothing to remark upon, even if he did have a civilian in tow.

That said, Hercules did pick up on the tension in a group seated on the other side of the bar in the corner to his right. But they behaved as if they were the hunted rather than the hunter.

It didn't take Hercules long to realise why his arrival had still gone almost totally unnoticed. There was something much more distracting, not to say appealing, on the semi-circular stage, beyond the bar, on the other side of the undercroft.

The dancing girls were in town.

DIETER VON STAUFFENBERG picked up his glass of schnapps from the age-blackened bar top, his gaze lingering a moment longer on the officer who had just entered the bierkeller, along with the black-suited civilian.

Moving away from the bar, casting as many furtive glances

around the undercroft as he did at the pretty girls parading themselves on stage, accompanied by the *oom-pah-pahs* of an enthusiastic, if less than perfectly in tune, brass quartet, he made his way as casually as he could to the table in the corner.

The three men already seated there looked up, their expressions drawn and pale, as he took his place among them.

"Gentlemen," von Stauffenberg said, smiling grimly.

The others nodded or grunted their greetings in return. Von Stauffenberg cast his eyes around the table. There was grey-haired Colonel Vogel, looking as if he were chewing a wasp. Next to him sat Major General Olbricht, teasing at his moustache nervously with one hand. Leaning back in the chair next to his was Lieutenant Griffin, the finest example of Aryan perfection von Stauffenberg had ever seen, while beside him, the less-than-perfect Major Schenk sat perched at the edge of his chair, compulsively polishing his spectacles with a monogramed handkerchief.

Vogel poured himself another glass of schnapps from the bottle in front of him, without offering anyone else any, and knocked it back in one go. "If we're all here, I'd like to make a start. This business is unpleasant enough without having to concern ourselves with it any longer than is strictly necessary."

Von Stauffenberg cast his gaze around the table once more and then again at the bierkeller beyond their conspiratorial corner. "But we're not all here. Where's Kemmler?"

"Kemmler's not coming," Vogel said.

"What do you mean, he's not coming?"

"There was an incident in Berlin. He's not coming."

"Then we have to stop this now," von Stauffenberg hissed. "If Kemmler's been compromised our whole enterprise could be in danger."

Von Stauffenberg moved to stand, as if the Gestapo were about to come through the door of the tavern right there and then, his chair squealing against the stone flags. Startled by the sudden noise, soldiers at nearby tables broke off from watching the six pretty girls cavorting their way through a can-can on stage, to look at them. Von Stauffenberg withered under half a dozen severe frowns.

"Calm down, Dieter," Vogel said, motioning with his hands that von Stauffenberg should remain seated.

"Calm down?" he hissed. "How can you be so offhand about all this? You do understand the consequences of what we're planning to do, don't you?"

Vogel shot him a weary glare.

"We're talking about taking down Hitler's regime, not going for a picnic at the park! We have to abort right now and regroup at a later date, only once we can be sure Kemmler hasn't told them anything."

"Things have progressed too far for us to stop now," Olbricht stated in a voice that was too unnervingly quiet and unnervingly calm, given the current topic of conversation. "The Icarus Project is nearing its final phase. If we don't act now there may never be another opportunity. Germany will win this war and then Hitler will march on Magna Britannia itself."

"Then we have to act now and act fast," von Stauffenberg said. "Are we ready to do that?" he asked, looking at Major Schenk.

Schenk looked worried. He opened his mouth to speak, but before he could say anything, Griffin interrupted him.

"Of course we're ready," Griffin growled.

Judging by Schenk's nervous demeanour, the logistics member of the team was anything but.

"No, I don't like the sound of this," von Stauffenberg murmured. "I don't like the sound of this at all."

He shot paranoid glances around the room, at the parties of enlisted officers, at the sweating, greasy barkeep, even at the pretty young things on the stage, as if expecting any of them to reveal themselves to be Gestapo plants or onto their rebellious plan at any moment. He got to his feet.

"I'm leaving. And if the rest of you have any sense, you'll do the same thing."

Vogel made to stand as well, hands raised once more.

The crash of the bierkeller door opening sounded like a thunderclap to von Stauffenberg, making him start, instantly dropping back into his seat. Vogel didn't move a muscle.

Von Stauffenberg watched Vogel and Olbricht as their eyes tracked whoever it was who had just entered the fug of the bar.

"Who is it?" he whispered through clenched teeth.

"Kaufman," Vogel hissed.

"Relax," Olbricht breathed between barely open lips. "You're going to draw attention to yourself otherwise. Just enjoy the girls like everyone else."

His heart racing, von Stauffenberg turned in his chair, draping an arm over the back in what he hoped was a suitably relaxed manner. It seemed to him that everyone in the bar was a little less relaxed than they were a moment before and he found his eyes inevitably straying to where a man in a black trench coat and wide-brimmed black hat stood flanked by two Schutzstaffel troopers.

"Keep your eyes on the dancing girls," he heard Olbricht whisper behind him, "and that way we might all just get out of here alive."

THE GIRLS CAVORTING about the stage, in sequin-embroidered bodices, feathered headdresses and long taffeta skirts, kept watchful eyes on the handsome new arrival and his companion as they barged their way between the crowded tables, searching for someone.

They spun and whirled to the parping of the tuba and as they ran together towards the back of the stage, accompanied by a *glissando* slide on the trombone, one of the girls – her raven-black hair tied in a long plait behind her head – kicked up her skirts and went for the pistol secured within its suspender-holster at her thigh.

At the same moment, a long-legged blonde gracefully glided over to her, putting out a hand to hold her back.

"Steady, Missy," the blonde whispered into the gunwoman's ear. "Not so fast. We don't want to blow our cover."

Missy let her hand slip from her thigh and the two girls spun away from each other with a renewed burst of whooping and scandalous, undergarment-revealing high kicks.

The blonde scanned the other girls' faces. Even as they continued with their routine, to the delight of the troops who had come to Alsenz for a little R&R, she could see that they were all keeping a weather eye on the SS agent and his bodyguard.

Cookie, she thought to herself, *you don't know what's going on between the Germans. Until someone starts shooting, it isn't your concern.*

The pug-faced Gestapo agent continued to ignore the girls' performance, peering myopically through the hazy curtains of tobacco smoke, his mouth screwed into a sour grimace, and passing the stage without so much as a sideways glance.

Cookie met the eyes of each of the other five girls in turn as they linked arms in a circle, spinning across the rattling boards of the makeshift stage, giving each of the girls a wink in turn that said, "Keep up the pretence a little longer but watch for my signal."

And with that Jinx and Cat parted and pranced backwards, moving away from one another, but keeping a tight hold of Dina and Trixie by the waist as they stretched out in a line across the stage. Once they were in a straight line again, the girls broke into another cancan, to the cheers and wolf whistles of those soldiers still absorbed in the show and lost in the moment.

"WHO ARE THEY?" Jekyll whispered, his stale breath rank in Hercules' nostrils as he leaned forward. The pale lager on the table in front of him remained untouched.

Hercules picked up his own glass and knocked back the measure of schnapps it contained, grateful for the heady alcoholic vapour as it swept away the stink of the defrosted doctor's cryo-sleep halitosis.

"The Gestapo," Hercules muttered out of the corner of his mouth, "Himmler's secret police." Nasty bastards, employed to make sure that the rest of Hitler's forces obeyed their Führer's implacable will, Hercules thought, his knitted brows betraying his dark thoughts.

Still facing the stage, Hercules stared at the glass he was slowly turning in his hand, but focused on the distorted reflection of the agent and his bodyguards.

"I don't like it," Hercules murmured, returning his gaze to the dancers on the stage.

"You think they're here for us?" Jekyll asked, a rising note of panic in his voice.

"I don't know, but I think it's high time we got out of here." Hercules slid his chair back carefully.

"No sudden movements now. Just finish your drink and make for the door."

The two men got up from their seats, Jekyll knocking back his lager, as Hercules began to ease his way through the crowd, with a ready apology in fluent German on his lips. "Entschuldigung. Entschuldigung."

"Stop! Halt!" came the harsh cry from the other side of the bar.

Moving with more urgency now, Hercules kept going for the door. He didn't dare look back to see what was going on, to even check if it was he who was being ordered to stop.

"Halt!" the command came again, stronger this time, so loud that the band burped and parped their way into silence.

Hercules ran for the door, only glancing back over his shoulder to make sure that Jekyll was keeping up.

The bierkeller entrance loomed ahead of him, as did the two muscle-bound young men in uniform who were striving to get there first and intercept him.

"WE'VE BEEN RUMBLED!" von Stauffenberg snarled, leaping from his seat and turning on Olbricht.

"Colonel Stauffenberg!" the bitter-faced Agent Kaufman called across the bar, turning to face the corner table.

"We have now, you bloody idiot!" Olbricht retorted as he too got to his feet.

As one, von Stauffenberg's co-conspirators leapt to their feet, chairs clattering to the floor as they went for their guns.

"For the Resistance!" Olbricht shouted, taking aim and firing.

CHAPTER TEN

All Hell

IN THE INSTANT immediately following the pistol shot, a fragile silence descended over the bar. Then it shattered as the bierkeller was subsumed by a cacophony of shouts, screams and breaking glass, tables overturning in the panic and confusion.

Von Stauffenberg followed the trajectory of the Major General's single shot, having to know if Kaufman had been eliminated or not.

Kaufman glared back at him, a blazing inferno of hellish hatred in his eyes. The bodyguard beside him had a hand to the side of his head, a disgruntled look on his face and blood pouring between his fingers from where half his ear had been blown clean off.

"Arrest them!" Kaufman screeched, pointing at von Stauffenberg and his companions.

Von Stauffenberg's pulse raced. He knew their situation was hopeless now, but that didn't stop the warrior within him wanting to fight his way to the end.

His own pistol – a Mauser C96 – in his hand, he picked his target and fired at the advancing soldier. The report was deadened by the acoustics of the crowded bierkeller, and he felt the kick of the pistol against his palm.

The bodyguard fell face first across a table, sending steins of beer and half-drunk bottles of wine tumbling to the floor, accompanied by the sound of breaking glass.

Von Stauffenberg levelled his pistol at the other approaching bodyguard.

But the rest of the bierkeller clientele had cottoned onto what was going on now. As von Stauffenberg tightened his finger around the trigger, a chair struck him solidly between the shoulder blades.

He stumbled forwards, reeling from the shock and pain of the blow. His aim suddenly awry, the gun went off in his hand, the bullet smacking into the solid stone flags at his feet.

Knowing that another attack must be coming, von Stauffenberg turned, swinging his gun around with him.

The chair connected with him again on the back stroke, its support struts breaking against his arm and sending the gun flying from his hand to land under a table.

Von Stauffenberg lost his balance altogether, falling backwards onto his arse amidst the sodden sawdust and spilled beer covering the floor. Unarmed and unbalanced, he prepared for the worst.

Another shot rang out and Agent Kaufman gave voice to an unnerving, womanly sound.

The soldier that had floored von Stauffenberg cast aside the broken chair and stalked towards the unarmed colonel, pushing up his shirt sleeves as he did so, ready to give the traitor the beating of his life.

But before he could lay a single punch against the debilitated von Stauffenberg, Griffin took hold of the soldier's head with both hands and, biceps bulging under his uniform, twisting sharply.

There was an audible crack and the thug's eyes rolled up into his head until only the whites were visible. As Griffin let go again, the man slumped lifelessly to the floor, half landing on top of von Stauffenberg.

Von Stauffenberg twisted round, wondering what had happened to Kaufman to make him cry out. And then he caught sight of the trench-coated agent, hunched over but still standing, his right hand clasped tightly to his left side.

It was only desperation that had driven Olbricht to start shooting, an undeniable knowledge that their endeavour was doomed. Months of planning and it had come to this. Perhaps he had seen no other option but to try to shoot his way out. Perhaps he had thought that if they were all done for, then he was going to try and take as many of the Führer's lapdogs with him as possible.

In the close confines of the bierkeller, the officers and soldiers were reluctant to arm themselves and join in the gun play – except for Agent Kaufman.

A slim black Walther P38 was gripped in the agent's hand now, its barrel pointed at von Stauffenberg. Not that von Stauffenberg knew that, not until he heard the muffled crack of the gunshot. Pain exploded through his head and the black gulf of oblivion took him.

"TAKE COVER!" COOKIE screamed at the dancing troupe.

The six girls threw themselves off the back of the stage and into the narrow crawl-space between the jerry-rigged platform and the wall.

Keeping her head down, Cookie glanced to her left and saw Dina, Trixie, Cat, Jinx and Missy all staring back at her, their eyes wide with the rush of adrenalin, ready to spring into action at a second's notice. Missy's pistol – a Smith and Wesson – was already in her hand. Cookie held her at bay once again with a simple wave of her hand.

Cautiously, listening to the crash of tables and glasses, the shouts of the startled men and the occasional sharp report of a handgun, Cookie dared to peek above the edge of the stage again at the bar beyond.

The bierkeller was a riot of chaos and confusion. As far as Cookie could tell, the Germans seemed to be fighting each other. The black-coated Gestapo agent was now engaged in a fracas with a group of apparently high-ranking Nazi officers.

On the other side of the room, the British spy and his companion were also facing opposition as they made for the door. She hadn't been certain it was them at first, but seeing how the British agent had blown his cover prematurely – even though there had been no need to do so – there was no doubt in her mind now.

"It's alright, girls," she whispered so all of them could hear, "we're good." The taut strings of a piano sang out as a stray bullet struck the ancient upright. "Our cover's still good. So, the plan is, we get out of here and prepare for the moment to strike, but not now. Follow me."

She turned and, crouching behind the makeshift stage, made for the door that led to the bar's back-room and freedom.

This wasn't their fight. Their fight was yet to come. And Cookie was determined that they would be ready for it.

HERCULES QUICKSILVER HAD hoped that the drama playing out on the other side of the cellar would cover his and Jekyll's escape. But the two well-built soldiers between them and the door advanced on them, hands going for their own holstered firearms.

Hercules decided that there wasn't time to draw his own pistol. To give him and the doctor the best chance of getting out of the bierkeller at all, there was nothing else for it.

He dived forwards, launching himself at the legs of the man closest to him. It was a rugby tackle his old games master at Eton would have been proud of.

The man went flying, arms flailing as he fought futilely to keep his balance. As he fell, he toppled into his fellow, sending the other man crashing into a table.

"Get his gun!" Hercules shouted as he fought to keep hold of the German's furiously thrashing legs. He didn't exactly know where to take things from here, but he reasoned that if Jekyll could grab the soldier's gun, it would give them a fighting chance of getting out of there alive.

Hercules swore as he wrestled the man's legs. Jekyll had been right; coming into the tavern had put the mission at risk all over again. He didn't know how viable it would be now – they hadn't even made the rendezvous at Darmstadt. All he was worried about right now was surviving for another second, and another, and the one after that...

Hercules glanced up at Jekyll. The wretch was still shuffling from one foot to the other indecisively, shooting longing glances at the exit as if wondering whether to abandon Hercules altogether, and leave him to sort out his own mess. But Hercules wasn't going to give him that option.

"Get his gun!" he screamed again.

A full-on fight had broken out in the bar, but who was to say how long it would be before the Gestapo managed to quell the disturbance again, leaving the agent and his men free to move on Hercules, his cover well and truly blown?

With a reluctant, almost repulsed look in his eyes, as if he were being asked to pick up a dead dog's mouldering carcass with his bare hands, Jekyll bent down and teased the man's pistol from its holster and pointed it shakily at the other man.

Hercules scrambled to his feet and the doctor's side, taking out his own gun.

As the two soldiers climbed to their feet, Hercules shouted at them in German: "Stay where you are. Try to follow us and we'll put a bullet through your brain!"

With the bierkeller dissolving into chaos behind them, the men did as they were told and stayed where they were.

"What did you say?" Jekyll asked in bewilderment.

"Come on," Hercules said, picking his purloined cap from where it had fallen on the floor during the struggle. "We're out of here – now!"

Guns trained on the two soldiers, with the rest of the Nazis preoccupied by the internecine warfare now engulfing the drinking den, the two British spies backed out of the door and into the cold light of day.

"Right," Hercules said as the door swung shut before them, "now we just need to find ourselves some more transport."

He was still turning from the tavern door when the heavy blow connected with the back of his head and he dropped to the ground, out cold.

*   *   *

TEN MINUTES LATER, with the situation inside the bierkeller under control, still clutching his bleeding hand to his chest – his coat hanging from his thin shoulders – Agent Kaufman emerged from the dingy undercroft to be presented with an unexpected prize.

He looked down at the unconscious colonel and then at the emaciated man now held fast in the grip of his driver. An ophidian smile spread across his thin, bloodless lips and a snort of triumph escaped his nose.

"What do you want done with them, Herr Kaufman?" his driver asked.

Kaufman grunted as he considered his prisoners, one conscious, one not. The man's suspicious behaviour in the cellar, and the determination with which he had tried to leave when the Resistance gave themselves away, had been enough to rouse Kaufman's own suspicions.

"Have them taken to Schloss Geisterhaus along with von Stauffenberg and the others. It would appear that I have a busy day ahead of me after all," he added, a malicious twinkle in his eye.

CHAPTER ELEVEN

Secrets and Lies

DIETER VON STAUFFENBERG blearily opened his eyes, and immediately wished he hadn't. Wherever he was, he was still in darkness, but on waking, his stinging headache had returned with renewed ferocity. The pain was focused upon his forehead.

He went to put a hand to his brow, only to find that his hands had been cuffed behind his back and secured to the back of his chair.

Through half-closed eyes, he took in the room in which he now found himself. He wasn't in total darkness. Light leaked in around a door set in an ill-matched frame and, as he became accustomed to the gloom, details begin to resolve themselves.

There were dusty, cobwebbed wine racks and heaps of forgotten coal. A bucket and mop stood in one corner, and he could hear water dripping from a tap or a pipe somewhere. The musty smell of damp was undercut with the ammonia reek of detergent.

Shifting his weight, he tried to shuffle the chair around to see what was behind him, but realised that his ankles had been secured to the chair as well, and the chair bolted to the floor.

Anger welled up within him. Kemmler must have betrayed them, whether willingly or otherwise. Back at the bierkeller he'd thought them all dead men once the shooting started, but here he was, chained up like an recalcitrant Rottweiler and still alive. And as long as he remained that way, he would fight for what was left of his life with every ounce of strength, determination and courage left inside him.

He jerked and thrashed against the chair until the sinews in his neck stood out and a vein throbbed at his temple. A howl of rage escaped his foam-flecked lips, as it all proved to be to no avail.

His body sagged, the fight gone out of him, for the moment. Sweat beaded his brow, his flesh goose-pimpling in the cold of the dank wine cellar. His head pounded.

Doing his best to ignore the pain, he turned his thoughts inward, trying to piece together the events that had brought him to this point.

He remembered the bierkeller, the sharp smell of tobacco in the air; he remembered meeting with the other members of the Resistance. Kaufman's sneering face swam into view and the gunshot echoed through his memory.

He knew how he came to be here, he just had no idea where 'here' was.

The sharp scrape of warped wood on stone and the squeal of rusted hinges made von Stauffenberg start as amber light, the colour of malt whisky, poured into the cellar.

A scarecrow figure stepped into the rectangle of light, silhouetted for a moment against the brightness behind, and then Agent Heinrich Kaufman entered the cellar alone.

Closing the door carefully behind him, he approached the chair, the *tap-tap* of his heels as loud as drum beats in the confines of the cellar. Von Stauffenberg saw that the man's right arm was now in a sling, the hand bound with bandages.

"So," Kaufman said, "you are awake."

Von Stauffenberg glared at him, eyes narrowed, cold hatred burning within the black pits of his pupils.

"Tell me," the Gestapo agent said, "how did you ever think your plan could possibly succeed?"

Von Stauffenberg snorted. "What plan?" His voice was cracked. His throat felt as rough as sandpaper.

"Come, come, Herr Colonel," Kaufman chided, a sneering smile creasing his bloodless lips. "You know that we know of your little plan, otherwise you would not be here."

"Then what are you doing here?" von Stauffenberg challenged. "If you know everything already, why come to me now? Why even take me prisoner? Why didn't you just kill me when you had the chance?"

The smile vanished from the agent's face. His expression hardened.

"Let us not play games, Herr Colonel. We are not children. Answer my questions and you can expect to be treated... mercifully. Resist and you shall suffer unending agonies, the like of which you have never known."

"Here's a thought," von Stauffenberg said. "Let me put it to you that you know next to nothing, and you only want me to believe the opposite to be true in the hope that I'll spill my guts to you and reveal all. Because – let me guess – I'm the only one you managed to take alive. Either the others managed to get away or those idiots back at the bierkeller killed them all, and I'm your only prisoner."

"Let me tell *you* something," Kaufman said, striding across the cellar, his back to von Stauffenberg. "It is a simple thing to cause a man more pain that he can endure. I would suggest you think on that before deciding how you will answer my next question."

The agent paced back across the room, heels clicking on the cold stone floor. He stopped in front of von Stauffenberg.

"Who else was involved in your little scheme? How far up does it go? I want names."

Von Stauffenberg glowered at Kaufman, his eyes smouldering with cold hatred.

"Alright," he said at last. "Assuming I had even the slightest idea what you were talking about, wouldn't you have got all this from Kemmler?"

Kaufman's ugly face remained an impassive mask. Slowly, and very deliberately, he pulled his Walther from its holster.

Von Stauffenberg couldn't stop the snigger of derision that escaped him then.

"And what do you intend to do with that? You missed last time, at near point blank range, and that was before you'd been shot in the hand yourself!"

Kaufman took a step towards him. Holding the pistol by the barrel, he brought it down sharply across von Stauffenberg's face with startling force.

He heard, as well as felt, the butt of the pistol break several of his teeth. Shock deadening the pain, he was taken aback by the amount of blood that welled up and ran from his broken mouth, down into his lap.

Just as quickly as the pain had dulled, his shock boiled into rage. But it wasn't a desperate thrashing anger. It simmered, tempered with hatred, and deep within himself, von Stauffenberg knew that one day – maybe long after Dieter von Stauffenberg was already dead – Heinrich Kaufman's time would come.

"You won't get anything from me," he growled, spitting half-congealed blood and enamel fragments from between swollen lips.

"Your loyalty and your stalwart attitude are commendable. It is only a shame that they are so misplaced."

Adjusting his grip on the gun, returning the butt to his hand, Kaufman peered myopically at his subject like a vulture trying to decide which parts of a zebra carcass to feast upon first.

"There are a thousand agonies that I could subject you to," he said, "and in the end you would say everything I wanted to hear, whether you actually knew the truth yourself or not. And so your reticence tells me far more than a confession extracted under torture ever could. You are quite right, Kemmler proved less... durable, shall we say...? and told us nearly everything we needed to know."

Kaufman lowered the barrel of the gun.

"But I have encountered your kind before, Colonel. I know when I am beaten. There is no point in me interrogating you further. That being the case, you may still be allowed to serve the Führer once again."

"Over my dead body," von Stauffenberg snarled, in a spray of bloody spit.

A slow, cruel smile spread across Agent Kaufman's lips once more. "Very well, if you insist."

Slowly he raised the gun again.

Von Stauffenberg started to laugh, great belly laughs that set his whole body shaking.

"You're going to shoot me after all?"

Kaufman took another step forward.

The laughter died in von Stauffenberg's throat.

"I can hardly miss now, can I?" the agent said, pushing the muzzle of the pistol into von Stauffenberg's stomach.

THE CRACK OF the pistol shot made the guard standing outside the cellar start and hurriedly come to attention again as he composed himself.

A few moments later the door opened and Agent Kaufman stepped out into the cold, dank passageway.

"Have the body sent to Darmstadt," Kaufman said. "Let's see if the Frankenstein Corps can't have this traitor fighting for the Fatherland again by the end of the week."

"Yes, Herr Kaufman." The soldier saluted and hurried to obey the Gestapo agent's instructions.

Not looking back once, Kaufman marched away along the corridor. They were under the house here. The manse's extensive cellars made for ideal holding cells.

The Resistance Movement had suffered a devastating set-back, thanks to his hard work. He need not concern himself with them any further. They were no longer a threat to the Third Reich.

He grimaced. His hand ached. He would have to get it looked at properly, but it could wait for the time being. Right now he was more concerned with the other two prisoners he had brought back to Schloss Geisterhaus after the raid on the Alsenz bierkeller.

What part had they to play in the rebels' meeting? Or had it been pure coincidence that had brought them to the same tavern, at the same time, on the same day? And if they hadn't been helping the German Resistance, what were they doing there, deep behind the German front line?

It had to have something to do with Darmstadt, Kaufman concluded. They were too close to the fortress-factory for that to be a coincidence.

THE MUFFLED PISTOL shot made Henry Jekyll start.

For a split second he was in another place, another time, the sound of a pistol shot echoing through his mind, knowing that he had been pointing the gun at himself. And then it was gone again.

Jekyll grasped the arms of the chair to which he had been chained, knuckles whitening as he tugged at the wood, the metal cuffs biting into the sparse flesh of his wrists.

His pulse leapt, his mind awash with questions. Who had fired the gun? Who had been shot? Was this the first sign of a rescue attempt? Or was it the first execution?

He cursed the moment Hercules Quicksilver had ever taken him from the facility in Edinburgh.

He pulled frantically at the chains securing him again, blinking frightened tears from his eyes as a whimper of desperation escaped his lips. If only...

No! He couldn't allow himself to think like that. After all, as he knew all too well, that way madness lay.

The sudden bang of the basement door opening made him start all over again.

Standing in the open doorway was the man who had had Jekyll and the unconscious Quicksilver brought here; the one the soldiers had addressed as Herr Kaufman.

"So." Kaufman peered through his glasses at Jekyll with a hungry, hawkish stare. "Doctor Jekyll, wasn't it?"

The man's English was good, but for an unmistakeable guttural accent.

Jekyll made another feeble attempt to free himself from his bonds.

"Planning on going somewhere?" the German mocked him, pulling up another chair and sitting down.

"I warn you," Jekyll said, his breathing fast and shallow, his heart pounding in fear now, "you don't want to make me angry." His warning had sounded less assured than he might have hoped.

"Angry?" Kaufman said, his bloodless lips stretching into a thin smile. "You're not angry, doctor. You're terrified. I can almost smell your fear. Or have you just soiled yourself?"

The slap came out of nowhere. Jekyll reeled from the blow, shocked into inaction.

"How are you feeling now?" Kaufman asked and hit him again. And again.

"How about now?"

A fourth time.

A fifth.

The agent opened his mouth, ready with another goading taunt, but hesitated, brows knitting, as he caught a flash of green fire in the black pits of the doctor's pupils. It seemed to Kaufman that the temperature in the cellar had suddenly dropped and there was a frisson of some untold power in the air.

When Jekyll spoke again his voice was like steel and had dropped an octave.

"You wouldn't like me when I'm angry," he growled as emerald lightning crackled across his eyeballs.

CHAPTER TWELVE

Breakout

"ARE *YOU* THREATENING *me?*"

The Gestapo agent could not help but raise his eyebrows.

Who did he think he was? He was chained to a chair, by both his wrists and his ankles, in the labyrinthine basement of a country manse with guards at every turn, occupied by the Führer's forces. And before the guards even became an issue, this skinny, unarmed man would have to overcome Kaufman, assuming Kaufman didn't gun him down first – which he would.

"You think you can escape? You are sadly mistaken, Herr Doktor. There will be no escape for you; none whatsoever. I don't like spies. But, before I have you shot – or maybe hanged, or perhaps even electrocuted – you will tell me everything; about your mission, your reason for being here, who you were here to meet and who was working with you."

"I warned you," the doctor growled, his voice deeper again.

Was it his imagination, a trick of the light, or was the prisoner larger than he remembered? Where before he had been sure the man's arms were little more than weedy sticks of skin and bone, he now saw muscles bunching and straining at the seams of his shirt sleeves.

Agent Kaufman felt the hairs on the back of his neck stand on end. There was something, some unknowable tingling in the air around him. Was it some sort of static charge, created by he knew not what, or was it something else, a sensation he hadn't enjoyed in a long time? Was it fear?

DOCTOR HENRY JEKYLL saw the room before him subsumed by a green haze, as if he was looking at the cell through an emerald lens. His whole body ached. Muscles and sinews tightened. His blood was on fire, as if it was liquid magma that coursed through his veins.

The door behind the Gestapo agent suddenly swung open. Standing there was a long-limbed woman, lithe and tall. She was dressed in the sinister black uniform of an officer of the Schutzstaffel, her blonde hair tied up in a plait under her hat. Her tailored jacket was buttoned up across her chest, whilst tight-fitting jodhpurs followed the contours of her toned legs.

Kaufman turned, surprised, ready to rebuke whoever had dared interrupt his interrogation.

Calmly, the woman raised her handgun and pulled the trigger. There was a muffled *pfft*.

The agent was thrown backwards off his chair, which clattered to the floor after him. Jekyll looked down at the body. The man stared back, the eyes behind the thin-framed spectacles as glassy as their lenses. There was a look of surprise etched forever on his ugly features now, his mouth forming an O of surprise, viscous black blood oozing from the neat hole in the middle of his forehead. He lay in the mess of brain matter, blood and bone fragments that plastered that floor behind him.

The emerald mist began to fade from before Jekyll's eyes. He sighed, the tension in his body easing, suddenly weak with relief.

"Quick, come with me," the woman beckoned from the doorway, glancing back over her shoulder, her gun ready in her hand, just in case.

He rattled his restraints, and she cursed and moved into the room. Her accent and her choice of expletive didn't sound particularly German to Jekyll. In fact they sounded more Eastern European than anything.

Crouching down in front of his chair she pulled at the manacles holding his ankles in place. He didn't know what she did, or what tools she used, but he heard the snap of a link breaking, followed by the rattle of chains falling to the floor. There was another sharp metallic snap and his other leg was free as well.

Rising, the woman seized hold of the restraining bracelet at his wrist.

She was close to him now, the scent of her, strong and heady as musk, arousing even in his current dire predicament, the swell of her bosom sending a pulse of excitement through his body.

He could see exactly what she was doing now. She took the bracelet in her hands and gave it a sharp twist. Incredibly, the metal gave and then snapped. She did the same with the other just as easily.

Jekyll's mind reeled at what he was witnessing. The manacles must have been old, the metal weakened by rust or age. Even so, they had remained resolutely unpliable even as he had felt the change begin within him. Perhaps that initial transformation had been enough to weaken the metal.

"Now," she said, narrowing her eyes at him. "Follow me."

Henry Jekyll's mind raced.

"Who are you?" he hissed, as he followed the woman into the warren of passageways beyond his erstwhile prison, rubbing feeling back into his aching wrists as he did so.

She fixed him with those piercing eyes again, silencing him. "I am – how do you say? – your ticket out of here."

Having looked both ways – Jekyll assuming she'd found the way ahead clear – she sniffed at the air sharply.

"This way," she said, leading them left past the T-junction.

At that moment, the bewildered Jekyll believed that he would have followed her into the jaws of Hell, if she had only asked him. He didn't know what kind of power it was that she had over him, but whatever it was, it was potent.

He followed her to another part of the cellars. Stopping at another junction she sniffed the air again, turned her transfixing gaze upon him once more and said, "Wait here."

And so he remained exactly where he was as she strode boldly through the brick-built archway into the passageway beyond.

He felt his pulse quicken as he heard a gruff male voice, and then felt his heart leap as he heard her issue a sharp command in perfect German. There was a brief exchange of words and then the sound of two sets of heavy footsteps receding up a flight of stairs and into the house above.

"Come," the woman hissed, poking her head around the corner once more.

Jekyll followed her into the better-lit passageway beyond. The guards were gone. He didn't bother to ask her how she had managed that; he already knew. He would have done anything she asked of him at that moment too – anything at all.

The passageway ended at a locked iron door. Somehow, the woman had already managed to procure a set of keys and was busy at the lock. A moment later, the door swung open.

The smells emanating from the room beyond were an uncomfortable marriage of damp and disinfectant.

A man, dressed in the now dishevelled uniform of a Nazi officer, had been chained to a chair in the middle of the room and the chair bolted to the floor. His chin rested on his chest. Jekyll wondered if Kaufman had got to him already.

Hercules Quicksilver looked up.

"Who... who are you?" he asked groggily.

Jekyll followed like an obedient puppy as the woman entered the cellar and set to work on Quicksilver's restraints.

"My name is Katarina Kharkova," she said as she worked. There was a *ping* of failing metal and she moved to free his other leg. "I am an agent of Imperial Russia and I am here to rescue you."

* * *

"WHY?" HERCULES ASKED, eyes half closed against the light streaming into the cellar. "What's in it for you?"

"We are allies, are we not?"

"Our nations are," Hercules confirmed.

"And it would seem to me that you need all the friends you can get just now."

"But what's in this for you?" Hercules pressed, as she snapped the last of the cuffs securing him to the chair, with her bare hands.

"How does the saying go?" she said, a distant look entering her exotic, aquamarine-coloured eyes. "You scratch my back...?"

Hercules' brow crumpled in confusion.

"I need your help," she said, making her point plain.

"*You* need *my* help?" Hercules asked, pointedly looking at the broken links and chains now lying on the floor at his feet.

"We cannot delay here any longer! We must away to Castle Frankenstein."

"Castle Frankenstein?" Jekyll gasped, appalled. "I don't like the sound of that. What on Earth for?"

"We have to rescue Prisoner Zero."

Hercules looked at the woman, making eye contact with her for the first time.

"Really?" he asked.

"Really," she said, transfixing him with her stare.

Hercules blinked several times and shook his head, as if trying to shake off the befuddling drowsiness that seemed about to come upon him.

"Right then," he said, suddenly jumping up from his chair, apparently no worse for his recent ordeal. "We can't waste any more time hanging around here. We need to be off on our way. It is this way, I take it?" he said, dashing over to the door and scoping the corridor ahead.

Hurriedly taking the lead once more, Katarina led the way for the two men to follow, up the steps after the two guards who had quit their posts at the Russian spy's instruction.

From the top of the stair, they followed what must have once been a servants' passageway through the mansion house, to which Hercules and Jekyll had been taken following their capture in Alsenz.

As they jogged along the echoing corridor after their devastatingly beautiful liberator, Hercules glanced out the tall windows over a cluttered courtyard.

The sheer weight of armour parked up outside took his breath away. There were troop transports, squad cars, munitions trucks, jeeps mounted with steam-powered Gatling guns and even a pair of steam-powered Jotun-class tanks. The heavy ordnance alone would easily have been enough to level a country estate – ornamental gardens, orangery and all.

They turned a corner and entered a passageway adorned with oil painted landscapes and the portraits of former margraves of the region, as well as the garish crimson pennants of the Nazi party. The hallway carpet deadened their fleeting footfalls. Ahead of them Hercules could see a black and white tiled hallway and polished ironwood double doors. A suited clerk was sat behind an unnecessarily large desk in front of an ornate marble fireplace.

On catching sight of the desk-bound clerk, Katarina Kharkova smoothly slowed her run to a walk, adjusting her uniform as she did so. She confidently approached the desk, her footsteps clicking in time with the clock on the mantelpiece above the grand white marble hearth.

The clerk looked up, and straight into the Russian agent's persuasive stare.

"Now listen to me very carefully," she said, and Hercules saw the feeble wretch wilt under her intense gaze. "My friends and I are walking out of here right now and you are not going to do anything to stop us, do you understand?"

The clerk nodded slowly in slack-jawed compliance.

"Very good." Katarina turned towards the closed double doors. "Let's go," she told the others.

As Hercules moved to follow her he was suddenly aware of an engine revving on the other side of the large ironwood doors.

With a sound like the crash of a cliff falling into the sea, the front façade of the house bulged and fell inwards, bricks and sundered stone tumbling into the atrium with all the noise and force of a landslide.

Hercules watched as the doors disintegrated, huge splinters of wood flying the length of the hallway. One of these struck the Russian, spearing her body and hurling her backwards, pinning her to the mahogany panelling covering the walls.

Hercules stared in horror as her body sagged, suspended a good twelve inches off the ground.

Frozen to the spot in shock, Doctor Jekyll cowering in fear behind him, Hercules looked from the transfixed Katarina to the bricks sliding into the hallway as he watched in disbelief.

The desk and the clerk were gone, buried under several tonnes of rubble and fine Rococo carvings. Poking from the juddering mountain of ruined masonry was the broad barrel of a gun six feet long.

Hercules could hear shocked, shouting voices from outside the breached building, getting closer with every passing moment.

Where the front wall of the house had been there was now only a broken hole, the occasional broken piece of baked clay clattering to the ground from the ruptured brickwork above. Pale sunlight poured into the atrium from outside.

The last thing he was expecting was for a hatch to squeal open near the top of the pile of rubble, sending a fresh fall of bricks tumbling to the cracked tile floor. And he certainly wasn't expecting a young woman to pop her head through it, but he watched her with hawkish interest as she brushed a tress of amber hair out of her face and hooked it behind her ear.

"I know you!" he gasped, in stunned amazement. "You were at the bierkeller."

"The name's Cookie," the young woman said, in a cut-glass upper-class English accent. "It's a pleasure to make your acquaintance at last, Mr Quicksilver."

"But what are you doing here?" Hercules was beginning to babble. "And in a German Jotun-class tank too!"

"I'm your rendezvous," she said. "Now, let's get you out of here before you get us into any more trouble."

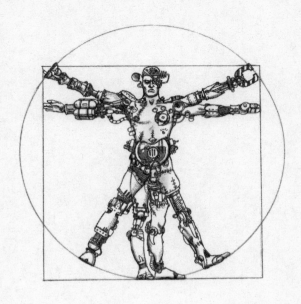

ACT TWO

Mission Impossible

*"Terrorism is the best political weapon, for nothing drives
people harder than a fear of sudden death."*

– Adolf Hitler

CHAPTER THIRTEEN

Aftermath

SCHLOSS GEISTERHAUS, ALSENZ, GERMANY, 1943

LATER THAT AFTERNOON the Devil descended upon Alsenz.

The Lieutenant-Colonel's staff car came to a halt with a squeak of brakes. The driver opened the door, and Engel Teufel got out.

Something crumbled beneath his jackboot and he looked down, a bored expression on his knife-sharp face as his eyes lighted on a powdered stone.

Major Isla von Haupstein at his side, he surveyed the scene of utter devastation that welcomed him.

Schloss Geisterhaus had once been a grand estate comprising some hundred hectares. The house itself was a fine example of Romanesque architecture, and boasted a dining room that some said rivalled the Hall of Mirrors at Versailles.

It had made the perfect base for the German army's 28th Panzer Division, and had been appropriated by the Nazi party when Hitler had set his master-plan in motion when he declared war on the rest of Europe. And it had looked glorious with its Romanesque façade draped with the flags and banners of the Third Reich.

Now it looked as though it had been the victim of a strafing run by the Magna Britannian Royal Aeronautical Corps.

The gatehouse was gone, little more than a pile of bricks and broken stone, the twisted and blackened remains of an exploded jeep lying amidst it. A few puddles of oil still burned, splashed over the spoil heap.

Taking careful steps, Teufel climbed the nearest mound of rubble to better survey the devastation beyond.

Much of the front wall of the main house was gone, the grand atrium behind it exposed like the innards of some gutted beast.

To his left, smoke coiled from the broken windows of the west wing. To his right, a row of burning vehicles filled the air with choking black smoke.

Standing at the Lieutenant-Colonel's shoulder, Major Haupstein cast her feral gaze over the ruins, as if searching for something. Then she paused, and sniffed the air, sharply, twice.

Behind him and around him, Teufel's own crack squad of Stormtroopers spread out to secure the devastated courtyard, scoping the piles of debris, on the look-out for danger, in case the ones responsible for the attack were still there, hiding in the ruins, a sniper's rifle aimed at the Lieutenant-Colonel's heart.

A shout from the house on the other side of the devastated courtyard. The Stormtroopers' rifles rattled as they were raised and trained on the meek-faced clerk – his hair grey with plaster dust – now standing in what should have been the doorway of the mansion.

His cry for help turned into a yelp of panic. He hastily raised his hands, shouting, "Don't shoot! Don't shoot!"

Teufel peered through the drifting smoke and brick-dust, his face an impassive mask.

"Bring him to me," he instructed.

"AND YOU SAY this was all done by one tank?" Teufel said, as though he couldn't quite take in what the wretched individual had just told him.

"Y-Yes, sir," the clerk stammered.

"One of our own, you say?"

The man nodded, unable to speak, his mouth suddenly dry.

Teufel turned his disconsolate gaze from the quivering clerk to his adjutant. "Major?"

"They were here," Isla von Haupstein said, inhaling deeply, her head jerking from side to side as she sniffed the acrid air. "Two males. One young and smelling of risk; the other smelling of anger and fear."

"I see," Teufel breathed.

The Lieutenant-Colonel and the Major descended the mound of rubble. "They weren't alone," Haupstein offered.

"They had help, I can see that," Teufel said.

Haupstein sniffed at the smoke-wreathed air again. "Females. I'm picking up several different scents."

"Driving a tank, no doubt," Teufel pondered, as he considered the possibility that the Resistance or another, as yet unidentified party of interested individuals were also operating behind the German front line.

The thought made him both unhappy and delighted at the same time. The thrill of the hunt to come filled him with a crackling excitement that energised every fibre of his being.

"Females, you say?" he mused, stepping through the crumbling façade of the house and into the partially-demolished atrium beyond. "Like this one, perhaps?"

The woman had been pinned to the back wall of the hall by a thick splinter of wood almost five feet in length.

Haupstein froze, a fearful hiss escaping her bared teeth. With a frisson of excitement, Teufel saw the stiff hairs on the back of her neck rising.

He turned his attention to the body pinned to the wall. "We should be grateful that the doors of Schloss Geisterhaus were made of natural wood," he said, smiling darkly.

Gesturing to two of his men he said, "Take the body down and burn it."

Teufel turned from the corpse, mounted on the wall behind him like a bizarre hunting trophy, and strode out of the shattered building, back into the sunlit courtyard.

So, their quarry had been here, but once again, they had caught up with them just a little too late.

They had followed a circuitous trail from the zeppelin crash-site, west of Valkyrie post 7, through woodland and rolling fields, as far as Alsenz. At Alsenz the local party official had informed Teufel that the men he was hunting had been taken to Schloss Geisterhaus by the Gestapo's Agent Kaufman.

Teufel, Haupstein and the rest of the hunting party had arrived at the manse only a matter of hours later. A pillar of smoke had led Teufel to the initial crash-site earlier that day, and another column of greasy black smoke had told him what awaited them at Schloss Geisterhaus; that their prey had already escaped.

Stirring himself from his reverie – seeing again the shattered gatehouse, the burning hulks of tanks and troop transports, the buckled, burning wreckage of other vehicles, the smashed masonry and collapsed façade of the house itself – a bitter grimace upon his face, he turned to his adjutant.

"They have escaped us again, my dear Isla," he said thoughtfully.

Her own expression set like concrete, as hard and as perfect as marble, the Major said, "They shall not escape us next time."

"Lieutenant-Colonel!" a private shouted, running over the rubble towards them from where their convoy of vehicles had pulled up beyond the broken gatehouse.

"You have them?" Teufel anticipated.

"Yes, sir. The fugitives have been spotted twenty miles east of here."

A slow smile spread across Teufel's lips. The cyber-eagles had done their job. "They're heading for the Darmstadt Dam," he muttered. "You are right, my dear," he said, addressing his adjutant again. "They shall not escape us a third time."

He turned to his men. "Radio the dam. Tell them the fugitives are heading their way. And signal the nearest Landsknecht squadron. Tell them to back up the forces at the dam and engage the enemy on sight. Tell them to look out for a Jotun-class tank and make it clear that they are permitted to shoot on sight."

Teufel shared an excited look with Haupstein as they climbed back into his staff car.

"No," he said, "they won't escape us again."

CHAPTER FOURTEEN

Monstrous Regiment

"WHAT ARE THOSE?" Cookie said, putting her binoculars to her eyes again.

Missy raised her sniper rifle and peered through its telescopic scope.

"Just birds," she said, lowering the rifle again.

The team leader turned her attention from the sky to the road ahead. The stretch of countryside through which they were passing was eerily quiet. The distant twitter of birdsong could be heard from the trees on the horizon, but there was no sign of another human being for miles around.

It was strange; if it had not been for the fact that they were making their way across Germany, behind enemy lines, with the intention of destroying a super-soldier manufactory, right at that moment she might almost have described their journey as pleasant. It was a little nippy, admittedly, but then it was October. And of course, being out here, even under these desperate circumstances, was better than the alternative.

No, Cookie thought, legs swinging over the edge of the tank's top hatch as if she was six again, she would savour this moment for as long as it lasted. After all, she never knew when she might get the chance again – if at all. Life was all about the little moments.

"You keep watch up here," she told Missy before climbing back into the cramped confines of the tank's interior.

The cabin rang to the clattering of the tank's steam engine and the rattle of its caterpillar tracks, as Jinx – seated up front and looking out at the road through a narrow slit in the plate-shielding at the front of the tank – fought its unresponsive controls to pilot the *Siegfried* towards their ultimate destination.

Cat and Dina had positioned themselves behind at the trigger paddles of the port and starboard sponson guns while Trixie was monitoring radio traffic on a portable receiver, headphones in hand.

They all looked very different from how they had been attired when the British agent had first arrived at the Alsenz bierkeller. They had exchanged the tight-laced corsets and flouncy skirts of the dancing troupe for more practical leather jackets and tight-fitting trousers. Judging by the looks he kept giving the other girls, the Department's man found their new outfits even more appealing.

Jinx was also wearing a peaked cap, to keep her shoulder-length auburn hair out of her eyes, or so she claimed. Cookie thought it more likely that she liked how she looked in military dress.

Jinx's shirt sleeves were also rolled up to the elbow and she was wearing thick leather gloves in case she ended up buried in the guts of the tank again, having to tinker with the engine as she had done twice already.

Cookie favoured the hat method of hair management herself. Leading a team of crack commandos behind enemy lines didn't allow much time for her to worry about her appearance although, perversely, it was precisely how her team looked that had got them all this far without attracting any undue attention.

That had been until the raid on Alsenz, of course. Now every Nazi for miles around would be looking for them. She only hoped that they could complete their mission before their pursuers could catch up.

Cat's long blonde hair was kept tidy and out of her face in a tight plait. It was as neat and controlled as the rest of her, matching her lithe grace and remarkable flexibility. These were what had made her a natural cat burglar – that and her spoiled, and ultimately unfulfilling, upbringing.

Of course Dina's dark hair was cut in a short bob, so that she didn't need to worry about how she was going to keep it out of the way. After all, she didn't list hair care as one of her hobbies; dynamite and primer cord were more her short of thing.

Trixie's mousey hair wasn't long either, but she still kept it tied back. It distracted her otherwise, and got in the way of her glasses. And when she was working against the clock to break open another vault, crack another safe, or hack into another Babbage Engine, distractions weren't an option.

It was only Missy who wore her hair down, a pair of goggles pushed up on top of her head, keeping the naturally curling tresses out of her face.

Cookie glanced back up at the sniper through the circle of the hatch in the turret of the tank. Missy had her rifle to her shoulder again as she scanned the rolling landscape through the scope.

"Anything?" Cookie called up through the hatch over the chugging purr of the engine.

"Nope," Missy replied without taking her eye from the scope as she continued to sweep the rifle left and right.

"Anything?" she asked Jinx, bending down.

"Not so far as I can see," the team's driver replied.

"Anything on the radio?" Cookie asked.

Trixie looked up through her large framed spectacles. "Nothing yet."

"I don't like it," Dina whispered, from her position behind the sights of the port-side sponson.

"I know what you mean," Cookie came back. "It's *too* quiet," she said, although having to raise her voice to be heard over the rattling tank.

"Too damn quiet," the explosives expert muttered to herself.

Cookie smiled. Dina preferred to be surrounded by noise –

loud as a landslide or an explosion in a munitions factory. That was more her style.

"So, what's the plan?" came a man's voice from out of the darkness behind her.

Cookie turned and, using the exposed pipework of the tank's cramped interior to support herself, made her way towards the back of the cabin. It was the younger of the two men who had spoken; the handsome one.

"That's on a need-to-know basis," she said, smiling, to Hercules Quicksilver. He was devilishly handsome. If they had met under different circumstances...

"This is our lives you're playing with," came another voice, tinged with discontent and a Scottish burr. "If we don't need to know, who does?"

Cookie silenced the other with a looked that could have curdled milk. "And have you not heard of culpable deniability?" she said. "If you're captured again by the Nazis you might spill the beans on the whole operation."

"What if they take *you* alive?" the doctor countered.

"With all due respect," the handsome one said, interjecting, "if we're captured this mission's as good as over anyway, so what have you got to lose?"

"I have my orders," Cookie pouted.

"And so did I," Quicksilver replied, "but I had to start improvising long ago. And I would hazard a guess that it's the same for you, since the good doctor and I missed our original appointment with you."

Cookie met his intense stare, her own eyes narrowed in suspicion.

"So come on, tell us," he said, smoothing his moustache with one hand. "I can be very persuasive."

"I'm sure you can," Cookie chuckled, registering the scowl Cat was giving the two of them.

"Can't we at least be on first name terms?" Quicksilver persevered as they were jostled together in the back of the tank, as the armoured vehicle bumped and bounced along the rutted road.

"I've already told you mine. I'm Cookie."

"Cookie? Really?"

"Really."

"Just Cookie?"

"Just Cookie."

"That's a codename, am I right?" he said. "Let me guess, you're the leader and you're called Cookie because you cook up all of your team's crazy schemes. Am I right?"

Cookie laughed. "And what sort of a name is Hercules Quicksilver?"

"A very fine and honourable name," he said, bristling, but with a twinkle in his eye.

Before Cookie could come up with a reply, all on board the tank heard the whistling whine coming from above, growing ever louder and lower.

"Oh –" Cookie began.

"– shit!" Hercules finished for her.

The bomb hit a split second later, the explosion deafening them with its primal, hungry roar.

And then bodies were tumbling about the confines of the cabin as the shock-wave hit the tank.

CHAPTER FIFTEEN

The Dam Busters

FOR A MOMENT the tank was powering forward on its right tracks alone. Drive-shaft squealing, it crashed back down onto the rutted ground as another bomb detonated at the road's edge away to the right.

"Floor it!" Cookie shouted at the driver. "Get us out of here!"

There were loud protests from the gearbox as Jinx changed gear and stamped on the accelerator with both feet. The chugging steam-engine gave a throaty roar and the tank took off along the road, throwing the already disorientated passengers backwards again.

Cookie tensed her grip on the bar she was hanging from to stop herself being thrown into Hercules' lap.

She glanced up and out of the hatch to see Missy, still somehow clinging onto the top of the tank, lining up the sights of her rifle on something above them. As the tank bumped through a pothole she caught a glimpse of a distant, black shape against the monotonous white of the washed-out clouds high above. It was unmistakeably a large bird; a raptor of some kind.

"Missy, get down here!" Cookie shouted over the growl of the engine as the dull sound of another explosion threw clods of black earth rattling against the hull of the *Seigfried*.

"I've almost got one," the sniper hissed back through gritted teeth, the scope of her rifle pressed tight to her eye. "If Jinx could just keep this bucket of bolts steady..."

If Jinx heard Missy's snide remark over the roar of the steam-engine, she clearly chose to ignore it.

"How many are there?" Cookie called back.

"Four that I can see."

The sniper's finger tightened about the trigger.

"Missy, come on. Leave it."

"Just one more second," the other hissed.

The knuckle of her index finger whitening, she squeezed the trigger very gradually.

Cookie felt her throat tighten as she saw one of the raptor shapes swoop past overhead, just as a bulbous object dropped from its hooked claws.

The tank jolted as it ran over a gouged rut in the road surface, accompanied by the crack of Missy's rifle. Several unbearable moments later, preceded by the same ominous whine, the third bomb hit the ground.

It hit the road behind them, detonating on impact. All on board the tank were thrown forwards, to a chorus of shouts and expletives as the explosion lifted the back of the armoured juggernaut clear of the ground. Missy fell into the tank, landing on top of Cookie. The hatch slammed shut behind her.

For them to be carried by the birds, or whatever it was that was hunting them, Cookie thought, the bombs couldn't be that large, but then they didn't need to be. One direct hit would be all it would take to put the tank out of action. And if one detonated inside the cramped confines of the cabin it would kill them all outright.

With a loud crash the back end of the tank made contact with the dirt road again, throwing up a great spew of mud behind it as the tracks regained their grip and the *Seigfried* shot forward.

The tank swerved sharply, but this time it was all down to

Jinx. The tracks rattled and bounced as the vehicle left the road. The nervous doctor gave a whimper of fear and clung to the access panel beside him. Quicksilver, meanwhile, had braced himself between the roof of the cabin and the floor, his face set in a grimace.

And then Jinx swerved again, changing gear as she did so and putting her foot down once more, sending the tank careening across the dirt track. She churned up the turf on the other side as she spun it round once again.

She was driving like a maniac, but Cookie never once doubted her decisions or her ability to keep control of the wildly zigzagging machine. Jinx knew exactly what she was doing, Cookie was sure of it. The crazed course was their best chance of avoiding the bomber birds.

"Dam!" Jinx suddenly shouted.

Cookie scrambled across the cabin to the driver's position in an instant. "What is it? What's the matter?"

"No, it's the *dam*. Dead ahead."

Cookie peered out of the slit in front of the driver's seat.

And there it was, around a bend to the right in the road ahead of them – the Darmstadt Dam. To their left the ground rose up towards the foothills through which this stretch of the Rhine tumbled over the mossy boulders of a limestone gorge. To the right, the land dropped away towards the forested depths of a steep-sided valley below. And here, where the river's current was at its most ferocious, the dam had been built.

It was a great black stone wall, two hundred yards long and almost a thousand feet high. Beyond it, a forest of steel pylons followed the rugged peaks of the hills, heading east. The unstable electrical energy generated by the dam's furious turbines supplied power to the corpse factory that lay another sixteen miles away, hidden among the wooded hills north of the industrialised town itself. The road crossed the top of the dam. To the right, beyond a low wall, lay the giddyingly deep gorge; to the left, behind a higher wall and the block of buildings that contained much of the dam's inner workings, the man-made lake behind the dam.

"We're almost there!" Cookie gasped, hardly able to believe that they had progressed so far with their mission.

The other girls allowed themselves a stifled whoop of joy, the thrill of the chase and the rush of adrenalin inside each of them setting nerve endings on fire.

"They won't dare bomb the dam, will they?" Dina said, suddenly breathless with excitement.

"Not a chance," Cookie said, with relish. "If they take out the dam they will have as good as completed our mission for us."

Dina looked at the squad's leader, grinning from ear to ear, a flicker like the spark of a burning fuse in her eyes. "Although that is something I'd like to see," she added, murmuring with almost festishistic delight.

"Me too," Cookie said with a smile.

"The Nazis may be many things," Quicksilver threw in, "but they're not stupid."

Cookie's face fell. "More's the pity."

"Bugger!" came the curse from the driver's seat.

"What is it?" Hercules asked, coming to the front of the cabin as Jinx directed the tank back onto the road, heading for the dam.

"Stalkers," Jinx muttered, eyes narrowing as she changed gear again, the tank's grumbling engine growling like a caged beast in response.

"Stalkers?" Hercules said, clearly unfamiliar with the term.

"Landsknechts," Cookie explained, her face slack with shock. "Which means we're all as good as dead already."

HERCULES PEERED THROUGH the viewing slit in the hull of the tank. There were three of them; a full squadron. They were lined up next to each other on the other side of the dam, their armoured might blocking the way ahead.

There would be no sneaking past them, or charging past for that matter. The only way for the *Seigfried* and its passengers to get any further was to go right through the middle of them.

"What are Landsknechts?" Doctor Jekyll asked from the rear of the cabin, his voice a high-pitched waver.

"Take a look for yourself," Hercules said, nodding towards the letter-box shaped slit.

Unable to contain his curiosity, Jekyll clambered across the rocking cabin to the crowded driver's position, having to bend down to see out of the viewing port. His croaking gasp, trailing off into silence, said it all.

The Landsknechts were walking machines, twenty feet tall, great armoured behemoths weighed down by their weapons. With their backward-jointed legs, they looked not unlike squat wading birds. The cab supported on top of the waist bearing, however, looked like a miniature tank, with its cannon sponsons and rotating turret gun. The ammunition hoppers mounted behind the cabs made them look hunchbacked.

Smoke came in gusts from the smokestacks in the top of the machines. One was rocking from side to side as it stamped its feet, like a horse impatient to gallop into the fray.

The tank began to slow.

"What do you want me to do?" Jinx asked, glancing at Cookie as the *Seigfried* approached the near side of the dam.

"Don't slow down," she threw back. "Keep going."

"Right you are," Jinx replied, a sinister smile spreading across her lips as she changed up a gear and put her foot to floor once more.

There was a dull boom from somewhere off to their right that echoed from the thick walls of the dam and away into the valley below. The resultant shockwave caught the tank and slammed it into the side of the low wall skirting the dam-road.

The *Seigfried* kept powering forward, gouging a groove in the stonework of the wall before Jinx was able to bring it back under control.

Jinx and Cookie looked at each other in surprise.

"You know how you said the Nazis wouldn't be so stupid as to bomb their own dam?" Hercules said, a wry smile curling the corner of his mouth.

Cookie nodded.

"On what were you basing that supposition, exactly?"

* * *

"Stop those birds!" Lance Corporal Riker screamed into the radio microphone in his hand. "By Thunor, somebody call those birds off before one of them blows a hole in the dam!"

"At once, Lance Corporal," a voice distorted by static crackled back through Riker's headset.

Commander Riker looked through the eyepiece of the periscope of the *Wotan*, the command vehicle, positioned between the *Donner*, with its thunder hammer cannon, and the *Blitzen*, with its flame-thrower attachment.

He angled the scope so that he caught the swooping cyber-eagles in his sights. There were four altogether and each of them had dropped one of the two spherical bombs they carried in their adapted steel claw-clamps.

He watched them anxiously as they came in low over the dam, as if preparing for another strafing bombing run. But then he relaxed as the avians peeled away, the lead raptor diving over the side of the dam as its electrode-plugged brain received the signal to cease-fire, the rest of the flock swooping after it and over the wooded valley below.

"Take aim and prepare to take out that tank on my command," Riker shouted into his handset, turning his attention away from the errant cyber-eagles and back to the approaching Jotun-class tank.

But something was wrong; either the last eagle hadn't received the stop signal for some reason, or its bomb harness was faulty. But whatever the problem was, as the bird swooped low over the dam, the second bomb it was carrying rattled loose of its claw-frame as the raptor turned and plunged over the edge of the dam after its fellows.

The bomb didn't have far to fall before it hit the road in front of the tank. Its detonation didn't seem loud but it hurt Riker's ears, blotting out all other sound.

Smoke and flame washed across the dam towards them and Riker felt the force of it through the trembling Landsknecht.

As the smoke drifted away on the breeze, Riker caught his first glimpse of the crater the explosion had excavated in the top of the dam. Six feet deep and three times that across, if it had exploded halfway down the dam, right now they would be plummeting into the river valley below – tank, stalkers and all – as the force of the Rhine tore the structure apart, carrying chunks of stonework as large as houses away in its white-water wrath.

They were safe, if only just, but the same couldn't be said for the traitorous tank. It was going too fast, its driver unable to bring it to a halt in time as it was consumed by the roiling ball of smoke and flame.

The armoured behemoth plunged nose first into the smoking pit. Tracks ground uselessly against the crumbling sides of the crater, the barrel of its main gun wedged in the bottom of the hole, leaving the *Seigfried* angled at close on forty-five degrees.

The spies wouldn't be going anywhere in a hurry now.

"Riker to all Landsknechts!" the commander spoke into the handset once again. "Take aim and, on my mark, hit that tank with everything you've got."

CHAPTER SIXTEEN

The Beast Within

THE WOTAN TREMBLED, with a reverberating *clang*, as something heavy landed on top of it. The whole machine shook, Riker dropping his precious handset in the process. He cursed loudly, as did the three crewmen locked inside the Landsknecht with him.

Riker grabbed the handles of the periscope and twisted it around, pushing his face up against the rubber-rimmed eyepiece again. Whatever it was that was on top of the Landsknecht, it was so close as to be blocking his view entirely. All he could see was indistinct darkness.

Suddenly the tube of the periscope twisted in his grasp, tugging him round and making him lose his footing. He slipped and the periscope twisted again, anti-clockwise this time, one of the handles catching him in the face as he struggled to keep his balance. The assault was accompanied by what sounded like a bullish snorting from beyond the carapace of the stalk-tank.

Blood pouring from his nose, on his hands and knees on the grilled floor of his elevated command position, the Lance Corporal found himself level with the pilot's reinforced view port.

The stricken *Siegfried* remained where it was, upended in

the blasted crater, forgotten about in the heat of the moment. The crews of the other two Landsknechts were still faithfully waiting for his command to fire.

His eyes fell upon the microphone, lying on the plates in front of him. Grabbing it, his words distorted by the injury to his nose, he gave the order: "Open fire!"

The air was suddenly filled with the clatter of the *Wotan's* paired Gatling guns running up to speed.

To the left of the command vehicle, the *Blitzen's* flame-thrower ignited. To the right, the gunner on board the *Donner* calculated firing solutions and cranked the thunder hammer cannon into position.

The *Wotan* rocked again. This time the pilot was forced to compensate, the stalker taking a stumbling step forward to avoid being toppled altogether. But whatever it was that had caused the heavy machine to stumble was ready and waiting.

Just when all of the bipedal walker's weight was over its right foot, the unseen assailant struck again. It hit the sturdy leg side on, turning the machine's great weight against it. The *Wotan* began to topple, slowly at first, and yet as unstoppable as a falling tree, colliding with the *Donner* to its right.

Its momentum was not enough to send the braced heavy weapons stalker toppling as well, but it was enough to knock its carefully-targeted cannon off target.

The thunder hammer fired, a split second before the *Blitzen's* flame-thrower sent a wave of burning naphtha washing towards the immobile Jotun-class tank.

TRAPPED INSIDE THE upended tank, Hercules Quicksilver and the others on board instinctively ducked on hearing the cataclysmic boom of the cannon, while Jekyll just screamed, overwhelmed by fear.

They heard the whine of the heavy projectile as it spun through the air, passing over the tank.

"How could they miss at that range?" Dina muttered incredulously.

There was a second distant boom of an explosion, this time somewhere above them.

"They hit something," Hercules added, glancing anxiously at the roof of the cabin.

A moment later they heard the crackle of flames as the flame-thrower vomited blazing naphtha over the hull of the tank.

"Is it me, or is it getting hot in here?" Hercules asked, rubbing a finger inside the collar of his shirt.

Abruptly the flames died.

"If I might make a suggestion," Hercules said, his voice loud in the eerie silence that had suddenly descended, "I think we should get out of here, and fast. We might not get a better chance than this one."

"EVERYBODY OUT!" COOKIE commanded.

Throwing open the hatch, taking in what was going on around them with only the most cursory glance, she led the way for the rest of them, leaping down from the top of the tilted turret onto the fractured tarmac surface of the road.

Their closest cover was the wall of the dam. Running to the wall, she stopped and looked again at the Landsknechts. The middle one had fallen against the machine to its right, effectively wedging it against the dam. The one to its left, however, was clanking towards them with bird-like steps, the blackened nozzle of its flame-thrower tracking them.

The flicker of a moving shadow on the other side of the dam, something moving behind the stalkers, distracted her. There was something else there with the Landsknechts. It looked like an impossibly large man.

"Quickly!" she shouted as Missy, followed immediately after by Dina, Cat and Trixie, clambered out of the top of the tank and ran to join her at the wall. Jinx was the last one out of the *Seigfried*, looking disgruntled.

Cookie leaned over the top of the wall, the curved structure of the dam sloping sharply down to the churning waters of the river below. Immediately on the other side of the wall there was a ledge at the same level as the road, a few feet in width. It protruded from the side of the dam above the precipitous drop. Gracefully swinging first one leg, then the other, over the wall, she lowered herself onto the ledge.

"Where's Quicksilver?" she hissed, peering over the top of the wall as the rest of her team joined her on the ledge.

And then she saw him getting out of the tank, having let all the women out before him.

"He's such a gentleman!" she heard Cat whisper. She caught the glint of desire in the burglar's wide eyes; the kind of look that she usually reserved for large cut diamonds or priceless antique crowns.

And she had to agree, he was.

The stalker was closing the distance to the tank with every clanking step. Cookie could hear the hiss of the flame-thrower's flickering blue pilot-light now.

"Hurry up!" she shouted.

A fleeting shadow caught her attention again and she shot a glance at the sky.

Now she knew what it was the shell had hit.

At that moment, the stricken cyber-eagle lost the battle to stay airborne and dropped like a stone, its one remaining bomb still clutched in its steel-trap claws.

"Get out of there!" Cookie screamed.

HERCULES REACTED IMMEDIATELY, twisting to look at her and then following her appalled gaze to the plummeting bomb-bird above.

There wasn't time to even swear. Half-jumping and half-falling from the tank – only dimly aware Jekyll's sweat-slicked hand slipping from his – Hercules dived at the wall as the eagle hit.

The great bird – its wingspan some fifteen feet from wingtip to wingtip – landed directly on top of the stricken tank, accompanied by the crash of buckling exo-skeletal mechanisms and the snap of breaking feathers and bones.

Hercules had already picked himself up and was running for the edge of the dam when the eagle's payload exploded.

The force of the explosion lifted him off his feet and slammed him into the low wall. As he half-fell over the other side, the girls of the Monstrous Regiment – as Hercules liked to think of them – grabbed him and pulled him to safety on the thin ledge beside them.

A roiling cloud of oily flames and greasy smoke rolled over them and was carried away on the cold autumnal breeze, the echoes of the explosion rippling across the wooded valley below.

Crouched on the ledge behind the wall, Hercules closed his eyes and put his head in his hands. He felt like weeping. Their mission had always been fraught with danger, but to have got this far, to have had Jekyll's hand in his, ready to pull him from the trapped tank, and now...

There seemed little point in going on now, even if he did have the Monstrous Regiment at his side. He had thought he had failed in his mission from the moment he landed in Hessen, but somehow Jekyll had survived, the cryo-pod perhaps sheltering his fall. And now he felt a thousand times worse. To have had his hopes raised, to have got this far, even having been captured by the Nazis once already, only to have them dashed like this. This was one disaster that Henry Jekyll wouldn't be walking away from, unscathed or otherwise.

But, Hercules thought, jerking himself out of his self-pitying stupor, if he could survive an airship crash...

The roar of rage that reverberated from the walls of the dam – surely amplified by the acoustics of the river gorge, for how else could it be so loud? – made him start. Had it really come from the wreckage of the tank?

Hercules joined Cookie in cautiously peering back over the top of the wall, the cold wind whipping about them. Thick black smoke was still pouring from the crumpled carcass of the tank and drifting across the dam, concealing the Landsknechts from sight.

With a screech of tearing steel, a huge fist punched its way clear of the twisted hole in the top of the tank.

The powerful fingers of a huge hand grasped the lip of the hatch and pulled. With a colossal noise, the whole turret section came free of the rest of the wrecked tank slid, with a crash, onto the road.

Two huge hands now appeared over the lip of the exposed cabin and a monstrous creature, twice as tall as a man, pulled itself out of the wreckage. Coils of smoke rose from its flesh, as the torn rags of a jacket and shirt fell, smouldering, to the ground. The monster climbed atop the remains of the *Seigfried* and raised its bunched fists to the sky, arms bulging with biceps the size of car tyres, the monster gave voice to a bellow of primal fury.

It bellowed.

"HYDE!"

CHAPTER SEVENTEEN

Battle Royal

THE MONSTER'S BULLISH roar was echoed by an answering howl of fury from the far side of the dam.

"Now what the hell was that?" Hercules muttered under his breath.

The ominous armoured forms of the Landsknechts emerged from the smoke as the breeze was blown clear. Standing atop the half-collapsed central stalker was another creature, a monstrous primate of a man. It had to be eight feet tall at least and almost as broad across the shoulders. The knots of corded muscle around its neck and arms were visible even under the long coat it was wearing, and Hercules could make out a mane of greasy black tresses whipping about its head in the breeze.

It was holding some part from the walker triumphantly above its head.

For a split second he found himself entertaining what seemed like a totally crazy idea. Was this second fiend on their side?

Hercules looked back at the first beast, still standing atop the tank. The creature's skin had an eerie emerald hue to it, as if the blood in its veins had been replaced with chlorophyll. The challenger had succeeded in grabbing its attention.

"I don't know about that one," Cookie said, indicating the second beast, "but I think this one over here is Doctor Jekyll..."

"But how...?" Hercules' voice trailed off in incredulity as he continued to stare at the creature now standing atop the wreckage of their tank. It looked as if it might start beating its chest like an enraged ape at any moment.

It was naked from the waist up, its monstrous musculature clearly visible under its weirdly green-tinged flesh. The trousers that Hercules had found for Jekyll back at the farm, which had been several inches too large around the waist, now clung to his expanded physique, looking like they might go at the seams at any moment. Bits of Jekyll's tattered jacket clung to its shoulders.

Giving voice to another mighty roar of rage, the second monster hurled the engine part, the greased steel spinning end over end, only for it to be plucked out of the air by the bellowing hulk of a man that – if Cookie was right – Doctor Henry Jekyll had somehow become.

Any thoughts Hercules might have had that the two monsters were actually on the same side were gone now.

"Now that's not friendly," the Jekyll-beast growled, and Hercules was surprised to hear it speak with a strong Cockney accent that boomed like crypt doors slamming shut. Grasping the broken piston like a club, the hulking thing brought it down hard on top of the tank, the impact sending shattered links flying from what was left of the tank's twisted caterpillar tracks.

Still holding the piston as if it were a cudgel, the thing-that-had-been-Jekyll tensed, muscles bunching, and then leapt towards the lank-haired creature, the frame of the tank buckling beneath it as it did so.

Howling with rage, the other creature kicked off from the stricken Landsknecht, sending the walking machine spinning to the ground with a crash, and freeing the trapped *Donner* into the bargain.

The two behemoths hurtled towards each other with horrific inevitability, the sound of their impact echoing across the dam like a thunderclap. The challenger's mighty meat-hammer fist connected with the face of the brutish Jekyll. Hercules saw the flesh of his face ripple beneath the punch, even as the transformed doctor's improvised bludgeon connected with the creature's ribs.

Hercules' gaze shifted between the two titans as they struggled. It was hard to tell which was the bigger of them, and from the way the battle was going, they appeared to be pretty evenly matched.

There were, however, distinctive differences between them. There was the unnatural greenish tinge to the flesh of the thing that used to be Jekyll, while the parchment yellow weathered skin of the other creature was criss-crossed by the white lines of old scars.

Both the brutes resembled men, but seen through a glass darkly. Jekyll was now a grossly bulging version of a man, like a freakishly over-enhanced body builder. Whereas the other creature, by comparison, gave the impression of being a patchwork of people, put together from bits and pieces of others, so that nothing quite matched or fitted together as it should.

Under the force of each other's blows, the two behemoths spun away from each other and came to ground with concussive force against the fabric of the dam. Jekyll slid to a halt on his back, the already fractured surface of the road gathering in great broken folds behind his shoulders, while the patchwork creature's flight was arrested by the opposite wall of the dam, the brickwork crumbling at the impact.

The Jekyll-thing sat up, shaking its head, looking like a punch-drunk prize-fighter as it tried to clear its befuddled mind.

And then a sudden, and horrible, realisation dawned on Hercules. This was undoubtedly the thing that had taken out an entire platoon of German soldiers after the *Baron von Richthofen* had crash-landed behind enemy lines. And he had been unwittingly travelling with the perpetrator of that atrocity ever since.

On the other side of the dam the scar-covered giant was struggling to its feet.

The hulking Jekyll did the same, and Hercules saw that the over-sized boots he had borrowed from the abandoned farmhouse were long gone, the ancient stitching having burst apart, unable to contain Jekyll's colossal feet.

"Pucker up, big boy," the green colossus rumbled, as it began to stagger drunkenly towards the lank-haired monster, the cracking of its knuckles like a salvo of cannon fire, "and kiss this."

With a deafening bang, the thunder hammer cannon spoke again. The spinning shell hit Jekyll in the stomach, blasting him off his feet and punching him clean into the wreckage of the tank, the *Seigfried* groaning and screeching as the huge body hit it with all the force of a crashing meteorite.

"Shit!" Hercules heard one of the girls gasp from where she was crouched somewhere on the ledge behind him.

"That's one way of putting it," he said, stunned himself. "Scratch one British secret weapon. I guess we can forget the mission after all."

"Wait!" Missy hissed, cutting Hercules off mid-sentence. "Look!" She was pointing at the wreck of the *Seigfried*.

All eyes swivelled back round to the crumpled chassis of the tank half-buried in the hole the errant eagle-bomber had blasted in the road. Huge fists gripping the sides of the tank, the thing that had been Jekyll pulled itself free of the wreckage once again.

"Amazing," he gasped, unable to believe his own eyes. There didn't appear to be a scratch on him.

"Now that *really* wasn't very friendly," the Jekyll-thing snarled, its voice heavy with malice. It was holding something in one ham-sized hand; something large, bullet-shaped and made of metal.

Back on its feet now, the scarred fiend gave voice to another furious howl. Its blood was up.

"Hold your horses," the Jekyll-creature growled, teeth bared at his opponent like an enraged chimpanzee. "You'll get yours in good time." It strode away from the other creature, towards the *Donner*, the stalker's crew working furiously to reload the thunder hammer before it was too late. The panicked shouts of the soldiers trapped within what had suddenly become a prison even reached the allies sheltering behind the wall at the dam's edge.

Hercules watched as the brute tossed the unexploded shell in his hand one more time, as if assessing its weight, and then, with a grunt, hurled it back at the machine.

The shell struck the Landsknecht, detonating on contact, and the percussion touched off the stalker's remaining payload. The force of the explosion obliterated the fighting machine, liquefying the tarmac on top of the dam and fusing what was left of the machine – its splayed, bird-like iron feet – into the surface of the road. A surge of flame washed back over the dam.

As the echoes of the *Donner's* destruction faded over the man-made lake, it was replaced by the beast's rumbling laughter.

The other creature's attack caught him off guard, the lank-haired monster covering the last ten yards in a single bound.

The two monsters went bowling across the top of the dam, only stopping when they hit the wall behind which Hercules and the others had taken cover.

Hercules felt the stones shift. A shower of broken mortar, loosened from between the bricks, tumbled away over the side of the dam.

"I think it's time we got out of here, don't you?" Hercules said, turning to the leader of the Monstrous Regiment.

"What about Doctor Jekyll?" Cookie asked, following Hercules on her hands and knees as he edged along the wall, heading for the opposite side of the megalithic structure two hundred yards away.

"I rather think he can take care of himself, don't you?"

The seven of them edged their way along, while the grunts and thunderous impacts of the two duelling monsters sent shockwaves shuddering through the Darmstadt Dam.

It felt to Hercules as if the entire structure was shaking beneath him. What with the eagle's bomb, the destruction of the Landsknecht and the tremors resulting from the monsters' prolonged battle, he began to wonder how much more damage the dam would be able to take before something catastrophic occurred.

There was a sudden violent *crack* and a section of the wall in front of Hercules exploded in a shower of brick dust and broken stones, as a huge misshapen head burst through it. For a moment Hercules found himself staring into the half-closed eyes of the stunned, yet still monstrous, Jekyll. And then it disappeared as Jekyll's opponent grabbed him by the hair and hauled him back to the fight.

Hercules watched, crestfallen, as a good twenty yards of the ledge underneath the fracture crumbled and fell away right there in front of him. They wouldn't be going that way now.

With the roars of the grappling giants ringing in his ears, Hercules couldn't help peering back over the wall to watch the battle unfolding between them.

"Looks like it's time Mr Hyde taught you a lesson," the hulking brute gloated as it seized the patchwork monster in a one-armed, crushing headlock, bringing its other fist around into its opponent's face. Hercules found himself vaguely wondering who this 'Mr Hyde' was.

Was this thing, now calling itself Hyde, Jekyll or not? If he wasn't Jekyll, then where had Hyde come from? There certainly hadn't been room inside the tank to keep a secret as big as that hidden.

So Hyde had to be Jekyll, but horribly transformed. But how?

And then Hercules found himself recalling the words of Professor Knox back at the Medical School in Edinburgh, before he had introduced him to the frozen Jekyll: "My colleagues and I have tried to continue the doctor's ground-breaking work, in our own small way."

Was Hyde what Knox had been talking about?

Hercules watched as Hyde hurled the other creature from him, only for the brute to come at him again, its massive hands twisted into savage, blunt-ended claws. Mr Hyde responded by beating his chest and tensing his biceps like some sideshow strongman.

And then, just as the scarred savage was almost on top of him, Hyde curled himself into a ball. The other creature went sailing over its target, only for Hyde to come out of his crouch at the last minute and grab a trailing foot. He yanked violently at the limb, halting the creature's flight and bringing its wrist in reach of his other hand.

"Time to dance!" Hyde boomed.

With one hand gripped tight about the monster's wrist and the other about its ankle he began to spin about on the spot, whirling his captive as if they were caught up in some rural folk dance, or as if he was preparing to throw the hammer.

As the creature howled and struggled to free itself of the hulking brute's grasp, Hyde completed one rotation, then another, speeding up as he did. With a guttural snarl, he hurled the creature away over the edge of the dam, towards the river gorge, the monster coming down into the black waters of the lake several seconds later and a good fifty yards downriver.

Cautiously rising to his feet, Hercules watched the ripples spread from the monster's splash. There was no sign of the creature for several seconds, and Hercules began to wonder if the hulking Hyde really had discovered the best way to defeat it.

An eerie calm fell over the dam, broken only by the crackle of flames and the hiss-clank of the last of the Landsknechts.

Suddenly aware of another presence nearby, the thing that had been Doctor Henry Jekyll turned to face Hercules. The brute's chest and shoulders heaved as he panted for breath after his incredible exertions. He glowered at the British agent in the Nazi uniform. Hercules smiled back weakly.

Hercules stepped through the gap Hyde's head had created in the wall, and thrust a hand towards the looming half tonne of muscle and pent-up rage. The beast stared back at him in incomprehension, as if they had never met.

"Quicksilver," Hercules said, frowning uncertainly. "Hercules Quicksilver."

Hyde's face held the surprised look of a hungry cat to whom a mouse had just held out its paw in greeting. He slowly held out his own massive, green-hued hand. "Hyde," he said, in his deep Cockney rumble. "Mr Edward Hyde. Pleased to make your acquaintance."

Hercules was suddenly conscious of the hiss of the flame-thrower's pilot light and the glug of naphtha sloshing into a pressurised propellant chamber.

Hyde's wary expression suddenly became a grimace of anger

and Hercules felt his own pulse quicken, preparing him for whatever was about to happen next.

Rather than take Hercules' hand and shake it, Hyde's own massive palm suddenly smacked the man aside, flicking him away as if he were no more than a fly.

A split second later, a torrent of incendiary naphtha gushed across the road, and splashed across the hull of the stricken tank.

The crew of the last Landsknecht had closed the gap between them and the *Seigfried* in a few clanking steps.

Hyde himself leapt clear but not before he was caught by the stream of blistering naphtha. Flames licked at his unnatural flesh, leaving it scorched black with soot but otherwise unmarked.

The stalker's secondary weapon opened up then, the rattling Gatling gun peppering the road surface with bullets.

From where he now lay flat on his back on the road – having been saved from the *Blitzen's* hungry flames by the hulking Hyde – Hercules was certain he saw several rounds hit Hyde himself, only rattle onto the road, leaving the green giant unharmed. However, the force of the fusillade sent the brute stumbling back towards the tank.

The flame-thrower was still throwing out a torrent of flame, the burning naphtha pouring over the dented wreckage of the *Seigfried* and into the crumpled crew compartment.

"Jump!" Hercules shouted, scrambling to his feet and running for the wall.

Cookie stared at him aghast and then at the tank and the licking flames streaming from the Landsknecht.

"Now!" Hercules screamed.

The woman's own instinct for survival – honed by military training and experience in the field, as well as the life she had led before taking on the moniker 'Cookie' – took over and she turned and leapt.

Hercules vaulted from the top of the dam a split second later, sailing out beyond her. And then they were both falling, dropping like stones.

Having worked out what was going on, the rest of the squad threw themselves after their leader and the British agent.

The fall seemed to last for an age. Focusing on the churning white-water below, Hercules prayed that they would hit the river and not the dam's massive stone footings.

They still had another two hundred feet to fall when the heat of the flame-thrower's caresses cooked off the munitions still locked inside the tank's magazine.

Spears of smoke and flame tore through the plate armour of the *Seigfried* as if it were no more than a model constructed from paper and card.

The tank was consumed by a ball of greasy smoke and retina-searing pyrotechnics that continued to expand, swallowing the top of the dam. Secondary detonations were swallowed by the vast roiling explosion, producing a fireball of extraordinary size.

And then the turmoil of the churning river was suddenly right there under them and Hercules and the others hit the water with a succession of splashes. The waters of the river closed over their heads and the powerful pull of the current dragged them away downstream between the steeply wooded banks of the valley below.

Fragments of blackened steel and shattered cogs rained down around them, hissing as they were cooled by the river, throwing up great clouds of steam.

Hercules surfaced moments later, gasping for breath and treading water, trying to gain some semblance of control over his careering course as the river dragged him further and faster downstream. He saw six other spluttering faces looking back at him, hair and make-up a mess after the impromptu dunking.

As the aftershock echoes of the explosion faded, another seismic rumbling took its place.

Hercules twisted mid-stream and stared in amazement as the top of the dam collapsed and the lake began to pour down into the valley after them in a Biblical flood.

The destruction of the tank had been too much for the Darmstadt dam, weakened as it had been by the assaults it had already had to endure.

Thousands of tonnes of water and rock tumbled down the cliff-like face of the dam's foundations. Colossal pieces of masonry bounced over the rough terrain to come to rest further downstream, where they proceeded to clog the river once again. The gushing waterfall now cascading from the shattered dam crashed down into the newly spreading pool, the river breaking its banks as millions of gallons of water went rushing through the valley below, uprooting trees and carrying boulders the size of jeeps before it.

Hercules stared back upstream at the approaching wave, stunned with horror and yet resigned to his fate, suddenly utterly helpless when faced by the full force of the one element that had shaped the very face of the planet – more than Man with all his machines and inventions could ever do.

"Hold on!" he shouted at the women riding the river behind him. "This could get a little rough!"

CHAPTER EIGHTEEN

The Hunting Party

THE CONVOY GROUND to a halt at the edge of the ruined dam, the jeeps and half-tracks unable to go any further as the River Rhine now tumbled unhindered in front of them. An explosion of clearly devastating force had ripped open the dam as if it had been no more than a sandcastle.

Lieutenant-Colonel Teufel climbed out of his staff car at the head of the hunting party. His jackboots crunched on the mess of shell casings and metal debris that littered the impacted road surface. He stopped, at a safe distance from the spot where the road surface had collapsed altogether, gazing at the hypnotic flow of water churning through the fissure. He watched as more of the crumbling dam was worried loose by the splashing waters and carried away by the river and over the edge of the new waterfall.

Teufel's eyes followed the stream as it disappeared over the brink and tumbled away into a fine white spray, shot through with myriad rainbows, as it cascaded down the cliff-like face of the dam. Down there in the valley, amidst the fractured stonework, he could see all that was left of a tank and a

Landsknecht, crushed by the cyclopean blocks of masonry that had come down on top of them.

A stretch of dam some forty yards wide had been wiped out by the devastating explosion. On the far side, its legs half hanging over the gulf, lay a fighting machine.

The Landsknecht lay on its back, its legs frozen as if in the act of walking, one of the piston-powered limbs twisted back on itself. The hull of the fighting machine was scorched, its Nazi insignia almost entirely burnt away.

Two men were standing beside the stricken machine. A third was slumped against it, his right arm trussed up in a makeshift sling. One of the other two – a lance corporal, judging by the insignia sewn onto the sleeve of his jacket – waved at them from across the divide, a handkerchief pressed against his mouth. Teufel could see congealed blood covered the man's nose and chin.

Isla von Haupstein joined him, as close as either of them dared stand at the edge of the precipice. "They were here," she said enigmatically.

"Yes, thank you, my dear," he said, enunciating slowly and clearly, "but I'd rather worked that out for myself."

Teufel glowered at the lance corporal, an expression of weary annoyance on his face. He turned from the waving fool to address his own team.

"Bring him," he said.

"So, Lance Corporal Riker," the Lieutenant-Colonel began, resting his steepled fingers under his chin, "you had the enemy in your sights and you let them get away?"

Riker sighed. He was tired and wet, having been thrown a line by the Devil's men, who then watched as he braved the freezing, torrent to get to them. Before he had even been given the opportunity to get dry again and make himself comfortable, he had been dragged before the old man to give an account of his actions and those of the men under his command.

Riker had heard of Teufel, the Devil. Everyone had. He was infamous among the officers of the German military.

"It wasn't like that, sir," he began.

"Oh, I'm sorry," the old man hissed, his voice dripping with venom. "I am mistaken, am I? It wasn't our quarry at all." He gestured at the hole in the dam and the metal debris scattered all around them. "It was the League of German Girls, was it?"

"No. I mean..." He faltered.

"Then why don't you enlighten us, Lance Corporal?" Teufel interjected. "Why don't you tell us what you *do* mean?"

Riker met the gaze of the Lieutenant-Colonel and his adjutant in turn. Unable to bear the force of their eyes upon his, he cast his gaze at the ground.

"We were attacked," he said.

"By our quarry?"

"No, Herr Colonel. It was something else."

"Something else, you say?" Riker could feel the Devil's black stare burning into him. "But what?"

"I... I'm not sure," Riker replied weakly.

Teufel said nothing.

Unable to bear the silence, any more than he was able to bear the Devil's eyes upon him, he gave voice to his own private thoughts, even though he knew that to do so would be to damn himself. "It looked like a man."

"A man?" Teufel hissed, his voice barely more than a whisper.

"A giant, I suppose," Riker went on, shoulders sagging, his tone resigned now, knowing that he had condemned himself through his confession. "That's what it looked like."

"One man did all *this*?" Teufel said, almost laughing, indicating again the ruinous damage caused to the dam with a wave of his gloved hands.

"Well no, not one man. There were actually two of them."

"*Two* men did this? Two men, between them, destroyed a tank and two Landsknechts, put another Landsknecht out of action and ended up tearing a hole big enough to drive a train through in the *Darmstadt Dam*?"

"They were big men. Really big," Riker persisted.

Teufel glowered at the downcast man, pure poison in his stare. "And where are these men now?"

"I'm sorry?"

"I said, where are they?"

Riker raised his head and met the Devil's penetrating, coal-black stare at last. "I... I don't know, sir. Gone with the dam, I suppose."

Teufel turned away from the dejected lance corporal. "Then you are of no further use to me," he said coldly. "On your knees!"

Such was the force of the Lieutenant-Colonel's command that Riker dropped to his knees on the hard, broken ground immediately.

All those present waited in silence as Major Haupstein placed a gun in the Devil's open palm. Without hesitation he turned it on the errant officer and fired a single shot, before the shocked Riker had taken in what was happening.

The report of the gunshot echoed from the walls of the gorge, over what remained of the draining reservoir. Haupstein picked up the body and threw it into the mouth of the waterfall, where it was carried over the edge of the precipice and out of sight.

The commander of Teufel's personal squad of Stormtroopers waited a respectful moment before asking, "Where do we go from here, sir? What are your orders?"

"I rather think it's time I sent Major Haupstein here to do what Lance Corporal Riker and his Landsknechts could not."

The Stormtrooper cast a wary look the Major's way.

"Well, you know what they say about a woman's work," Haupstein said, a predatory smile forming on her lips.

"If you would be so kind, my dear?" Teufel said, a beseeching look in his eyes.

"For you, Lieutenant-Colonel," she purred, "anything."

Without another word, pausing only to sniff the air once more, she turned and sprinted back to the near end of the dam. Once there she began to scramble down the rugged slope, and the craggy cliffs of the river gorge, into the valley below.

"I should have done this long ago," Teufel confided to the Stormtrooper, never once taking his eyes off the dwindling figure of Major Haupstein as she bounded over the mossy rocks with the grace of a panther.

CHAPTER NINETEEN

The Strange Case of Dr Jekyll and Mr Hyde

"ARE YOU ALRIGHT?" Hercules asked as he hauled the young woman from the shallows of the river and up onto the bank.

Cat looked up at him and smiled. Her long blonde ponytail had become unravelled and now hung in lank, dark tresses, framing a heart-shaped face with fine cheekbones and the most striking green eyes.

"I am now," she said, holding his hand for longer than was strictly necessary.

Hercules felt his cheeks redden, despite being soaked to the skin and feeling as cold as ice after his prolonged dip in the river.

"Hey!" Cookie shouted down to them from further up the bank. "There's a house up here!"

Cat released Hercules' hand but held his gaze a moment longer as she turned and climbed the slope into the stands of copper beech and ash beyond. He couldn't help noticing the way her wet fatigue trousers clung to her well-toned thighs and the proud curve of her buttocks.

"So, are you going to help me too, or what?" a fierce voice called, while Hercules enjoyed the view a moment longer.

"Yes, of course," he said, blushing again and reaching out a hand to help Dina to safety.

The surge of floodwater unleashed when the dam burst had carried them much further downstream than Hercules had first anticipated. Fortunately the surging torrent had also kept them clear of the rapids that littered the river further downstream in the densely wooded valley below. As soon as he was able, Hercules had fought the current to reach the northern bank of the river as the flood swept them around another bend, finding shelter within a swirling pool separated from the rest of the river by a natural rocky barrier. The others had followed his example. Free of the full force of the river, from there he had been able to scramble clear of the water at last, helping his new companions to do likewise.

Once they were clear of the river's chill clutches, the dishevelled party eventually re-grouped above the water-line, further up the slope within the bounds of the forest.

"There's a house, did you say?" Hercules asked, joining the squad's leader.

"Look." She pointed.

He could see it now. Half-hidden by the pine trees higher up the slope, the place looked deserted. The forest lodge had been constructed from the same trees as those that surrounded it, keeping it from prying eyes. There were no lights visible in any of the windows, no tell-tale curls of woodsmoke rising from the chimney, and no other signs to indicate that the place was anything other than deserted.

Hercules scanned the eager faces of the young women encircling him.

"First things first," he said, "we need to get into the dry, get out of these wet things" – he blushed – "and work out where we go from here."

"Agreed," Cookie said, her expression stern. "But I don't want to take any chances. We haven't managed to keep operating behind enemy lines for the last three months by being slapdash."

"*How* long?" Hercules asked, taken aback.

"You heard. And that's a long time to be stuck behind enemy lines, I can tell you."

"And you've been passing yourselves off as a dancing troupe all that time?"

"No. Not the whole time. We've been the secretarial staff of a strategic centre and a medical team working out in the field as well."

"So the Karlsruhe Incident?"

"That was us."

"And the Stuttgart factory explosion?"

"Yup. Us too."

She turned to her team now.

"Missy – skirt around and cover our approach from the other side of the house. Cat and Dina, I want you two to come in from the east. Trixie and Jinx – you'll come in from the west."

"And what will you be doing?" Cat asked, glancing at Hercules with envious eyes.

"Hercules and I will cover the approach from below."

"Yes, ma'am," he saluted, coming sharply to attention and grinning cheekily.

Cookie smiled back at him.

"Oh, 'Hercules' is it now?" he heard the blonde mutter as she strode away with the team's demolitions expert, checking the load on her revolver as she did so.

If Cookie heard her, she chose to ignore it – and wisely so, in Hercules' considered opinion.

Hercules turned and gave the quietening waters of the river one last glance, before setting off up the densely wooded slope after the young woman. It was then that he spotted the body.

It was drifting face-down in the river, arms and legs bobbing on the water like a limp doll, and it was wearing nothing but a torn pair of black trousers.

"It's Jekyll!" Hercules shouted, the girls all snapping their heads around in shock and alarm at hearing the shape-changing doctor's name again. Hercules was already running back down the slope to the pebbled foreshore of the river. "Help me!"

None of the women moved.

Hercules splashed into the shallows, great strides taking him waist deep in a matter of moments.

"Help me get him out!" he shouted again in frustration.

Grabbing hold of the drifting body by an arm, he hauled it into the shallows, dragging it up onto the pebbles, rolling Jekyll onto his back as he did so.

Jekyll's eyes were closed, his mouth hanging slackly open. And it *was* Jekyll, not the hulking monster with green-tinged blood; but the question was, was he alive or dead?

Urgent fingers found the man's carotid artery. Hercules held his breath as he waited to feel the pressure of a pulse at his fingertips.

And then it was there, weak but steady. The wretch was still alive, but only just.

Hercules leant over Jekyll, putting the damp skin of his cheek over the doctor's mouth. He couldn't feel anything; the man wasn't breathing.

"Damn!" Hercules swore. Then, taking a deep breath, he clamped his own mouth over Jekyll's and breathed out, forcing air into the doctor's water-logged lungs.

With a sudden convulsion, Jekyll's body heaved. Hercules broke contact as a disgusting mix of river water and vomit fountained from the doctor's mouth.

Rolling Jekyll onto his side, so that the watery gruel might drain from his body the more easily, Hercules sat back on his heels and waited.

Jekyll started to cough between snatched gasps as his body expelled more of the river from his body.

Eventually he rolled onto his back. The women had joined them at the water's edge. They were watching Jekyll suspiciously, weapons held loosely in their hands but ready to fire in an instant should matters dictate.

Jekyll opened his eyes. His swimming gaze found Hercules' own stern stare.

"What happened?" he wheezed.

"You mean you don't remember?"

"Remember what?" Then cold realisation dawned in the doctor's eyes. "Oh no," he said, his voice a broken whisper, turning his head away in shame. "Not him. Not again. After all this time…" Facing Hercules again, he said, "So, I take it you met Mr Hyde."

"Come on," Hercules said with a resigned sigh, rising onto his haunches and offering the shivering Jekyll his hand. "Let's get you somewhere warm and dry. You and I have a lot to talk about."

"Right, as you were," Cookie told her team and they moved off again up the slope.

"AND SO," DOCTOR Henry Jekyll said later that day, when the party were gathered in front of a roaring fire in the central room of the deserted lodge, "without access to my laboratory or my potions, knowing that Hyde would return – and doubtless all too soon – I wrote to my friend Dr Lanyon."

He stared into the fire, his voice a gentle Scots brogue once more. "The transformations were occurring all the more frequently; I had realised that stress and fear, or rage, triggered my metamorphosis into the incorrigible Mr Hyde. I was hunted by the police as a murderer – wrongly, I might add, for all those crimes of which I was accused were the work of that devil – and eventually run to ground. But when the police tried to take me into custody, Hyde made his inevitable appearance and clearly, as I was to learn later, fought his way free. He was responsible for the deaths of ten policemen and a flower seller that day."

Jekyll shuddered as he recalled the nightmare he had been forced to live through all those years ago, pulling the drape closer about his scrawny frame.

Looking at him now, Hercules still found it hard to believe that this was the same man who had transformed into the massively powerful Mr Hyde when they were cornered atop the dam.

"Not knowing what else to do, I fled to France, then to Italy," Jekyll went on. "I made my way to Rome, but after Hyde made his presence felt there too, I was finally snared in a honey trap, given chloroform whilst I slept in a whore's bed after Hyde had apparently availed himself of her services the night before."

"So how did you come to be in cryogenic stasis beneath the University Medical School?" Hercules asked, intrigued.

"It was the only way to bring Hyde's rampage to an end."

"Why not simply execute him?" Missy asked.

"Oh they talked about it, believe me; endlessly, if I remember rightly. But there was always the fear that if they tried to harm me in any way, Hyde would simply resurface and make even more trouble for them.

"Knox said that they'd tried to continue with your ground-breaking work," Hercules put in, recalling his meeting with the eccentric professor back in Edinburgh.

"I bet they did," Jekyll grumbled. "But it didn't work, did it?"

"From the fact that you're here, I would presume that it didn't," Hercules agreed.

"Of course it didn't!" Jekyll gave a snort of derisive laughter. "As it turned out, the original batch of my elixir had been tainted. Even I couldn't reproduce its effects.

"So now my secret's out, and you all know the truth behind my strange story," Jekyll said, the final words of his speech underlined with a heartfelt sigh.

His tale told, the tension seeped out of him. It seemed that, in Henry Jekyll's case at least, confession really was good for the soul.

But, a tense silence had descended over the rest of those present, the only sound the pop and hiss of the logs burning in the grate. His mere presence had the women on edge now.

"And we were supposed to deliver you to Castle Frankenstein." Cookie's voice was no more than a horrified hush.

"Except we weren't," Hercules contradicted her. "Unknowingly, we had all been tasked with delivering *Hyde* to the castle; including you, doctor.

"Yes," he said, leaning back in the chair beside the fire and taking another sip from his hip flask. "I think I fully understand the purpose of your mission now."

"I can't believe they'd do that to us," Dina said, her face pale. "They were prepared to let us march in there with Jekyll, knowing what would happen... We could have been killed."

The others all turned and looked at her, disbelief writ large on their faces.

"You're not serious?" Trixie said.

"Have you not heard of the term 'collateral damage'?" Missy laughed mirthlessly.

"Acceptable losses," Cat muttered.

Hercules looked on the girl more kindly. "Desperate times call for desperate measures, I suppose."

"So, what do you suggest we do?" Cookie challenged him. "Seeing as how you seem to have all the answers."

"We continue with the mission – as originally planned."

"Precisely as planned?"

"Well, with a few modifications."

Hercules turned to Jekyll.

"You up for that, doc?"

Jekyll fixed him with a cold stare. "Do I really have a choice?" he said, darkly.

"Great!" Hercules clapped his hands. "Then let's get started!"

CHAPTER TWENTY

Suicide Blondes

"So LET ME just check I've got this straight," Cookie said, once they had all dried out, got dressed and gathered again in front of the roaring fire. "You're suggesting that we infiltrate Castle Frankenstein and unleash Hyde once we're inside?"

"I'm sitting right here!" Jekyll grunted disconsolately.

Hercules glanced his way but chose to ignore him. "That's right," he said.

"And how do you propose we do that?" Cookie asked.

"Well, I was actually going to leave the details to you. After all, you know what your girls are capable of better than me. And, anyway, isn't that what you do? I'm sure you'll be able to cook something up between you."

"But it'll be suicide!"

Hercules gave her a smile and a wink. "I thought suicide missions were your thing."

Cookie weakened at that, unable to help but smile. "Very well, Mr Quicksilver, we'll do it your way. But if Jekyll, or Hyde, or whatever he is, ends up getting us all killed, I'm going to haunt you for the rest of eternity."

"Is that a threat or a promise?" Hercules smiled.

"Touché, Mr Quicksilver."

"I need some fresh air," Jekyll muttered, getting up and making for the door. Not one of the others moved to stop him.

"Don't go running off now," Hercules called after him.

"Where would I go?" the doctor growled in response.

The front door of the lodge banged shut behind him.

"Talking of the good doctor," Dina said, now that he was out of earshot, "are you sure it's a good idea – taking him with us, I mean?"

"We've managed to bring him this far," Hercules pointed out, "and against the odds, I might add. You yourselves risked life and limb to rescue us from Schloss Geisterhaus."

"But Dina's got a point," Missy said, backing up her friend. "I mean Hyde's hardly shown himself to be the reliable type, has he?"

"Yeah, he's unpredictable at best," Jinx threw in, "at worst…"

"I know," Cookie said, butting in, "and I hear what you're saying, but orders are orders. We haven't got this far to give up now."

"I wasn't suggesting we should," Dina threw in.

"The doctor comes with us, okay?" Cookie cast a furious gaze around the group. Dina and Jinx suddenly found the knotty holes in the floorboards at their feet inexplicably interesting, while Missy met her leader's stare defiantly. "Okay?"

There were murmured mutters of assent, while Cat – her hair tied in a tight ponytail again – nodded enthusiastically. "If Hercules thinks that's best," she added.

Trixie threw her a bored scowl.

"What? If those are our orders…"

"You could at least keep him guessing a bit longer," Trixie muttered. "At least until the mission's over."

"You know what they say?" Cat said fiercely. "*Carpe diem*!"

"Right," Cookie said loudly, in an effort to regain order, "so here's the plan…"

*   *   *

ISLA VON HAUPSTEIN sprinted through the woods, bounding over the fungus-infested trunks of fallen trees and leaping over boulders, revelling in the freedom to run free, unrestrained by orders or convention. The thrill of the hunt thumped in her veins, her mind heady with the rush of scents and other, subtler sensations that her altered physique could detect.

She crossed the forested slopes with long, leaping strides, relishing the rush of adrenalin flooding her bloodstream and bringing her to the verge of the change.

Her quarry had been carried away several miles downstream by the force of the swollen river some hours before the convoy had even reached the dam. But some trace of them lingered.

She saw the scents as colours and patterns, a visual cacophony that only she could make sense of. Strongest of all were the bilious yellow of fear and the deep crimson of unrestrained rage.

But this was the one thing that Isla couldn't work out. Those two contradictory fragrances seemed somehow inextricably linked, as if they came from the same source; as if there were two separate identities inhabiting the one body.

And now she could smell wood smoke, the diluted scents of her prey mingling with the aroma of resin, painting an impossible rainbow of colours across her cerebral cortex and helping her to refocus.

She raced on, her body on fire with vitality.

She tensed suddenly and, landing in a thicket of thorns, froze. The curious yellow dread, with its almost overpowering undercurrent of fury, was suddenly stronger.

Carefully moving aside a trailing bramble, Isla von Haupstein peered through the encroaching darkness, her eyes instantly alighting upon the thin-framed figure standing there, shivering in the twilight, his breath misting in the chill air.

Silent as a hunting wild cat, she padded towards the lonely lodge.

JEKYLL STARTED, SHOOTING panicked glances into the encroaching gloom, turning his head left and right trying in vain to see anything at all through the encroaching dusk. He had thought he'd heard the snap of a twig underfoot.

"Who's there?" he hissed.

There was a rustle of leaves nearby.

And then his already quickening pulse skipped a beat altogether as a raven-haired goddess stepped into the light from the undraped windows of the lodge, like some Wagnerian Valkyrie.

Transfixing him with her piercing stare, she tilted her head back, exposing the swan-like curve of her neck. Nostrils flaring, she savoured the scents on the air.

"Who are you?" he croaked, his voice a cracked whisper, backing across the veranda towards the door.

The woman replied with a strong German accent. "I think the real question is, *what* are *you*?"

HERCULES OPENED THE door and stepped out onto the veranda. There was no one there.

"Jekyll?" he called into the encroaching night. And then again, louder: "Henry! Henry Jekyll!"

Leaning over the edge of the veranda he listened, absorbing all the sounds of the night before trying one last time. "Jekyll!"

Moments later he returned to the warmth of the lodge, looking pale and drawn.

The Monstrous Regiment turned, their expressions darkening as they saw the desperate glint in his eye.

"He's gone," Hercules said bluntly.

"What do you mean gone? He can't be gone!" Cookie challenged him. "I mean, where would he go?"

"Take a look for yourself then," Hercules said, stepping away from the open door and gesturing for her to go through it.

Intrigued, the group gathered at the door as their leader joined Hercules outside on the veranda.

"You're sure?" she said, looking at him with plaintive eyes. "I mean people don't just vanish."

"You're sure about that, are you?" Hercules said, recalling the empty farmhouse he had raided for supplies not long after arriving in Germany. "This is a country under military rule; anything could happen."

"So where's he gone and run off to?" Cat asked, staring at Cookie and Hercules in bewilderment.

"I don't believe he ran off anywhere," Hercules said, now crouched on the dirt track in front of the lodge, peering at the ground by the light spilling from the open front door.

He rose and turned to face the women waiting on the veranda, seeing that Missy had a pistol ready in her right hand.

"There are two sets of fresh prints here – other than ours, I mean," he said. "It looks to me like he was taken."

"Taken?" Dina laughed. "But Hyde would hardly have let that happen, would he?"

"That a very good point."

The party looked at each other, the concern writ large upon their faces. In the silence that fell between them, Hercules suddenly dearly wished to hear the crash of undergrowth and the bullish roars of the enraged Hyde again.

"This is worse than I thought," he said.

"This is bad," Cookie said, putting into words what they were all clearly thinking. "Very bad."

What could have befallen Jekyll that prevented even Hyde from coming to his rescue?

"Sorry, girls," Cookie said, addressing her crack team. "Looks like the mission's off."

"It most definitely is not!" Hercules railed. "We go ahead as planned."

"You can't be serious."

"We have to rescue Jekyll," he said, rounding on her. "Don't you see? Just because a bunch of half-senile surgeons back in Edinburgh couldn't successfully recreate Jekyll's experiments doesn't mean Hitler's pet geniuses in the Frankenstein Corps won't be able to. And if they get their hands on the secret of Jekyll's success, it can only end badly for our side."

Cookie nodded slowly, saying nothing.

"But how can you be sure he's been taken to Castle Frankenstein?" Jinx challenged.

"Where else would they take him?"

"So, what do you suggest, Hercules?" Cat asked, ignoring the disapproving *tut-tut-tut* that escaped Trixie's lips.

"We go with the plan as agreed," Hercules said, "only now we have two objectives; to destroy the facility and rescue Jekyll."

Cookie turned to him, a look of begrudging admiration on her face. "Anything else?"

"Yes. We go tonight."

CHAPTER TWENTY-ONE

The Best Laid Plans

THE NIGHT WAS cold, the sky clear, the moon a portentous presence in the heavens above, bathing the fortress in its ethereal light. Private Scholz scanned the vista beyond the perimeter of Castle Frankenstein, flexing his gloved hands about the trigger paddles of the Czechoslovak mounted in the gun emplacement, his fingers aching from the cold. He had lost all feeling in his toes as well. He didn't know who he had pissed off to end up on look-out duty during the graveyard shift, but he was sure he was paying the price now.

Castle Frankenstein never slept. The production line of the corpse-factory worked day and night to reanimate the dead and send them back to the front line – a forest of chimney stacks belching smoke and steam into the chill mountain air – but from midnight to dawn, the fortress was at its quietest. The motor pool and inner courtyard were as quiet as they ever got, while the scientists and flesh-wranglers of the Frankenstein Corps worked by the electricity that powered almost everything within the castle, from lighting the laboratories to reanimating the reconstructed Prometheans improved by the Corps' flesh-smiths.

But since the destruction of the dam earlier that day, the supply of electricity from the power station had dropped off considerably. While the engineers were struggling to repair the dam as best they could, the castle was running on reserve power, the massive machines employed by the production line steadily draining the acres of reserve batteries buried beneath the castle in their lead-lined vaults.

The pylons stretched away west towards the dam – skeletal figures, black against the velvet blue of midnight – connecting the turbine halls there with the castle, the power-lines they carried crackling with the weak bursts of electricity the dam could still provide.

Ever since the attack on the power station, and then the arrival of the Devil himself, along with the rest of his cavalcade, the whole castle had been on edge. The British agent's secret weapon might now be in Nazi custody, but there was a rumour among the men that there was a crack commando unit still out there somewhere, on the loose in the forested hills of Hessen.

Private Scholz, however, was confident that no matter how elite and deadly they might be, they wouldn't dare launch an attack on Castle Frankenstein.

He glanced to his right, to the adjacent gatehouse watchtower. The other look-out, Weber, had his eyes locked firmly on the road winding up from the valley below, around the curve of the hill to the castle gates. The echo of a round being chambered reached Scholz's ears.

Scholz followed the other look-out's gaze down to the approach to the castle, and then he saw what Weber must have seen too, and had the sights of the Czechoslovak gun trained on the target in a moment.

There were two of them, limned in the silvery light of the moon.

Squinting through the sights, releasing the left hand trigger paddle, Scholz reached for the tower's telephone handset and cranked the handle – doing everything one-handed – and waited for his counterpart in the other tower to pick up.

"What do you make of that?" Scholz asked.

"An officer – a colonel, by the looks of it – and a lone prisoner," Weber's voice crackled back over the line. "Must have become separated from the rest of the Lieutenant-Colonel's party."

"You're sure?" Scholz challenged.

"Let Voight and Ziegler deal with them," Weber said, casting a glance at the gate below before returning to scanning the night beyond.

"COLONEL MERKUR TO see the commandant," the approaching officer announced, pushing the bound woman before him with the barrel of his Luger.

"I'm sorry, Colonel Merkur, but Colonel Kahler is occupied at present," said the gate guard, his greatcoat buttoned up against the cold and his helmet pushed down firmly on his head.

"I'm sure he is, private," Merkur said, "but he'll want to know about this." The officer prodded the woman again with his gun. "I've captured another one of them."

Voight looked the young woman up and down. Her svelte figure was clad in dark, tight-fitting fatigues, her wrists tied with what looked like one of the Colonel's bootlaces.

Private Voight hesitated for a moment, uncertain what to do. He didn't want to disturb the commandant's meeting with the Devil, but if Colonel Merkur had caught up with another enemy spy, the others should probably know about it too.

"Yes, of course, Herr Colonel," he said, turning back to the gateway behind him, signalling for his companion on the other side to raise the checkpoint barrier and open the gates. "Right away."

The Colonel pushed his captive towards the gate once again, causing the woman to stumble and fall against Voight.

Before the private could even utter a grunt of surprise, his own gun was pulled from his hands and his legs kicked out from under him.

He fell to the ground, landing on his hands and knees. And there was the girl standing over him, her hands somehow free, and his gun in her hands.

There was a muffled report and the other guard dropped to the ground, groaning softly, his hands to his stomach.

In the instant it took the private to realise what was happening, there was another gunshot and Voight never heard anything else ever again.

As soon as he heard the first muffled shot from below, Scholz leant forward, aiming his gun at the wan pools of light cast by the flickering lanterns on the gate below.

There was a second shot as he struggled to focus on what was going on down there. His eyes fell on the two prone figures lying on the ground in front of the checkpoint.

They had been duped. But the infiltrators wouldn't get past the gate – Private Scholz would see to it personally.

There was the *pfft* of a silenced gunshot from somewhere amidst the inky shadows among the trees beyond the castle, followed by a faint moan from the nearest watchtower.

Caught off guard, Scholz glanced to the right, his heart pounding against his ribs. There was no sign of Weber.

He snapped his view back to the impenetrable treeline, the enemy below forgotten as his natural instinct for survival tried to pinpoint where the sniper's shot had come from, painfully aware that he could be next.

As a result, he was taken completely by surprise when an attacker swung down from the lip of parapet above him, planting two feet firmly in the middle of his chest and sending him stumbling backwards to the floor of the gun-nest, beside the Czechoslovak, and a svelte form landed cat-like on top of him.

One hand closed over his nose and mouth and the other plunged a knife up to the hilt into his kidney. His gasp of shock and pain was muffled by the smothering hand, which held firm as a cold numbness rapidly spread throughout his body.

"Any problems?" Missy asked Cat as the two passed each other on the tower stairs.

"Like taking candy from a baby," the assassin purred. "You?"

"Bulls-eye," Missy said, forming an imaginary pistol with her right hand and miming taking a shot.

As the sniper took her position as look-out at the top of the sentry post, Cat joined Hercules and Cookie in the shadows beyond the gate, and Trixie, Jinx and Dina jogged from the cover of the trees and up the road to join them.

"So far, so good," Hercules whispered as they came together at the checkpoint. "Now the fun really begins."

"You all know what you have to do," Cookie said, checking the load on her gun, "so let's do this."

Hercules watched as the women melted away into the darkness, following Cookie and Trixie, the code-breaker, as they made for the nearest guard-post.

JINX FROZE AT the sound of tramping footsteps and crouched down in the lee of the canvas-covered truck. Keeping her breathing deep and slow to still her racing heart, she listened intently as the footsteps passed by her and receded into the distance, heading in the direction of the inner courtyard.

Once she was sure she could go about her business again undisturbed, she let out her breath noisily, rose to her feet, and tried the passenger door of the cab. It wasn't locked, but then nobody inside Castle Frankenstein would have suspected anyone already inside the castle of wanting to steal one.

Climbing inside, she pulled the door gently shut behind her, listening as the door catch caught with a click, and then slid across to the driver's seat. She was almost disappointed when she pulled down the sun-visor and the keys to the ignition fell into her open hands. She had been secretly hoping she was going to have to hot-wire it.

DINA HUNG BACK by the gate, laying out a length of fine fishing line, looping it around the supports of the checkpoint itself before attaching it to the firing pins of a pair of grenades at each end.

The trap set, she ducked between the serried rows of parked vehicles that filled the outer courtyard of the castle. Crouching down in the lee of a jeep, she secured a device of her own invention – comprising a couple of sticks of dynamite, a length of primer cord and a remote trigger – under a wheel arch. The trigger itself was safely stowed within the harness she wore like a waistcoat, along with half a dozen small, short-fuse grenades.

Brushing a stray strand of dark hair out of her face, Dina moved on through the darkness, looking for another suitable place to set a booby-trap.

"HEY, WHAT'S –" WAS all the guard managed to say before Hercules brought the butt of his pistol down hard across the back of his head. With a stifled groan he slumped forwards onto the Enigma terminal.

Cookie pulled the unconscious man from his seat and hurriedly hauled his body under the table while Hercules moved back to the door to keep watch, Luger in hand.

Trixie filled the now vacant position and set to work, her fingers moving in a blur of speed. One security barrier was breached after another as the code-breaker's counter-cyphers systemically overcame the Enigma engine's defences one at a time.

"I'm in," Trixie declared triumphantly a few minutes later, pushing her glasses up onto the bridge of her nose again.

"Well done!" Cookie said, giving her a well-deserved pat on the back. "Now pull up a schematic of this place and find out where the good doctor's being kept."

EASING OPEN THE door in the east wall, Dina peered into the gloom beyond. She could see very little. She waited a moment longer, listening, but she could hear nothing, either. Stepping through into the passageway beyond, she was hit by a waft of surprisingly warm air.

Closing the door carefully behind her, she set off into the dirty orange light cast by a string of naked electric bulbs, following them until she entered a room smelling of damp rust. It was unpleasantly humid within the chamber, which seemed stifling after the chill night she had left on the other side of the door.

Thick steel pipes, orange with rust, ran the length of the wall and ceiling, penetrating the walls and floors of the castle above like the roots of some pernicious iron weed; but they all emanated from one source.

Following the winding course of the knotted pipework, Dina came at last to a sweltering basement, empty apart from a huge boiler the size of a house. The furnace that would have to be kept stoked in order to keep it in operation must have been another level deeper, but this would do perfectly.

Listening to the hiss of venting steam and the drip of condensation – and for anything that would betray the presence of another human being there with her – Dina set about planting her explosives.

HERCULES WATCHED WITH barely hidden awe as the svelte cat burglar shimmied up a drainpipe and clambered in through a window above the arched gateway.

The Enigma device had told them what they needed to know – that Doctor Jekyll was indeed being held within the depths of the castle, in the dungeons beneath the thirteenth-century keep – and they now needed to gain access to the inner courtyard and the buildings beyond.

Cookie and Trixie waited in the shadows on one side of the gate, whilst Hercules hid himself on the other.

Moments passed. The longer they waited, the more anxious Hercules felt. Had Cat run into some kind of trouble?

With a sharp rattle and a click, the door set into the gate opened. Hercules tensed, his finger on the trigger of his pistol.

A heart-shaped face appeared, ghostly white within the deeper shadows of the gateway.

"Are you coming or what?" Cat hissed.

* * *

MISSY WATCHED COOKIE and the others disappear through the door in the inner courtyard gate through the sights of her Lee-Enfield rifle. Unlike the guard she had replaced in the look-out post, her attention was focused wholly *inwards* at the castle courtyard.

She would be ready, no matter how the mission went. Either she would be picking off German soldiers, as Cookie and the others made their escape with the shape-changing doctor in tow, or she would be laying down covering fire for her companions if it all went tits up.

And right at that moment, Missy couldn't be certain how things would pan out.

THE LAST OF the devices secured to the side of the massive boiler with the aid of more fishing line, her harness empty apart from a few hand grenades, Dina made her way back through the warren of tunnels and passageways. Ever watchful, she followed the traps she had laid, like Hansel and Gretel after a trail of breadcrumbs, back the way she had come to the entrance and out of the east wing.

From the rust-red gloom of the electric-lit passageway, she ducked into the darkness that would lead her back to the castle's outer courtyard.

The blinking of the lights within the passageway startled her almost as much as the clatter of guns being aimed and primed.

Three soldiers had her in the sights of their rifles. Slowly raising her hands above her head, she gingerly turned her head in an effort to see behind her. Three more soldiers blocked the other end of the passageway.

"Bollocks!" she swore under her breath.

"THIS WAY," HERCULES whispered, beckoning the other three forward.

The heavy oak doors barring the way into the corner keep of the castle were before them now.

As the armed foot patrol passed by their hiding place, turned and proceeded to make their way back towards the west wing of the castle, Hercules led them out of hiding and right up to the deep-set doors. Having evaded the last patrol, nothing now stood between them and the keep.

He tried the door. It remained firmly shut. Glancing at the door jamb he registered a combination lock built into the doors.

"Damn!" he hissed at the darkness.

"Don't worry," Trixie said, suddenly at his side, "I can do this." Crouching down in front of the lock she set to work, one ear pressed against the mechanism as she manipulated the tumblers with her fine fingers.

"Quickly," Cookie hissed from her hiding place behind a barrel a few paces away. "They're coming back."

"Did you hear that?" Hercules hissed, crouching down beside the code-breaker. "The patrol's already on its way back."

"I heard," Trixie whispered curtly. "Now, if you'd just let me get on with my job we might actually be able to get through these doors before the patrol gets here."

Hercules said nothing but shuffled over to the piles of crates where Cat crouched, waiting to pounce.

"There," she whispered, leaning in close over his shoulder, her breath warm in his ear.

"I see them," Hercules returned – the heady aroma of the woman's hair sweet in his nostrils – and took careful aim. If their plan was about to go all to hell, then he would do everything in his power to get the girls out of this nest of Nazis alive.

There was a dull click and he heard Trixie proudly announce, "We're in."

With a sigh of relief, Hercules returned to the porch, where Cookie and Cat joined him, the former pushing open the door with the muzzle of her machine gun.

Light bled out into the darkness beyond. Hercules winced, his eyes closing against its brightness.

Hercules was the first to see the object of their rescue mission, bound to a chair in the middle of the tapestry-draped hallway beyond.

It took him a moment longer to realise that the doctor was not alone within the hallway. From every archway and alcove protruded the muzzle of a pistol or a rifle or a machine gun, all aimed at the keep's threshold.

"Damn!" he cursed, half under his breath, as his companions stifled gasps of shock and alarm. "I knew it had all been too easy."

CHAPTER TWENTY-TWO

Of Mice and Men

FOR SEVERAL LONG moments nobody moved, as both sides faced each other down, guns poised and at the ready, between them a wan-looking Doctor Henry Jekyll.

A figure stepped out of the shadows, his boot heels clicking on the stone flags of the ancient hall. He was dressed in the uniform of a colonel as well, only his was in a markedly better state than Hercules'.

"Hercules Quicksilver, I presume," the man said, in flawless English.

Hercules could see that Jekyll was looking at him, his face pale and drawn as he mouthed the words, "I'm sorry."

Hercules scowled. "You would appear to have me at a disadvantage," he returned, keeping his gaze and his pistol targeted on the colonel. He heard the clatter of other guns in the room being cocked, and knew that they were pointed at him.

"In more ways than one," the German officer said, a wry smile curling his lips. "I am Colonel Kahler, commandant of this facility, but such details are unimportant right now. What I want to know is what you are doing here."

Hercules glanced at Cookie. She met his gaze, eyes wide with fear, pupils dilated from the rush of adrenalin now coursing throughout her body.

"Ah," the colonel said, noting their exchange, "whatever it is you're planning I suggest you forget it. You can't get away. There must be – what? – at least twenty guns on you. Such a strategy – whatever it might be – would surely be suicidal."

Hercules looked at Cookie again, reassuringly, urging her to stay calm. Understanding his intention, Cookie nodded.

He turned his head to check on the others. Cat met his gaze, her lips pursed, whilst remaining perfectly still, but Trixie was another matter.

Hercules could see her panicked look and tried to catch her eye. But it was all to no avail.

Even as he was about to tell her to calm down, the woman whimpered, turned and bolted.

"Hold your fire!" Kahler commanded, then calmly raised the Mauser HSc that was suddenly in his own hand. "I could do with the practice."

Hercules' face fell and he turned, throwing himself after the fleeing Trixie, diving at her legs in an attempt to rugby-tackle her to the ground, even as the single pistol shot rang out in the confines of the stone-walled entrance hall.

He brought her crashing to the floor, but from the lamp way the girl landed, without so much as a grunt, he knew with a sinking feeling that Kahler's shot had found its mark.

She was already dead.

HEARING THE CRACK of the lone pistol shot, Missy found the doors to the keep through her sights in time to see Trixie fall through the open double doors and down the steps beyond, Hercules clinging to her legs. Hercules remained where he was, laying half on top of her as Cookie and Cat ran hell-for-leather out of the keep, diving for cover behind a carefully stacked pile of barrels and tarpaulin-covered boxes. Hercules finally scrambled after them himself, but Trixie remained where she was.

With Trixie framed in the sights of her rifle, the code-breaker's body splayed like a rag doll across the steps, Missy was forced to blink away the hot tears that were now obscuring her vision, so as not to lose any potential targets.

And barely two seconds behind the others came the enemy. Sniffing away her tears, Missy took aim and opened fire.

A German soldier fell screaming, a bullet through his knee. The second made not a sound, Missy's shot punching straight through his left eye. The third was hurled backwards as a round took him in the chest.

Missy lined up her sights on another burly specimen and pulled the trigger, only to be met by a hollow *click*.

Her face impassive, she let the rifle fall from her hands – thudding against the rough-hewn boards of the sentry post – and took hold of the paddles of the Czechoslovak mounted there. Taking hold of it in both arms, with a roar of grief and frustration, she tore the bolts holding it to the floor free of the warped wood and yanked the weapon round so that it now pointed into the inner courtyard of the castle.

Soldiers were swarming out of the keep now, like furious, scalded ants. Taking a deep breath, she vented her grief and pain on the Nazis as she opened fire, shredding bodies in a lethal lead bullet-storm.

"TAKE OUT THAT gun-emplacement," Kahler said, snatching a glance through the open doors. "Deal with it!"

Two men hurried forward at his command, carrying a sturdy metal tube between them. As the first crouched down on one knee, still within the shelter of the doorway, his companion loaded a missile into the tube, patted the other on the shoulder and took a step back.

"Fire in the hole!" the launcher's operator announced and Colonel Kahler covered his ears. With a sound that Kahler felt through his feet, the rocket launcher fired.

The missile shrieked across the courtyard, corkscrewing its way towards the watchtower, trailing dirty smoke.

Moments later it reached its target and the storm of bullets abated as the gun position was consumed by a ball of greasy smoke and hungry, promethean flame.

"No!" Dina screamed as the top of the gatehouse blew apart. The explosion had made her captors jump too, but she was too shocked to make the most of the opportunity.

"*Weitergehen!*" a gruff voice behind her growled, making the point plain by shoving his gun barrel against her spine.

Dina took a stumbling step forwards.

"*Hände hoch!*" the officer shouted.

Pulling herself up straight, suddenly numb at having witnessed her friend's death, she kept striding forwards, proud, determined, not letting the Germans think for one minute that they had beaten her.

The command came again, louder this time, and the ever-present gun barrel prodded at her arms, trying to push them upwards. "*Hände hoch!*" She put her hands on top of her head.

As the soldiers marched her towards the gate dividing the two courtyards, Dina heard an exchange of gunfire from the other side. It was the staccato crack of carefully selected shots, as opposed to the white noise roar of the bullet-storm Missy had unleashed into the killing ground of the inner courtyard.

A firm hand suddenly pulled her to a halt as a pair of soldiers ran ahead of her, the two members of her escort taking point, ducking down behind the open door set into the inner courtyard gate and following the gun battle in an attempt to pick their own targets. Carefully, the two marksmen took aim.

With a sooty cough, one of the trucks from amongst the throng parked behind them roared into life. Headlights lit up the courtyard as the truck turned towards the inner gate, the soldiers throwing up their hands against the magnesium glare.

Germans scattered before the speeding truck like rats before the rising tide.

"You don't get away that easily, you Nazi bastards!" Jinx snarled, as she hauled the steering wheel around, turning the truck towards the archway, and put her foot to the floor.

She had seen what had happened to Missy and knew that the plan was no longer in operation. Priority one now was to get the rest of them out, as quickly as possible.

The last to realise what was going on were the two gunmen who were already half through the door in the gate as the truck caught up with them. Jinx was aware of a sudden scramble of movement, but they were too late.

The was a *crack* and another soldier went spinning from the bonnet as she clipped the wretch with the bumper, sending him whirling out of the way, his gun flying from his hands and shattering one of the truck's headlights into the bargain.

The gate disintegrated around her as the truck smashed through it, splinters and pieces of planking flying in all directions. Men howled as they were skewered by the splintery shrapnel, or screamed as they fell under the truck's wheels, or grunted, winded, as they bounced off its bonnet.

As HER GUARDS scattered before the speeding truck, Dina made the most of the second opportunity fate – or rather Jinx – had presented her with, and sprinted for cover.

But as she made a break for it, one last desperate soldier, reacting on instinct and not knowing what else to do, made a grab for her, focusing on the last orders he had been given – the only thing he had left to hold on to in this suddenly uncertain world. Desperate fingers snagged the harness she was wearing and snagged the loop of a firing-pin as the man lost his footing and fell.

JINX DUCKED DOWN inside the cab, still clinging onto the steering wheel, as the windscreen shattered above her under the torrent of machine-gun fire that greeted her arrival.

There were more cries of alarm, and the truck bounced over

the body of another soldier. She caught a glimpse of Dina as she stumbled, one of the enemy falling on top of her.

Keeping her head down, she spun the truck around, skidding across the courtyard towards the keep. If she could create an effective barrier between the escapees and the enemy, some of them might yet make it out of there alive.

THE PIN PULLED free.

"No!" Dina screamed, understanding all too well the fate that was heading her way. She desperately scrabbled at the buckles to free rid herself of the harness.

And as her frantic fingers failed to release the buckled clasps, the tears flowed freely, a wail of dread escaping her clenching throat.

THE SHOCKWAVE OF force that rippled outwards from the epicentre of the explosion, where Dina had been standing, sent soldiers tumbling before it, guns flying from their hands, and shredded the stacked barrels and crates.

The force of the blast treated all alike, regardless of which side they fought on, throwing Hercules, Cookie and Cat – and even Trixie's limp body – back through the open doorway behind them.

JINX FELT THE force of the blast as the window of the driver's door shattered, hurling shards of razor-sharp glass into the cabin with her, nicking her skin.

She felt the power of it as it lifted the turning truck into the air, flipping it onto its side, the battered chassis kicking a trail of sparks from the cobbles of the courtyard, like a miniature firework display.

Jinx lay there, in a tangle of limbs, every part of her aching, hearing nothing but the muffled *thrub-thrub* of her pulse in her ears, temporarily deafened to all else by the blast.

Slowly she became aware of crunching footsteps coming towards her. The footsteps stopped and then she felt rough hands seize her wrists and drag her unceremoniously clear of the wreckage of the cab through the shattered windscreen, her rescuers deaf to her breathless whimpers of pain.

HERCULES OPENED HIS eyes and looked up into the cold, hard face of a German soldier. The muzzle of a machine-gun was pointing directly into his face.

He tried to sit up and winced as a crimson spear of agony lanced through the back of his skull, forcing a cry of shock, as much as pain, out of him.

He automatically put a hand to the back of his head. It felt hot and tender to the touch and his fingers came back red and sticky.

"You!" the soldier snapped in German. "Get up!"

Wincing from the pain of the blow he had received to the head, his vision swimming in and out of focus, Hercules struggled to his feet. Now under armed guard, he and the other survivors of the Monstrous Regiment's ill-fated assault on Castle Frankenstein – Cookie, Cat and Jinx – were dragged back inside the keep.

Henry Jekyll was still slouched in the chair in the centre of the room, but behind him, Colonel Kahler had been joined by a black-suited SS officer and a raven-haired woman with a lean, hungry physique that matched her predatory flint-grey eyes.

"So these are the 'men' you have been hunting, Lieutenant-Colonel?" Kahler said, addressing the man in black.

"Indeed," the other replied.

"And they've been giving you the run around for how long?"

The SS officer gave the commandant of Castle Frankenstein a sharp, venomous look.

"We have them now," he said calmly, "that is what matters. And we have their secret weapon too." With one leather-gloved hand he patted the squirming Jekyll on the shoulder.

"So, do you wish to interrogate them, Lieutenant-Colonel Teufel?" Kahler asked.

"We have their secret weapon," Teufel repeated. "Do with them what you will. I have no further need of them."

"Take them away," Kahler instructed the prisoners' armed guard. "I'm sure Doktor Folter will find a use for them."

"Don't worry, we'll get you out of here," Hercules called back over his shoulder to Jekyll, as they were led away.

Kahler's laughter sent an chill tingling down his spine.

"Who did you think it was who betrayed you?"

Hercules felt his cheeks redden in anger. "Only under duress," he hissed.

"Under duress?" Kahler snorted. "Listen to yourself. You've seen what happens to the good doctor here when he's put under pressure."

Hercules could feel the colour draining from his cheeks as he understood the full implication of Kahler's words.

"The monster he hides within would have torn this castle down brick by brick, stone by stone."

"I don't know what it is you have over him but…" Hercules faltered as he realised that he couldn't imagine what Kahler could possibly have on the 'good' doctor. "But he would never have betrayed us willingly."

"Oh?" Kahler laughed. "You really think that, do you?"

Hercules turned imploring eyes on Henry Jekyll now. The doctor was sweating, his skin having acquired an unpleasant waxy sheen. "Could you?" he said weakly, the words almost sticking in his throat.

Jekyll swallowed hard, the lump of his Adam's apple bobbing as he did so.

"Why?" Hercules asked. "We came to rescue you!"

"They can cure my condition," Jekyll replied.

"Cure you?" Hercules retorted. "When the greatest minds of Magna Britannia couldn't?"

"They can cut Hyde out of me."

That was it then, Hercules thought. Jekyll's betrayal was complete.

"Judas!" Cookie spat.

At that, Kahler snorted in derision once again. "Welcome

to Castle Frankenstein," he half-chuckled. "I would say enjoy your stay, but you won't."

And with that the survivors of the raid on Castle Frankenstein were led away, now prisoners of the Third Reich, their fates sealed.

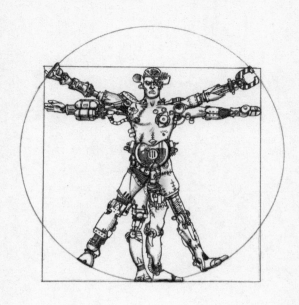

ACT THREE

Frankenstein's Children

"Society's needs come before the individual's needs."

– Adolf Hitler

CHAPTER TWENTY-THREE

The Man in the Ion Mask

CASTLE FRANKENSTEIN, DARMSTADT, GERMANY, 1943

THE MAN CAME to, to find himself being slapped repeatedly across the face.

Blearily he opened his eyes, struggling to focus on the person in front of him. There was the impression of an armoured helm, but that couldn't be right.

Fighting unconsciousness, he drifted out again for a moment.

"Wake up!" a voice snapped. It sounded as if the voice was coming from another room.

He struggled to open his eyes again but his eyelids felt as heavy as lead.

"I said wake up!" the voice came again, louder this time and accompanied by a mighty blow across his face that snapped his head round and shocked him into opening his eyes properly at last.

The chair he had been tied to rocked on its legs, threatening to tip over.

There was blood in his mouth. Mustering what strength

he could, he spat a great gobbet onto the stone-flagged floor. Probing at the inside of his cheeks with the tip of his tongue, he felt a molar give within the gum and wondered how many more blows it would take before it came out altogether.

A claw-like hand grabbed hold of his chin and pulled his head round. He winced, half-closing his eyes again under the glare of the lamps positioned behind his interrogator. All he could see of the gravel-voiced individual now was a silhouette of a hooded figure, almost monastic in appearance.

Blinking as his aching eyes slowly adjusted to the brightness of the arc-lights, he tried to focus on the shaded face in front of him.

It was metal; he was sure of it.

"What's your plan, eh?" the helmed figure demanded.

He stared at the metal mask in confusion and bewilderment as he struggled to recall who his interrogator was, where he was, what he was doing there, and why he was being interrogated at all.

His memories were a muddied blur, like the grains of sands in a tide-churned rock pool.

He remembered *the dome cracking apart like an egg as it was assaulted by the unreal energies unleashed by the whirling Sphere... His hideously-deformed nemesis turning and leaping into the ball of pulsing light...*

He remembered *scrambling up to the top of the twisted dais, hesitating before the malevolent machine... Following his enemy through... The unimaginable power of the forces unleashed by the device, the thunderous power of the vortex tearing an opening through time and space, joining two realities that Time and Nature had never intended should meet...*

He remembered *falling through time, the past, the present, the future... a myriad possibilities... an infinite number of potential realities... briefly bearing witness to the entirety of God's grand design, enough to drive a sane man out of his mind and make a madman lucid again...*

He remembered *a ball of incandescent heat, like a captured sun, falling through the years like a blazing comet, the chronosphere leaving a trail of unresolved potentialities as the tapestry of time unravelled in its wake, with him cocooned at its centre, shivering as impossible fractal patterns of frost etched their way across his exposed skin...*

He remembered *the tamed sun evaporating, melting away like ice on a magma floe, and feeling vitrified earth beneath him, as hard and as smooth as glass that splintered and cracked even as he warily rose to his feet, not knowing where – or when – he was...*

He remembered *feeling unbearably hot, as he was plunged into darkness, where before, trapped beneath the chromosphere of the miniature sun, he had felt so unbearably cold...*

He remembered *the acrid stink of burnt hair and the orange glow of scorched fibres at the elbows of his environment suit...*

He remembered *the sudden cold gust of air that took him by surprise, inhaling a great lungful of the pine-scented air, underlaid with the suggestion of damp and leaf mould...*

And then *torch beams stabbing the darkness... the roar of an engine... the harsh glare of searing sodium headlights... the clatter of rifles taking aim and cries of "Halt!" and "Sieg heil!"*

After that one moment of clarity, everything became muddy again, one day of imprisonment within the bowels of the castle blurring into the next, the interrogations becoming confused, until he could barely remember who he was, let alone what he had told his tormentor. Only it obviously hadn't been what he wanted to hear. But he remembered now.

Peering up through eyes blackened and swollen from the beatings he had received, he saw the metallic faceplate now. He saw the thin slit it bore in place of a mouth through which the desperate man's rasping words came, and the rectangles cut for his eyes, that the man inside might look out upon the world. It was lit from within by an eerie ice-blue glow as the ion mask struggled to stabilise the cellular structure of his face and prevent it from collapsing altogether.

"Daniel Dashwood," he said, a chuckle flavouring his pronouncement.

"What was the plan?" his interrogator demanded once again.

Ulysses Quicksilver laughed at that, more bloody spittle

flapping from his lips. "There wasn't any plan. There's never a plan. Haven't you heard? I make it up as I go along."

The robed, masked figure took a step back, raising a gloved hand as he did so, as if he were about to strike Ulysses unconscious. But then, suddenly and unexpectedly, the furious tension left the man's body and he lowered his hand.

"No matter," came the rasping voice from behind the mask. "There'll be no-one coming to help you this time. You will remain here, in this squalid dungeon, to end your days in misery, knowing that there's nothing you can do to stop me. The Führer's armies will win the war and turn Magna Britannia into part of the Über-Fatherland."

"What, with you as its puppet prime minister?" Ulysses mocked. "Think your face will fit?"

"If the Führer wills it."

"Magna Britannia shall never belong to Germany," Ulysses snarled, although he would have liked to have been more convinced himself.

"Oh, come now, Quicksilver. Magna Britannia's been German since the Hanoverian Succession of 1714. Hitler's just finishing the job, forging the two nations into one great empire – the greatest power the world has ever seen! One that will be undefeatable!"

"They said that about the Roman Empire too."

"Words," Dashwood spat, retracting a twisted skeletal claw that had once been a fine, firm hand. "Just words."

The Nazi was but a shadow of his former self, of the handsome man in his prime Ulysses had met at the séance to raise old man Oddfellow's ghost. But then, he had endured years of torment and suffering, having been cast into the time-stream by Ulysses' actions.

"That's all you have," he hissed, his voice a disgusting slobbering sound, as if he couldn't clear his mouth of saliva.

Ulysses lifted his head. As sense and feeling returned to him, he immediately wished it hadn't. He could feel every strained muscle, every throbbing bruise, every cracked rib, with every breath he took. The vertebrae in his neck protesting, he regarded the shrouded figure – looking like some iron-masked grim reaper.

"And what do *you* have?"

Dashwood laughed at that. "You remember the Icarus Cannon, don't you? That cocky bastard Shurin couldn't resist showing it off to you, and then faking his own death within its beam. The thing about death by heat ray, of course, is that it leaves behind nothing that can be used to tell you anything about a body, other than that it was carbon-based."

He hesitated, and Ulysses heard the slurp of his indrawn breath.

"And then there's the cavorite. Imagine what the world would be like if the Nazis were to have the first colony on the Moon. And advances in Babbage engines that men in this day and age could only dream of. And half a dozen other future technologies, existing here and now in 1943; a gift to the Führer from the future."

Dashwood suddenly leaned in close and Ulysses saw the scarred eyeballs behind the mask – irises and pupils split and twisted – bathed in the eldritch blue light, his nose wrinkling at the miasma of ozone and decay that Dashwood carried about him like a shroud.

"And do you know what the best part about it is?" he hissed.

"If I'd known you'd only come to gloat," Ulysses muttered, "I would have –"

"No!" Dashwood snapped, cutting him dead. "The best part is you won't be able to do anything to stop me. You'll die in this place knowing that I beat you!"

"So this is personal now, is it?" Ulysses said. "And here I was believing that you were motivated by some misguided sense of Aryan superiority, a warped wish to see a better world, free of conflict and suffering. And yet all along, all you were really interested in was getting one over on me."

This time, the force of the blow sent the chair toppling sideways, Ulysses hitting his head on the floor so hard it nearly knocked him senseless again.

"You're no threat to me now, and I can see that you're not going to tell me anything I don't already know," Dashwood scoffed. "You have outlived your usefulness."

He turned and marched across the room to where the outline of a door showed, delineated by a thin crack of light. There, he stopped and turned the expressionless plate of his mask on Ulysses one last time.

"But I'm sure the Frankenstein Corps will be able to make something of you. If you know what I mean."

And with that, the cackling gargle of a chuckle trapped in his throat, the twisted, revenge-driven monster that had once been Daniel Dashwood left the cell, leaving Ulysses Quicksilver to contemplate his fate.

CHAPTER TWENTY-FOUR

Being Inhuman

A THIN COLUMN of smoke was still rising from the battlemented and machine gun-encrusted walls of the fortress-factory when Katarina Kharkova emerged from the treeline at the top of the westerly escarpment overlooking Castle Frankenstein.

And it was an imposing place indeed. Along with the soaring towers, the high walls and the looming keep, the fortress bristled with gun emplacements and look-out posts. The snaking trail of pylons that she had followed from the devastation of the Darmstadt Dam continued into the complex of the corpse-factory, coils of humming power lines spooled between them like crackling Christmas tree decorations. Radio aerials and broadcasting transmitters rose amid the smoking chimneys of the fortress itself.

The external walls of the castle might be in shadow, but it was lit from within by a pulsing infernal glow, like some demonic throbbing heartbeat, as if the place that changed the dead into the living – and vice versa – was some hellish, living thing in its own right.

She had heard the sounds of gunfire, revving engines and

explosions before she even crested the rise of the hill. Arriving in the aftermath of the assault, she had decided to wait awhile before proceeding with her own plan. Things had not gone as she might have hoped up until that point. But it was barely past midnight; so what difference would another hour or two make? She just had to make sure that she was done before daybreak.

Of course, at one stage, it had been touch or go whether she would even make it this far.

After her attempt to liberate the British Agent from Schloss Geisterhaus was thwarted by a tank and five-foot-long splinter, Katarina hadn't come to again until after the Nazis had removed the spear of wood pinning her to the back wall of the atrium. Even then, she had remained semi-conscious.

As they carried her out into the sunlight, her skin began to itch, as if she was suffering from a chronic case of sunburn or had fallen into a bed of nettles.

It wasn't until they were preparing to throw her onto the hastily-constructed funeral pyre they had created for her – at the Devil's behest – that she managed to muster enough of her strength and her wits to fight back.

If only Teufel himself had stayed behind to make sure that his orders were carried out properly. Instead he and his bitch had raced off in pursuit of the British agent and his secret weapon.

The bonfire had been assembled from the debris of the entrance hall, but at the back of the house, thankfully out of sight of the rest of the Germans swarming over the ruination at the front.

As it was, she broke free of the two striplings who had been set the task of burning her body, killing both of them. Pulling their bodies into the shade of a pergola, she drained them both dry, setting herself on the path to a swift and full recovery.

Before anyone else was aware that she had escaped, she was already on her way to catching up with the British spy and the secret weapon.

Going by foot and not at the peak of fitness either, she had reached the Darmstadt Dam after dark. From there – following signs that Teufel had already been there before her – she followed the trail his entourage had left into the hills and practically to the gates of Castle Frankenstein.

She barely registered the cold wind against her cheek, but felt it in the hollows of the healing wound in her chest, its frosty breath a discomforting splinter of ice that went all the way through to the bone and knitting muscle of her shoulder socket.

Thankfully the haphazard stake had not damaged any of her major organs; although a great deal of blood had been spilled, the truth was that none of her injuries were life-threatening. She would recover from them soon enough and her body would heal itself completely, given time.

Cat-like eyes taking in what little light there was, Katarina studied this side of the castle in intricate detail.

She took in the smoking ruin of one of the gatehouse watchtowers, the open checkpoint below, the looming pylons penetrating the fortress itself, the electrical cables descending to the transformers of a sub-station somewhere within the complex, and the soldiers now scurrying about all over the battlements like swarming ants.

She grunted in annoyance and frustration. Once again the crude methods of the girl-soldiers were hampering her own rescue efforts.

As she continued to survey the fortress, she penetrated the fortress with preternatural senses beyond those possessed by mortal beings. She knew he was there; the taste of him was on the air. It was only a faint trace, but it was there nonetheless.

And, of course, she already knew that Prisoner Zero was there too, incarcerated somewhere within the castle's walls, and that if he were not saved... From what she had been told, the consequences didn't bear thinking about.

However, the conventional route she would have preferred to take to gain entrance to the castle was closed to her now. Had that been the only way in, then things might well have been tricky for her now. Except that she had visited the castle before, long ago, when she was still newly born to her twilight existence.

Descending from the wooded crags, shadow-swift, Kharkova skirted the southern perimeter of the castle, moving through the knotty undergrowth with barely a sound. Her progress unhindered by the darkness, she kept a watchful eye on the imposing silhouette atop the bluff above her.

And there at last, half a mile from the fortress on its eastern side, in an overgrown hollow in the tangled woodland, within earshot of a raging river, she came upon what she had been looking for.

If she hadn't known it was there she would never have found it; but she did. To any casual passer-by it would have been dismissed out of hand as just another animal burrow – if that. But Katarina knew better.

Pulling aside a screen of knotty brambles and woody creepers, she exposed the entrance to a shallow cave. Crouching under the natural screen and stepping through the dark hole, she made her way further into a tunnel descending through the hillside, the ceiling rising above her until she was able to walk upright again.

The darkness was all-enveloping, but Katarina knew where was she was going. Cosseted within the damp earth confines of the tunnel, she followed the stone-lined passageway as it turned west towards the roots of the crag upon which stood Castle Frankenstein.

Isla von Haupstein started, suddenly bolt upright, ears alert, darting glances around the room in which her master was now ensconced, as if seeing things that others could not.

"What is it, my dear?" Lieutenant-Colonel Teufel asked from the desk at which he was working, the hairs on the back of his neck rising in anticipation.

"She's here," his adjutant hissed. Isla inhaled deeply. "I can smell her."

"Who?" Teufel asked, regarding her with darkly hooded eyes.

"The vampire," she replied, turning eyes wild with feral hunger on her master. "She's still alive."

"Good," the Devil said, a death's head leer on his pale face. "And there was I, fearing that things would be boring from here on in. I do so prefer the thrill of the chase to the actual capture. Don't you?"

CHAPTER TWENTY-FIVE

The Prisoner

THE SUN WAS a ball of molten iron hanging in a blood-red sky. Ulysses could feel every square inch of his skin blistering at its cruel caress, burning away every nerve ending. His very existence was pain given flesh.

And then he woke up.

ULYSSES GASPED FOR breath. He felt a chill on his brow.

Anxiously he looked around him. He soon realised he was only using his left eye. The right seemed to be covered with something. He tried to blink, but his right eye stubbornly refused to respond.

He was in some kind of laboratory – that much was plain. A flickering, inconstant blue-white light, like sparking bursts of ball-lightning, lit the chamber, revealing bare stone walls, banks of primitive Babbage engines, and workbenches supporting a plethora of glass tanks containing a soupy yellow-green fluid. And suspended inside that murky miasma...

A host of hideous memories – or were they hallucinations? –

suddenly assailed his mind: flashes of images of masked surgeons; glinting razor-sharp scalpel blades; the glare of arc-lamps; and fingers probing where fingers were never supposed to go.

Ulysses gasped in shock and tried to sit up, but felt leather belts dig into his bare flesh as he strained against the harness securing him to the operating table.

He could move his head, but that was all.

Ulysses started to panic. He had been somewhere like this before. Memories of an operating theatre, its tiled walls crusted with dried bloodstains and worse. His heart quickened, and his breathing became shallow.

It was said that after it was gone, a man did not remember the pain he had once had to endure. And it was a good thing too, otherwise Ulysses would have gone mad from it, he was sure.

He was, however, aware of a dull ache in his face. It was his eye. It felt sore. He went to rub it, before remembering that he couldn't move his hands.

Tensing his arm again, Ulysses tried once more to extricate himself, gritting his teeth as the leather cuff around his wrist rubbed the sparse flesh raw. But it was no good; no matter how hard he tried he wasn't going to be able to free himself that way.

He stopped and tried to relax, hoping to clear his mind so that he might come up with a way out of his current predicament.

The last thing he remembered clearly – before the tormented visions of scalpel-fingered surgeon-torturers slicing him up – was someone entering the cell, in which he had been interrogated by Daniel Dashwood on and off since he had first been brought to Castle Frankenstein, and roughly clamping a rag soaked in chloroform over his nose and mouth.

Tied to the chair and unable to resist, other than for his semi-dream of demonic doctors, the next thing he had been properly aware of was waking up in a horizontal position, strapped to a gurney of some kind and unable to move, his eye aching horribly. It was like having a piece of grit in his eye that he couldn't blink clear or even rinse away with his own tears.

As he lay there, pondering his predicament, the sounds of the lab filtered through to his conscious mind.

He could hear the rising hum of electrical capacitors culminating in a crackle of discharging energy. He could hear the wheeze and hiss of a bellows, the rattle of an Enigma engine processing data somewhere in the background, and the *glub-glub* of air bubbles in a tank of fluid. There was the clatter of surgical instruments in a kidney dish and a murmur of voices. It took him a moment to tune into the fact that they were speaking German.

"He's awake, doctor," a voice said. It was male, young and subservient. It also sounded strangely familiar.

"Is he now?" came another voice, this one more thickly accented and cracked with age. Or possibly by insanity, Ulysses thought. It was certainly a possibility in a madhouse like this.

There was a metallic crash as something was dropped into a pan and then the sound of footsteps ringing from the floor of the laboratory. Moments later a figure was there at his side, looming over him.

Ulysses stared up at the emaciated spectre. It was wearing a blood-stained surgical gown. Several bright red traces were horribly fresh.

"Ah, so he is." It didn't come as any surprise to Ulysses that the broken voice belonged to the horrific creature. Various lenses, offering different degrees of magnification, were mounted on a metal clamp around his head.

Pulling his surgeon's mask away from his mouth, he revealed a disquieting leer. The freak was smiling at him.

"Good evening," he said in carefully enunciated English. "How are you feeling?"

Ulysses stared at the man in abject horror. How was he feeling? What kind of a question was that?

And then he was seized by a moment of doubt. Having thought he'd known, with horrible certainty, what was going on here, he now began to question his original assumption. Perhaps he had been injured and the surgeon was fixing him up. Perhaps the restraints were for his own protection. Perhaps he had been rescued whilst unconscious and he was in some safe house somewhere operated by the German Resistance. Hope blossomed like a winter snowdrop.

And then the reality of his situation came crashing back as the deathly surgeon continued. "But how rude of me. I have not yet introduced myself. I am Doctor Folter of the Frankenstein Corps, and I shall be your surgeon for the duration of this procedure."

Ulysses swallowed hard. It felt as though there was a hot stone in his stomach, melting through the tangle of his intestines.

"Procedure?" he managed at last, his tongue thick in his mouth, his mind eye's replaying the nightmarish images of ghoulish cadavers with finger-knives poised ready to slice him limb from limb.

"But of course. It is a long time since we have had any spare parts of such quality to work with, even despite the injuries you have sustained since being brought here," he grumbled, obviously unhappy at how his latest specimen had been treated. "But thankfully most of that is only surface damage. Your left arm especially," he said, almost hungrily. "Such strong and supple flesh. So young and fresh."

"My eye," Ulysses mumbled, painfully aware of the throbbing coming from the middle of his face. "What's happened to my eye?"

"This eye, you mean?" Folter said casually, holding up a pair of forceps. Gripped within its metal teeth was a glistening ball of white jelly, shreds of fine muscle still attached.

Ulysses stared into the small, dead pupil of his own right eye and was unable to stifle the scream of horror that burst from him then. It felt as if his eye-socket was on fire.

As terror seized him he tried to form a question between his howls of horror.

"You want to know why?" Folter asked.

Ulysses nodded furiously, unable to stop his remaining eye flicking from the monstrous surgeon to his grisly prize and back again.

"I would have thought that was obvious. But here, let me show you. Seziermesser?" the surgeon called to his assistant, the two of them turning Ulysses' gurney about.

And as the bed rotated, the arc-lamps spinning past above

him, Ulysses wondered wildly. Had he heard correctly, or had he imagined it? Had Folter really called his assistant Seziermesser?

"There," Folter said proudly.

From his new position, Ulysses could see the arcing capacitors now, bursts of chained lightning coursing between them, filling the air with the tinny stink of ozone and static electricity.

But it was the contraption standing in front of it – like some macabre medieval torture device – that seized his attention and wouldn't let go.

It was a huge rusted iron frame, stained red with rust, and other things besides. It was covered with a plethora of leather restraining straps, chains and cable-spun electrodes. Chained to it now was a monster of a man. At least it must have once been a man, but was now definitely all monster.

It had to be at least seven feet tall, its height and breadth across the shoulders bulked out by the addition of an extra pair of arms, and the bones and muscles needed to support them. Livid scar lines showed where the pieces of – by the looks of it – at least three different bodies had been sutured, stapled and bolted together to create this abomination. Parts of the body were textured a bruised purple, shot through with visible green veins. Perhaps this discoloration was the residue of the chemicals the body parts had been kept in until they were needed. Or perhaps it wasn't blood that was running through the creature's veins anymore.

As well as the flesh of three dead men, Ulysses could see where the madmen responsible for this monstrosity had been forced to resort to using mechanical components in place of missing human parts. No doubt the addition of hydraulic joints at the knees and down the length of the monster's spine were to help it cope with the additional musculature that had been stitched onto the body to support four huge arms instead of the more conventional two.

The features of the face hung low between its massive shoulder blades might once have been considered handsome, but not anymore. Aside from the thick stitches, livid purple scarring and dried blood caking its broken nose, there was a hole where the thing's right eye should be.

"I know," Doktor Folter said, following Ulysses' appalled gaze. "Magnificent, isn't it? I might even go as far as to say *wunnderbar!*"

He admired his creation for a moment, lost in silent rapture.

"Why copy the Creator's pattern when one can do so much to improve on what is, at best, a primitive design? We were so limited in our aspirations at first; wanting to do nothing more than mimic the great man's work. But we have a much greater understanding of human anatomy and mechanical science now; modern medicine is capable of so much more."

The monster sagging within the chains securing it to the frame, like some grotesque parody of Leonardo da Vinci's Vitruvian Man, looked like anything but the paragon of human perfection; more like some hellish abomination dreamt up by a madman, which was what it was.

"My masterwork!" Folter declared with a flourish of his arms.

Beyond the frame, Ulysses could see other corpses in various states of reconstruction. Through an archway in the wall beyond that, he saw shelf after shelf of giant preserving jars containing all manner of human limbs, internal organs and even the occasional pickled brain.

"We have done as much reconstruction as we can," the surgeon said, dragging the despairing Ulysses' attention back to the corpse-hulk hanging from the rusted steel frame, "but there's nothing like the real thing, and you have provided us with exactly what we needed, and for that I thank you." Absent-mindedly, Folter twizzled the forceps holding the eyeball between his forefinger and thumb.

Still smiling, he turned to Ulysses. "Perhaps you'd like to see how your sacrifice is helping to create something that is... almost divine."

The man was clearly insane; to think that Ulysses would really be interested in seeing how his own mutilation was benefitting the Nazi war effort.

"For what we practise here is truly an art, and is not art an expression of the divine within us all?"

Ulysses could bear it no longer. As Folter and his young assistant set to work, attaching his stolen eyeball into the monster's empty eye-socket, merciful oblivion overcame him and he blacked out.

PULLING THE NEEDLE from the thick thread, Folter tied off the end and then descended the step ladder in front of the undead hulk and regarded his creation.

"A masterpiece," Folter said, his voice barely more than a whisper.

"Yes, doctor," the young Seziermesser sycophantically agreed.

"It's only a shame our guest could not appreciate the wonder of what we are doing here. To create life where once there was only death. Are we not as unto the Great Creator Himself?"

"*You* are, Doktor Folter," the young man said obligingly.

"Thank you, Seziermesser, thank you," Folter said graciously. "Now it only remains for us to bring our creation to life. Prepare the galvanic radiation."

"Yes, doctor. At once, doctor," the other said, hurrying to carry out his master's wishes.

Standing in front of a bank of imposing machinery, the younger man began to tug at a series of levers and in response, accompanied by a rising hum, the electrodes began to pulse and spark more rapidly.

"Raise the frame!" Folter commanded, lowering a pair of tinted goggles over his eyes as he did so, transfixed by the crackling bursts of tame lightning now arcing around the domed roof of the chamber, lighting everything with their flickering blue-white glow and casting deep black shadows at their passing.

Locking the first set of levers in place, the young man then set about heaving on a second set, sweat beading on his brow from the sheer effort.

With a grinding rattle, the entire frame on which the corpse-thing hung spread-eagled rose towards the roof of the chamber.

When the steel rack was a good fifteen feet clear of the chamber floor, the rising mechanism ground to a halt, swinging gently.

Folter now turned from delighting in his marvellous creation and took up a loop of chain, which was also suspended from the ceiling, in his thick rubber gloves.

"Engaging probe now!" he declared, shouting to be heard over the furious snap and crackle of discharging electricity.

As he hauled on the chain, a Y-shaped piece of metal bound with coiled copper wire descended from the vaulted roof, lining up with the galvanic radiation emitters and the top of the steel frame. As it drew closer, the probe became wreathed in crackling corposant.

And then the connector fell into place.

Lightning leapt from the electrode emitters to the frame, twisting all over the steel scaffold and around the body secured to it, like a writhing serpent of capricious power.

The body was immediately wracked by violent convulsions, the thick trunks of its legs kicking at the frame and setting it jangling again – so much so that young Seziermesser looked up at it in alarm. The great arms tensed and thrashed against the manacles holding the altered body to the framework. The face contorted, giving rise to all manner of grotesque grimaces, teeth clenching, jaw twisting from side to side, eyelids flicking open one moment only to be squeezed tight shut the next.

But then it was always like this. A birth was never an easy thing.

"Enough!" Folter shouted, worried that the newborn might burst its staples or stitches if it kept thrashing in such a violent manner.

Seziermesser threw the levers, breaking the connection between the capacitors and the frame. The body twitched once more, an expression of primal pain on its face, and then it sagged within its bonds and was still.

As the noise of the machines died, Folter and his assistant waited with bated breath. This was always the worst part, waiting to see if the galvanic process had been a success.

And then his creation's chest heaved and it took its first ragged breath.

"It's alive!" Folter cried with something like paternal pride, as the monster's eyes flickered open, and regarded him with blank incomprehension.

He turned to Seziermesser.

"Bring it down," he instructed his subordinate, "and prepare it for imprinting."

He looked again at the monstrous thing hanging from the frame and felt pride swell within him.

It didn't matter how many times he brought a new life into the world; every single one was special, every one unique. Every one attested to the legacy of the primogenitor of them all, the great man himself, the legend that was Viktor Frankenstein.

They were all Frankenstein's children.

CHAPTER TWENTY-SIX

Tabula Rasa

"Don't delay now! Be quick about it," Folter called after Seziermesser.

"Yes, doctor. At once," the young man called back, making a curious bowing motion as he backed towards the archway leading to the supply room.

Folter turned back to the bank of machinery beside him...

...and came face to face with a porcelain-skinned beauty, with high, sculptured cheekbones, a delicate mouth and lips full and red. He gave a faint gasp of surprise. For someone who could find beauty in something as grotesque as the thing still bound to the frame behind him, Doktor Folter found the woman's natural beauty unnerving.

The second thing he noticed about her was the congealed bloody hole in the breast of the tunic she was wearing.

She smiled at him and the last things he noticed about her were the gleaming points of her unnaturally elongated canines.

Without saying a word she grabbed Folter by the lapels – even though he loomed over her like some silver screen Nosferatu – and with one fluid action hurled him bodily between the crackling spires of the still active galvanic electrodes.

There was a *crack* as loud as a thunderclap, and an explosion of light, and the laboratory was bathed in flickering incandescence.

Folter hit the floor still twitching, a residue of discharging energy wreathing his body, the cooked flesh of his face and heat-fused lips smoking gently.

On the other side of the archway, Albrecht Seziermesser crouched, nearly paralysed by fear, praying that he would be able to keep quiet and not give himself away.

"PRISONER ZERO?"

Hearing the honeyed, accented voice, Ulysses opened his eyes, as gentle hands shook him awake.

"Hm?" he murmured, focusing on the vision of loveliness appearing in front of him.

Was he dead? Was this vision of crystallised beauty an angel, come to carry him over into the next world? Had he in fact died back there in the psychotic surgeon's operating theatre?

"Are you Prisoner Zero?" the angel asked him again.

"Am I?" he slurred, struggling to get his left eye to focus properly. But as he did so, bewilderment creased his face. "Katarina?"

"You know who I am, then?" she said as she set to work unstrapping him from the gurney.

"It *is* you," he mumbled. "My, but this is turning out to be a day for renewing old acquaintances. We have to stop meeting like this," he rambled on as she laid his left arm across her shoulders and hauled him into a sitting position, as easily as she would a tailor's mannequin.

"Come on," she said – and Ulysses only realised then that she was in fact speaking English, despite her strong Eastern European accent – "we have to get you out of here."

Ulysses staggered willingly to his feet, his legs promptly giving way beneath him. But his saviour was there with a steadying arm around his waist, practically holding him upright.

"Now why would you want to do that?" he murmured, still drunk from the shocking revelation of what had been done to him.

"Because whatever it is you know is of paramount importance."

"But I don't know anything!" Ulysses protested, immediately on the defensive, as his blonde-haired rescuer led him towards the door out of the insane laboratory, and ultimately to freedom.

"You better had," she chastised him with a smile, "otherwise I've ruined a perfectly good jacket for nothing."

Ulysses studied her fine porcelain features by the epileptic light of the shorting electrodes.

"It is you, isn't it?" he said. "Katarina Kharkova. Agent K?"

"A pleasure to meet you," she replied. "And you are?"

Ulysses opened his mouth to answer her and then stopped himself just in time, as his mind cleared at last. Here he was in 1943, along with Katarina Kharkova, whom he had first met back in 1998. But in 1943, she hadn't met him yet. The consequences of that, he decided, he could deal with another time.

"You said it. Prisoner Zero," he said chirpily, trying to pass the moniker off as if it were nothing of importance.

The echo of a siren sounded from somewhere else within the complex, making the woman start.

"Rasputin's beard! I had hoped it would take them longer to realise what was going on..."

"What *is* going on?" Ulysses asked her.

Shifting his weight, she said, "Explanations will have to wait. Right now I have to get you out of here."

And with that, they left behind the lab, the smouldering corpse of Doktor Folter, the thing bound to the rusted metal frame, and the hidden, panic-stricken Seziermesser.

THE NEWBORN STARED vacantly into space through mismatched eyes, gasping for breath after the unexpected exertion of its re-birth.

And then, slowly, its eyes came into focus, as did its thoughts.

To begin with they were a soupy miasma, a syrupy mess of congealed reminiscences and degrading memories. But as it hung there from the frame, this amorphous cloud of recollection condensed into remembrances of taste and touch, of sights and smells and sounds that were so distinct as to be almost tangible.

It could recall a time before this one, before now, memories of another life lived, hopes and fears, betrayals and bonds of trust and friendship broken... loves found and lost... a wife, a child... people and places... laughter... desire... desperation... and a name.

There was a sudden scraping sound and the newborn focused on the darkened archway on the other side of the laboratory. Someone was coming, crawling back into the laboratory like a beaten cur.

SEZIERMESSER LOOKED UP at the four-armed abomination, mouth agape, still in a state of shock after the way the SS officer had gained entry unannounced and proceeded to murder Doktor Folter.

"Dee..." the brute beast still shackled to the tarnished steel frame mumbled.

Seziermesser tensed. Had he really heard the thing speak? Or had it merely been an unintelligible grunt, like the incomprehensible gobbledygook mewling of an infant?

That must be it, he tried to convince himself. When the creatures were awoken their minds were akin to those of newborn babes, hence their designation when in that unimprinted state. It was only the process of imprinting that gave them any wits at all. Until then, their minds were a blank slate, a *tabula rasa*, waiting to be written upon by the Enigma machines. Pure chance – that must be it.

His master was dead – murdered – and Prisoner Zero had escaped, aided by the traitorous SS officer, or imposter, or whatever the witch was in truth. It was his duty to report the incident to the facility commandant Colonel Kahler, but not before he had completed what Folter had started in creating the super-soldier. After all, with a mad killer loose in the castle, what better bodyguard could there be than a four-armed Promethean with the strength of ten men?

The most basic imprinting was all that was necessary and would not take longer than thirty or forty minutes – an hour at most – and then he would show the Colonel that he, Albrecht Seziermesser, Doktor Folter's protégé, was the great man's natural successor. It would then be but a small matter to convince Kahler of his suitability to take command of the Frankenstein Corps' scientific division. He just needed to get the imprinting process under way and then report the incident before anybody else could tell him otherwise.

Ducking back into the storage chamber, Seziermesser returned with a trolley bearing a pair of goggles, attached to a metal frame atop a portable transfer unit. All he had to do was link the transmission lenses to the lab's Enigma engine, place them over the newborn's eyes and initialise imprinting.

"Dee," the creature said again.

Seziermesser froze. That was twice now. Could it really be a coincidence? They said lightning never struck in the same place twice, but the work carried out within the walls of Castle Frankenstein, by those men inspired by the work of the originator of their science, had already proved that wasn't the case. So could it really be a coincidence?

Despite knowing for a fact that the newborns retained no memories of their previous existence – or *existences,* in some cases – Seziermesser couldn't shake the feeling that the monster's mumblings were more than some freakish fluke. He knew it was the nature of the human brain to look for patterns in things and make connections where, in reality, there were none – like seeing shapes in clouds, or faces of Christ in the bark of a tree – but in this case, his scientific instinct told him that it was something more than mere random happenstance.

He regarded the purple-skinned brute with the appraising stare of a scientist.

"Dee..." it said again, and then, "Diet... Dieter."

Seziermesser could not suppress his growing astonishment any longer. The creature had quite clearly been struggling to vocalize a name. "Dieter?" he repeated, hoping against hope that this wasn't merely some glitch of the galvanic process the body had just undergone.

"Dieter," the thing said again, more clearly still.

THE MONSTER STARED down at the man in the blood-splattered surgical robe. The doctor was shivering, not with fear, but with excitement.

That was it – Dieter. It remembered now.

Dieter; that was who it had once been in what now seemed like a brief period lost in the never-ending mists of time. In another life, lived before this one, it had been called Dieter – Dieter von Stauffenberg.

"Get me down," the newborn gurgled, its voice thick with coagulated blood and saliva. "And find me some clothes."

CHAPTER TWENTY-SEVEN

Two Minutes to Midnight

THEY DIDN'T STOP to rest until they were two miles from the entrance to the forgotten escape tunnel, taking shelter at last among the neglected tombs and tumbled headstones of a ruined graveyard that lay deep within the forest east of the castle. It seemed to Ulysses somehow appropriate.

Blaring klaxon-cries ringing from the walls of the castle, they had made their way deeper into the dungeons, going Ulysses knew not where, until they came upon the loose flagstone in a web-strewn corridor and the steps that lay beneath it.

The adrenalin rush of their escape had given Ulysses the strength he had needed to match the vigour of his rescuer. But now that they were well clear of the castle, he was glad of the opportunity to rest and succumb to the come-down that inevitably followed, sitting with his back to a crumbling crypt.

He felt cold as the sweat evaporated from his goose-pimpling skin, and pulled his prison fatigues about himself.

And then, of course, there was the eye-patch – or rather the combination of bandage, wadding and gauze covering his gouged eye socket.

Agent K turned her eyes from the star spattered sky above to her shivering charge.

"Here," she said, slipping off her jacket, "put this on."

"But won't you be cold?" Ulysses asked, taking the proffered jacket and putting it on nonetheless.

"I don't feel the cold," she replied.

Rubbing at his arms in an attempt to bring some warmth back into his body, Ulysses stared intently at his saviour with his one remaining eye. It still felt strange to view the world in this slightly off-centre way. He kept feeling like someone was going to jump out at him from his left. He realised he was over-compensating by turning his head slightly to the right to give himself – what he considered to be at least – a more balanced view of the woman.

She looked no different to the last time he had seen her, except that she was keeping her hair in a slightly different style, and she hadn't just had her throat torn out by a raging lycanthrope.

And yet he knew that she was more than fifty years younger than the last time he had met her and fought alongside her, and she had yet to meet him.

Looking at her now, he found himself thinking of Emilia again. He had thought about her a very great deal in the weeks since he had been taken captive by the Nazis and taken to Castle Frankenstein. He'd thought about how he'd been forced to leave her behind. The last he'd seen of her and her father was the two of them running from the fracturing dome of the moon base, being led to safety by someone who had seemed strangely familiar and yet whose face, seen only in shadow, Ulysses still could not place.

And he had thought a lot about Nimrod too, his ever loyal manservant, faithful even unto death, and whose fate, even now, he was uncertain of. As he had stepped into the whirling sphere of light and been transported across time and space to war-time Germany, he had promised the old boy he'd come back for him. There had been many occasions during the last few weeks when he had wondered whether he would ever be able to make good that promise. But at this moment, shivering in the dark of a derelict cemetery, it actually seemed a real – if faint – possibility. He just didn't know how he was going to do it yet.

He'd pondered the idea for hours on end in the silence and isolation of his prison cell, but the only recourse he had been able to think of – other than building himself another time ship in which he could travel back to the future, which didn't seem likely somehow – was to write a letter to his lawyers with instructions that they hire someone, at a future date, to save his friends at the crucial moment. After all, now that he was trapped in the past, who was to say that it hadn't been that very man – who he would one day have instructed by his lawyers – that Ulysses had witnessed come to their aid at the eleventh hour? Putting those instructions in place now would simply close the loop and make the future match what he had already witnessed.

"So," she said, feeling his eye upon her, "tell me; what is it that you know, that the Nazis would interrogate you for so long?"

He looked at her and gave a heartfelt sigh.

"Come on, you can trust me."

"Yes," he said, purposely turning his gaze from hers, to prevent her from mesmerising him, as she had once before, "I know." He looked to the ground and the carpet of moss covering the broken ground of the graveyard. "But the truth is I don't know anything – at least nothing that they didn't know already."

"Then why didn't they hand you over to the Frankenstein Corps sooner?"

"Dashwood only interrogated me for so long because of his own paranoia. His mind's completely gone now. He's utterly mad, but he seems to have got the Nazis here on side."

"Tell me then. What is it you know and the Colonel Kahler knows that Mother Russia and her allies don't?"

Ulysses gave another weary sigh. Where only a moment before had been a renewed sense of hope, now overwhelming despair came crashing back in. For how could the two of them – a half-dead vampire and a half-blind prisoner of war – stop the Nazis from putting Dashwood's plan into operation?

"Project Icarus was what they called it," Ulysses said, vacantly staring into the middle distance. "Although Armageddon or Doomsday would all do just as well."

Katarina looked at him, her face an inscrutable mask. Her manner implied that she had heard of, or even been party to, plenty of apocalyptic scenarios in the past. For all he knew, she might well have already lived through the First Great European War and the Crimean, maybe even going back as far as the Black Death that ravaged Europe during the fourteenth century.

"So, what is this Doomsday weapon?" she asked.

"Fire from heaven," Ulysses said. "That's pretty much it, really. The last time I ran into Dashwood he was calling it the Icarus Cannon."

"The last time?"

"It's a photonic accelerator," Ulysses went on, more like his old, verbose self now. "It harnesses the power of the sun itself, turning it into a beam of super-heated energy that will vaporise organic matter in an instant and even melt through rock, given time. And it is now in the possession of the Führer's forces."

Katarina continued to regard him with the same expressionless stare. "And where did this Icarus Cannon come from?"

"Ah, now that's where this all gets a little tricky," Ulysses said, grimacing as if in embarrassment or actual discomfort.

"How so?"

"I really don't know how to put this," Ulysses faltered.

"Is it Magna Britannian technology?" she pressed, totally uncompromising.

"No," Ulysses answered, possibly just a little too hastily. He felt himself blush and then felt ridiculous for doing so. "I mean, sort of... but no." He stopped, took a deep breath, and tried again. "That's not the problem. The problem is the technology shouldn't even exist in this day and age."

"What do you mean?" Katarina asked him. He could feel her aquamarine stare boring into him.

"I mean it's from the future."

At least that provoked a reaction, an eyebrow arching in unspoken disbelief.

"And how do you know this?" she asked. He was glad she wasn't dismissing the idea out of hand. But then, being a vampire herself, she should be open to ideas that might sound far-fetched to the rational mind.

Ulysses met her gaze at long last. "Because I'm from the future too."

"I see."

"That's what I know. You did ask."

Katarina said nothing.

"But whether you believe me or not, I assure you that Germany now has all it needs to construct its own Icarus Cannon, a weapon capable of wiping out whole cities!"

Ulysses sighed.

"Whichever way you look at it," he said, glancing at the ghostly lantern of the moon high above, "the clocks are set at two minutes to midnight. Doomsday is coming, and things aren't looking too good for the Allies."

"Very well," Katarina said, sitting up against a shattered memorial, "assuming that you are telling the truth, we must get you to Allied Command as quickly as possible."

"There's no time!" Ulysses protested. "Any delay at this stage could cost us the war and re-write the course of history altogether. No, something has to be done now!"

"Then what would you have us do?"

Ulysses took a deep breath. "You're not going to like it," he warned her.

"Try me."

"We have to go back to Castle Frankenstein. We have to find Daniel Dashwood and stop him. We kill him and then raze the whole place to the ground."

"Then what? Sow the ground with salt?" Katarina scoffed.

"I said that you wouldn't like it."

"We are an army of two," the vampire pointed out. "A man tortured to within an inch of losing his sanity and a vampire who's been staked once already since this – how do you say? – debacle began."

Ulysses made a point of casting his gaze around the broken

tombs and ivy-clad crypts. "I don't see anyone else here who could help us, do you?"

"So when do you suggest we embark upon this suicide mission?"

Ulysses stared at her intently. "Right now."

"But of course."

Katarina gave an exasperated grunt and fixed Ulysses with her penetrating glare.

"You're serious about this, aren't you?" she said.

"Deadly," he replied.

Katarina got to her feet and started checking the selections of firearms and throwing knives pocketed within the bandolier she had been hiding under her stolen SS uniform.

"We won't be able to get back in the same way we got out. I think it likely they will have discovered our escape route by now."

"Oh yes," another feminine voice growled from behind them.

The two of them whirled to face the voice. Standing beside the broken boundary wall of the cemetery was another woman clad in the funerary black uniform of an officer of the Schutzstaffel.

The woman took a step forward into the moonlight and smiled, the silvery luminescence picking out an elongated canine as her lip curled back.

"You can be sure of that," said Major Isla von Haupstein.

CHAPTER TWENTY-EIGHT

Things That Go Bump in the Night

"I WONDERED HOW long it would be before I had the misfortune to run into you again," Katarina said, in German.

"And I you," Teufel's adjutant snarled.

Katarina tensed, unconsciously forming her hands into clawing talons. "How did you know?"

"That you were still alive?" the other woman purred, pulling her jacket open with a flourish and shaking it free of her shoulders, the muscles of her arms and shoulders rippling as she did so. "The corpse stink of you is hard to miss."

"So you followed us," Katarina said, hands poised over her weapons.

"Yes, to see if the prisoner revealed anything more to you than we already knew."

"Which he didn't."

The other smiled. "Disappointingly, no."

"So now what? You intend to talk us to death?" Katarina challenged. "Because I don't believe for a moment that you plan on taking us prisoner again." Her hands moved slowly towards the bandolier belt slung across her chest.

"Oh, come now," von Haupstein said. "We're not going to resort to such primitive tools, are we?" She sounded almost disappointed. "Not when we have the opportunity to really test ourselves?"

"Katarina, don't be taken in by her," Ulysses warned, unconsciously speaking in the same language.

Von Haupstein snapped her head round.

"Wait your turn!" she snapped, glaring at Ulysses as she kicked off her boots. "I'll get to you after I've killed this bitch."

Ulysses clambered awkwardly to his feet, his every movement causing him pain. The eye-socket behind the thick bandage throbbed viciously.

"So," von Haupstein said, turning back to Katarina. "Are you going to do this or what?"

"Why not?" the vampire replied, pulling the bandolier over her head.

"Katarina, don't be swayed by her," Ulysses protested, as his rescuer cast her weapons belt aside. "You're injured. Now isn't the time to worry about your pride."

Katarina narrowed her eyes, settling into a fighting stance. "One on one, just you and me, to the death."

"Yes. Yours," von Haupstein snarled, springing up onto a tilting headstone and then, barely hesitating for a moment, leaping at the vampire.

Ulysses gave a cry of alarm as, flinging herself through the air, arms outstretched in front of her, von Haupstein began to metamorphose.

Hands became savage claws, bloody talons bursting from the ends of her fingers. Thick hair sprouted from every inch of her exposed skin and even her spine arched and twisted as she changed shape. Gone was her luxurious mane of hair, replaced by a thick mane of coal-black fur. Her ears narrowed to arrow-tip points, her sinisterly beautiful face elongating, a muzzle distorting her features.

Katarina met the snarling, spitting lycanthrope's attack with claws raised. The momentum of the monster's attack knocked her off her feet.

The two of them went tumbling backwards through swathes of fallen leaves, the vampire rolling onto her back, using the force of the werewolf's attack to bowl the creature over her head, planting both feet in the creature's midriff and kicking upwards as she did so.

All Ulysses could do was watch – helpless as he was, barely able to stand – as the two unnatural things battled each other.

The lupine thing went flying through the air, less gracefully than before, and into the side of another crumbling tomb.

There was a resounding clang as the wolf hit the railings surrounding the crypt, one of the rust-worn barriers giving way, the spear-tipped poles clattering to the ground amidst the growths of brambles and thistles.

But the monster was on its feet again in a moment, lips curled back, fangs bared and already bloody from its cruel transformation.

Katarina launched herself off the ground and impossibly high into the cold night air as the SS werewolf pounced again.

It snarled in rage as its prey escaped it a second time, swiping upwards with a savage claw before it came to ground again, catching the vampire by an ankle and sending her spinning away through the air to land atop another broken crypt.

On the ground now and on all fours, the werewolf briefly turned its lupine head towards Ulysses, growling like a mastiff, long strings of bloody saliva drooling from its jaws. Then – every muscle and sinew in its body tensing – it launched itself, bounding across the cemetery.

Atop the tomb, Katarina prepared to meet the animal's charge.

Snarling like a hyena, the wolf sprang to the top of the tomb, but once again the vampire was ready for it. She twisted her body out of the way with preternatural speed, grabbing hold of great tufts of the creature's mane.

The two of them went sailing off the top of the crypt and crashed to earth on the other side. Ulysses heard a distinct snap that made him wince and which was followed by an animal howl of pain.

Katarina Kharkova suddenly came flying back over the top of the tomb, arms flailing, trying to twist in mid-air.

Before she even touched the ground, the wolf was springing back over the tomb after her, eyes aflame, a snarl of savage rage in its throat.

The beast – all muscle, sinew, teeth and rage – landed on top of Katarina as she landed on her back, its paws pinning her to the ground. She wrestled her arms free of the beast's hold, and caught its snapping muzzle in her hands just in time to prevent the werewolf from ripping out her throat.

We've been here before, Ulysses thought. Or at least we will be, if she ever survives this encounter.

In the stark monochrome moonlight, Ulysses saw the teeth marks in the wolf's warped shoulder and the ragged flap of torn flesh, the creature's blood glistening nearly black.

The wolf yelped again as Katarina raked her fingernails across the soft flesh of its muzzle.

Snarling in rage and pain, the wolf arched its back, pulling its head free of the vampire's grasp, and lunged again, trapping Katarina's shoulder in its vice-like jaws.

Katarina screamed in pain. Ulysses jumped at the sound, feeling his own abused nerve-endings flare in sympathetic, half-remembered agony. Tortured or not, he could not stand by and let the wolf go unchallenged any longer.

He stumbled past the grappling monsters to the fallen fence and picked up one of the railings, staggered back across the cemetery, holding his improvised spear in two hands, and thrust it into the werewolf.

The beast howled again, throwing itself from the mauled vampire like a scalded cat. The railing spike slipped from its body even as it was wrenched from Ulysses' hands.

As Katarina lay writhing on the ground in agony, the werewolf turned its burning gaze on Ulysses. Utterly defenceless now, and not knowing what else to do, he began to back away as the beast stalked towards him. He shot anxious glances to either side of him, looking for anything that he could use as a weapon, but could see nothing other than rocks or broken masonry.

A skull, lying amidst the mouldering earth and bones that had tumbled from another shattered tomb, crumbled under a heavy paw.

Eyes on the wolf, he thought he saw a shadow moving through the darkness towards him. But then his attention was fully back on the beast as, a guttural growl building in its chest and its body tensing, it prepared for the kill. And Ulysses knew that nothing could save him now.

Hatred burning in its near-human eyes, the wolf sprang, muscles uncoiling like wound watch springs, a mass of muscle and rage launching itself towards him.

A huge hand emerged from the shadows between two tombs, snatching the leaping wolf out of the air by the scruff of its neck.

The changed von Haupstein snapping and writhing within its unrelenting grasp, a thing that could only be described as a monster stepped out of the darkness and into the moonlight.

It was at least eight feet tall, Ulysses judged, and immensely broad. Its face was a brutal mess of old scar tissue, and in the moonlight Ulysses took in the sallow complexion of its waxy skin and its misshapen nose. The bulk of its body was hidden beneath the long, battered travelling coat it was wearing.

Ulysses and Katarina both stared at the giant, paralysed by shock. Neither of them moved.

The creature looked down at the wolf snarling and twisting within its grasp, as if having forgotten that it was there. Clamping the lycanthrope's snapping jaws shut with one hand and taking it by the shoulders with the other, it gave one sharp, brutal twist.

"Bad dog," it said.

CHAPTER TWENTY-NINE

Adam

THE MONSTER CASUALLY let the limp body of Isla von Haupstein drop to the ground.

Both Ulysses and Katarina remained where they were, staring up at the brute, not daring to move lest they draw the giant's attention onto themselves.

The monster slowly looked from the paralysed Ulysses, then to the prone Katarina, and back to Ulysses.

"I could not help but overhear your conversation," the giant rumbled, speaking English with a strong Austrian-German accent. "And I will help you."

Ulysses stared at the creature in shock and awe, taken aback not only by the fact that the brute was articulate, but that it hadn't tried to kill Katarina and him as well.

"Help us?" he spluttered, even the pain of his missing eye forgotten for a moment.

"Yes. I will help you." The creature said, reiterating its point. "For no one does anything from a single motive."

Ulysses stared at the brute, utterly dumbfounded. Had it just quoted Coleridge?

"You want to enter Castle Frankenstein, do you not, with the intention of razing it to the ground?"

"Yes. That's right," Ulysses murmured.

"Then what is the point in sitting in darkness here, hatching vain empires, when we should let not England forget her precedence of teaching nations how to live?"

"*Paradise Lost*," Ulysses mumbled, utterly astonished. The monster spoke like a poet philosopher, but in the manner of a punch-drunk Bavarian prize-fighter.

The creature smiled, displaying too many teeth that appeared strikingly white in the silvery moonlight. "You know your Milton."

Here was a creature that could quote Milton and Coleridge, and wring a werewolf's neck without a second thought. It was something truly unique. And yet Ulysses had seen its kind before.

Ulysses glanced back at the body then. It had lost some of its wolfishness and now resembled a near-human von Haupstein, although her face retained a certain snout-like quality, elongated fangs, and the sort of facial hair that many a member of the Hirsute Gentleman's Club would have died for.

He turned back to the brute that had killed her then and found himself studying the crazed contour-lines of scars that traced the lumpen topography of the monster's face – the yellow, near-translucent skin, the watery eyes, the lank hair.

"You are, and please excuse me for stating the obvious," Ulysses began, "but you're a product of the Frankenstein programme, or Project Prometheus, or whatever it's called, aren't you?"

"No, I am not," the creature said, and Ulysses heard an undercurrent of anger in the monster's voice for the first time.

Ulysses continued to stare at the creature in bemused fascination. "Then, if you don't mind me asking –"

"What are you?" Katarina butted in, coming to the point.

She was sitting up now, applying pressure to the bite on her shoulder. Three savage slashes across her belly glistened, bright crimson against her alabaster skin.

The creature looked at her from beneath a beetling brow with darkly hooded eyes.

"I was the first," it said simply.

"The first?" Ulysses couldn't help but interject.

"The original, if you prefer. I am Viktor Frankenstein's son, his original creation."

Ulysses gasped. "I read Captain Walton's account of your story," he gabbled, "or rather Frankenstein's story, as dictated to him by Viktor Frankenstein himself, I suppose. Shelley's adaptation."

The monster tutted. "I have read it too. Far too melodramatic for my liking; and I could not understand why she felt the need to transplant Castle Frankenstein from Germany to Switzerland. But the bare bones of the story are there."

Glancing behind it first, the monster sat down on top of a tumbled tombstone, as if in an effort to make itself comfortable.

"Although, if I remember rightly, that version of events concluded with you going to your death in the Arctic Circle," Ulysses said, taking a seat on a hummock of grass.

"Ah yes," the creature said, staring into the night beyond the bounds of the cemetery. "So it did."

"So, what happened?" Ulysses pressed, his curiosity piqued.

"You really want to know?"

"Yes!" Ulysses said, suddenly feeling more alive than he had since coming to, under Castle Frankenstein. A sparkling glint lit his remaining eye and a delighted smile curled his lips.

"Then I shall share my story with you."

The monster paused and cleared its throat.

"Shelley is right in that I was overwhelmed by grief on discovering my father dead aboard Walton's ice-bound ship. Our cat-and-mouse adventure – that had lasted so many years and taken us all the way from central Europe to the Orkney Islands – was over and the only family I had ever known was gone. And no matter whose fault it might have been to begin with, at the end I had driven my own father to his death in his pursuit of me."

The creature carefully locked its knuckles together on top of its knees and looked down at the calloused skin of its hands.

Ulysses felt cold to the pit of his stomach. Incredibly, he could empathise with the creature. He too had lost his father when he was only fifteen years old. Although more than twenty years had passed since then, it still felt like there was a hole in his heart.

"Swallowed up in my own grief and self-pity, I did seek to end my own life, planning to travel to, as Shelley put it so quaintly, 'the Northernmost extremity of the globe,' and throw myself upon my father's funeral pyre.

"And there, on a raft of polar ice, I built my father's pyre from the wreckage of the jolly boat I had taken from Walton's ship. Using the oil from the broken storm lantern and the flint from a tinderbox I set it ablaze. But, coward that I was, as the fire rose to claim my father's body, I could not bring myself to leap into those purgatorial flames. The instinct to survive was simply too strong within me. It was as if the very flesh that formed me rebelled against my intentions, determined that it would not die a second time.

"Slowly the fire burned down until there was nothing left of my father but bones and ash, and me, still standing there, drifting amidst the frozen fog. I stayed like that day after day – for I know not how long – going over and over again the events in my life that had led me to that time and place.

"But time had no meaning there. The quality of the light and the colour of the sky never changed. It was a world of never-ending, impenetrable white.

"Eventually the Arctic currents carried the ice floe, and me with it, to the Norwegian coast. From there, having been prevented, it seemed, from bringing an end to myself, I set out instead to roam the wilderness, far from the lands of men, keeping clear of the borders of civilisation, knowing not where I was going, nor what I would do when I got there."

Ulysses continued to stare at the creature in stunned amazement. "How did you survive?"

"On roots and berries. Rats and voles. Anything I could catch. I ate whatever I caught raw."

"But that was years ago, wasn't it?" Ulysses went on. "Surely time itself would have begun to have an effect on you eventually."

"It seemed not," the spawn of Frankenstein said. "I did not appear to age. I never got ill. I could survive extremes of cold.

Any injuries I did sustain – such as when I fell into the crevasse atop a glacier – simply healed themselves over time. I would seem that I am, for all intents and purposes, immortal.

"And so I continued like this for the best part of a century, steadily venturing ever closer to civilisation. But war came to Europe for a second time, more terrible than any that had come before, and I began to hear my father's name mentioned for the first time in a hundred years, around campfires at night, while I listened from the shadows. Intrigued, I made my way home for the first time in decades. And the further I travelled, the more I learned of the Frankenstein Corps and what had become of my ancestral home."

"The corpse-factory," Ulysses muttered.

"It was then that I had my epiphany. I had fully intended to kill myself so that no-one would ever create another abomination like me, and yet here was an entire military division dedicated to doing just that, over and over again, with the sole purpose of working evil.

"Those bodies brought back from the dead by the Frankenstein Corps – how dare they corrupt my father's name so?" he spat. "They are no better than slaves. They do not have a voice. They do not have anyone to speak for them. And so it falls to me, to become the saviour of those made in my image, and free them from their bondage."

Ulysses was unable to tear his eyes from the creature now, the cold fires of hatred burning within the black pits of its eyes.

"So," it said, "I will help you."

Ulysses inhaled, slowly and deeply, as he processed everything the creature had told him and all that he had seen for himself. Just judging by the size of him, it seemed to Ulysses that having the brute on their side would make it a good deal easier to break back into Castle Frankenstein. And if he really was Frankenstein's original creation as he claimed, and he had truly lived for more than a century without injury or even aging, then it was even more the case.

"What do we call you?" Ulysses asked. "It wouldn't feel right calling you 'creature' or 'monster.'"

"Call me Adam, for that is my name," the giant rumbled.

"But I did not believe your father ever gave you a name."

"No, none, other than 'fiend' and 'devil' and 'wretch.' So I named myself Adam, for I was the first of my kind."

Ulysses considered this for a moment, and something about it irked him.

If Shelley's account of Frankenstein's story was correct, as the creature now calling itself Adam claimed it was, then Ulysses already knew that the monster was dangerously unpredictable, capable of sudden outbursts of extreme violence.

Adam had already made it clear that he had his own agenda, which just happened to coincide with what Ulysses and Katarina wanted to achieve in the short-term. He certainly had the will and – judging by the way he had dealt with the werewolf – the means to achieve it. But Ulysses also suspected that he would have no regard to the cost to others or who would be sacrificed along the way.

And, if Adam succeeded in his plan, and unleashed the re-made Prometheans of the Frankenstein Corps on the world, what might he do with an army of such beasts at his command?

If they were going to do this, they had to bear in mind that such an alliance could only ever be temporary. He would worry about how he would muzzle the beast again later.

"Very well," he said, carefully offering the giant his hand, making a deal with the devil. For a moment the brute looked at his hand curiously and then, the harsh expression on his deformed face relaxing slightly, took it in one huge meaty paw and shook it firmly, clearly taking care not to crush every bone in Ulysses' hand. "It would be an honour to have you at our side."

Ulysses looked to Katarina, meeting her dark stare.

"Now we are three."

"Perhaps not," she said.

"What do you mean?" Ulysses bristled.

"I mean, we may already have allies on the inside too."

"Excellent!" Ulysses declared, beaming. "Then the game is most definitely afoot!"

CHAPTER THIRTY

Enemy at the Gates

THE GROAN OF twisting metal made the guard atop the remaining gatehouse sentry post turn in suspicion. He snapped his gun around and trained it on the direction of the sound.

Against the velvet blue of the night sky, he saw the skeletal silhouette of a pylon start to fall.

There had been no detonation, no crash of a collision, and no rumble of subsidence, so there could only be one explanation for the buckling pylon's imminent collapse.

"Spotlight!" the sentry shouted to the arc-light operators on the tower at the corner of the castle and pointed towards the pylon's footings. The men manning the spotlight heard his cry and turned its beam on the hillside.

And then they all saw it: a looming gorilla-like shape, taller than a man. A colossus built of muscle and rage, it had its shoulders pressed against the structure, its huge hands crushing the metal supports between them.

The sentry put his rifle to his shoulder and took aim.

Strong hands grabbed his head from behind and gave a sharp twist. There was a *crack* and the man slipped silently to the floor.

Shouts of alarm were now coming from the spotlight emplacement, accompanied by the sounds of a gunman somewhere letting off a few rattling shots in the direction of the target. But it was too little, too late. With a groan of buckling metal, the pylon came crashing down, trailing sparks. Actinic bursts of electrical discharge erupted from the power lines as they were pulled taut and broke free, whipping around the castle battlements as the structure hit the spotlight.

Men screamed and died, their flesh cooked by the raw energy the power lines had carried into the castle. Lights winked out throughout the fortress complex as the little power still trickling through to the facility from the devastated dam bled away into the night in a coruscating fireworks display.

Muffled shouts of surprise rose from within the fortress-factory's flesh-smithies, laboratories and production line. Moments later, soldiers began to pour from the castle's interior, swarming over the battlements, barely able to believe that they were facing a second attempt to the storm the castle in one night.

Roaring like a lion, Adam leapt onto the toppled pylon now leaning against the side of the castle and scaled the twisted steel framework to the wall. He swung himself down onto the battlements in front of a gaggle of startled troops, rifles in hand, not one of them ready to face the raging beast. Below them, the mustering soldiers were hampered by the whipping, crackling cables still flailing across the courtyard.

With an enraged bellow, the brute grabbed the two nearest soldiers and smashed their heads together, fracturing both their skulls. While they were still falling, twitching, onto the stones, Adam picked up another man and casually tossed him into the nest of sparking cables below, the wretch managing one last scream before he became little more than a blackened, smoking skeleton.

A fourth soldier went over the wall the other way, landing in a tangle of broken bones and wheezing, punctured lungs.

Rifles were brought to bear at last, but too late. Adam charged the soldiers crowding the narrow walkway, slamming into them and pushing them backwards without slowing.

More men went tumbling from the battlements, screaming in terror, falling to their deaths below.

The soldiers scrambling up the stairs to bolster the defence of the battlements, as yet unaware of the mayhem they were about to join, suddenly found bodies falling on top of them and sending them tumbling backwards down the stairs to land in a heap at the bottom.

STEPPING OVER THE sentry's cooling corpse, Katarina Kharkova siezed the rope attached to a grappling hook embedded in the turret wall and heaved at it, speeding her companion's ascent to the top.

"This way," she said, as Ulysses swung his legs over the ledge of the parapet at last, gratefully dropping down into the look-out's position. She opened a trapdoor in the floor of the sentry post and slipped through it, disappearing into the darkness below.

COOKIE STARTED. "WHAT was that?" she said, stopping abruptly as she paced the straw-covered floor, anxiously looking at the ceiling of the dungeon cell.

Hercules Quicksilver followed her gaze from where he sat slumped against one damp wall, his manacled hands resting on his knees. "I don't know."

Another reverberation rumbled through the foundations of the keep.

"Gunfire," Cat declared confidently.

"The castle must be under attack," said Cookie.

"What? Again?" Jinx challenged. "Who else, other than us, would even attempt such a thing?"

A thought suddenly struck Hercules. He stroked his moustache thoughtfully as he met Cookie's eyes.

"The monster?" she whispered.

"The one from the dam, you mean?" Cat queried.

"Yes, the savage," Hercules pondered. "I mean it's certainly possible. The brute's certainly mad enough."

"But why?" Cat asked, bemused.

"Well there was certainly no love lost between the beast and the German Landsknechts last time we met," Hercules pointed out.

"But the explosion," Jinx said, "back at the dam. Surely... I mean it would have... I mean..." She faltered.

"How could anything survive that?" Hercules finished.

"Yes."

"Doctor Jekyll did, or Hyde at least."

"Traitorous bastard!" Cookie hissed.

"We don't even know the other monster was on the dam when the tank's magazine went up," Hercules reasoned. "The last I saw of it was when Hyde sent it flying into the lake."

The survivors of the Monstrous Regiment looked at each other.

"This attack, so soon after ours... you don't think...?" Cookie began.

"No, it couldn't be," Hercules interjected. "It couldn't be looking for us. I mean, why would it?"

There came another resounding crash that shook dust from the cracks between the stones of the vaulted roof. That one had sounded much closer, too.

"Could it?"

There was a sudden rattling at the door to their cell and they scrambled to their feet.

The rattling abruptly ceased, replaced by the crack of fracturing mortar. With a sudden tremor, the cell door was pulled clean away, dust and stone chips flying into the room in its wake, forcing those inside to cover their faces.

As the dust began to clear, Hercules lowered his arm from in front of his face and peered at the monstrous silhouette filling the passageway beyond. It was still holding the dungeon door in its huge hands.

Hercules reflexively went for his gun, but of course he was unarmed.

"Gentleman," the monster said in English, albeit with a Germanic accent, bowing slightly to Hercules. He shifted his gaze and bowed again, acknowledging the women this time. "Ladies. We're here to rescue you."

CHAPTER THIRTY-ONE

Like Father, Like Son

ULYSSES STEPPED OVER the body of the guard – whose head Adam had smashed into the wall hard enough to knock his eyeballs out of his head – and squeezed past the hulking giant to the threshold of the cell, and there froze.

He opened his mouth to speak but found he couldn't.

The young man standing in the middle of the room gave him an appraising look and then, smiling, took a step forward, offering Ulysses his hand. Ulysses just stood staring at him, utterly dumbfounded.

He had seen the young man's photograph a thousand times – with his instantly recognisable bushy moustache and strong jawline – and the painting that had once hung on the wall behind his desk, back in his study at his home in Mayfair. And most importantly, his own memories of the man. He had never looked this young, of course, but the man was still, unmistakeably, his father.

"Quicksilver," the young man said, Ulysses dumbly taking the proffered hand and shaking it. "Hercules Quicksilver."

Ulysses mouthed the words as his father spoke them, continuing to stare at the haggard-looking man in stunned amazement.

"And you are?"

"What?" Ulysses mumbled, shaking himself out of his stupor.

"Your name; what is it?"

Ulysses' mind raced as he tried to think of what to say. He couldn't tell the young man his true name, could he?

No, he determined, he most definitely could not. That was a whole can of worms he didn't want to get into right now – there wasn't the time to explain.

"Shelley," Ulysses suddenly blurted out.

"I can honestly say that I am *very* pleased to meet you," Hercules said, shaking the older man firmly by the hand – the son he did not know he would have.

Ulysses continued to stare at him, open mouthed and tongue-tied once again.

"Now, if you'll pardon me for saying so," Hercules said, taking charge, "if this is a rescue, shouldn't we be about escaping?"

"This way," said Katarina Kharkova, appearing within the devastated doorway herself.

"You're... you're alive?" Hercules gasped. "But I saw –"

"Yes, clearly I am alive," Katarina said curtly. "Now, if we could be on our way?"

Hercules stumbled towards the open doorway in a state of shock. "Excuse me," he mumbled, giving the looming giant a wary glance as he squeezed past.

The other occupants of the cell – young women, dressed in dark-coloured clothes – hurried after him, following Katarina along the passageway, through the castle dungeons and, hopefully, ultimately to safety.

Still in a state of shock, Ulysses – unrecognisable now, thanks to his emaciated appearance, the prison fatigues he was wearing, his filthy mop of hair, a thick growth of stubble and a bandage across his eye – turned to follow.

Adam put out a hand. Ulysses stopped and looked up into the monster's grotesque visage.

"I have helped you," he rumbled, "now you must help me – as we agreed."

Still completely overwhelmed at discovering that their allies on the inside included his own father, Ulysses did not respond immediately, staring deep into the creature's watery eyes.

"Of course," he said at last, with a forced laugh. "What, did you think I'd forgotten?"

"The guards will be expecting us to retrace our path through the keep," Adam said.

"And the barricade you erected will only hold them back for so long," Ulysses added.

Turning, the monster strode off along the corridor in the opposite direction, indicating that the others should follow him. "So we go this way."

THE FIRST RESISTANCE they ran into was in an adjoining corridor, but the preternatural speed of a vampire, the brute strength of the creature and the determination of a desperate group of survivors offered a second chance at freedom was too much for two already unnerved soldiers.

And so the party continued, Hercules still wearing the dishevelled uniform of a Nazi officer, but now carrying an MP40 sub-machine gun, as were Cookie and Shelley.

At the top of a flight of stairs from the dungeon into the lower levels of the keep, they were confronted by their next challenge; four troopers covering behind a statue of a lion.

This time it was a liberal dose of bullets and abject panic that did the job. The Germans didn't stand a chance.

And so it was that they pushed through another set of doors and entered the colonnade-cum-hangar beyond with their team now fully armed and ready for anything.

Ready for anything, perhaps, apart from a gigantic brass and steel effigy of an eagle.

"Oh my god," Hercules gasped staring up at the huge machine.

It was standing upright, as if on its perch, wings outstretched on either side, extending the width of the hangar in which it stood.

It looked just like the angular stylised raptor that appeared in so much Nazi symbolism, only with a wingspan somewhere in the region of one hundred feet.

"What is it?" Cookie whispered at his shoulder.

Hercules took in the cockpit bubble of the eagle's eyes above him, the articulated wingtips, the cantilevered doors in the eagle's breast, the access hatch at the top of its tail ramp.

"It's a flying machine."

"What?" Cookie exclaimed. "Like a dirigible, you mean? But how can tonnes of metal like this ever get airborne? There's not a gas balloon in sight."

"It's the future."

At that, they all turned.

Shelley was staring up at the monstrous metallic creation, an expression of horror on his face and in his single bulging eye. It was the first thing he had said since they had fled the dungeons under Castle Frankenstein.

"What do you mean?" Hercules demanded, his eyes narrowing in suspicion.

"I mean this... it shouldn't be here."

Shelley sniffed the air, Hercules copying him, curious as to what he might find. There was something about the atmosphere of the hangar, a metallic tang in the air, like molten lead.

"How long has it been?" Shelley said to himself. "If they've already started cavorite production on a significant scale here, what else have they achieved? How much longer has Dashwood been here than me?" he added, half under his breath.

"What are you saying?" Hercules challenged the man who had been designated Prisoner Zero. "What do you mean? Speak plainly now."

Shelley looked at him, a stony expression on his face and a flinty look in his uncovered eye.

"It would take too long to explain. I know we've only just met, but you have to trust me on this one – we must raze Castle Frankenstein to the ground and destroy everything hidden within."

Hercules regarded the wretch suspiciously. "Agreed," he said at last, "but I would know who you really are, Mr Shelley."

"Later," Shelley said, flashing Hercules a strangely familiar grin.

"Very well, so be it."

Adam's hulking form suddenly loomed over them, casting them in shadow.

"If we're done here, might we be about our business?" the brute rumbled. "After all, time and tide wait for no man."

Hercules was still confused. He turned his suspicious gaze from Shelley to the giant he and the Monstrous Regiment had first run into battling the Landsknechts on the Darmstadt Dam; the monster who had been so instrumental in rescuing them from the castle dungeons after Jekyll had turned traitor and yet who had taken Hyde on in an epic fist fight back at the dam.

"Absolutely," he said, checking the load of his MP40.

"Then we go this way," the giant said, turning and striding across the hangar towards an arched doorway.

Giving the giant iron eagle one last awed glance, Hercules followed, leading the rest of the party after the lumbering creature and out of the hangar.

CHAPTER THIRTY-TWO

Pandemonium

COLONEL WOLF KAHLER looked up, hearing the crash from the other side of the steel door at the far end of the long vaulted chamber. So did every scientist, engineer and Enigma machine technician working on the production line.

It was as if an eerie silence had fallen over the room, even though the rattling mechanisms were still running, straining the coal-fuelled back-up generators to the point of failure. No one spoke, but all shared the same unease.

A second later, with another resounding crash, the steel door at the end of the chamber buckled and exploded inwards, iron hinges tearing free of the stones.

As the buckled steel clattered down the iron staircase, coming to rest noisily on the stone flagged floor, Kahler stared out of the observation booth at what could now be seen framed within the doorway, one foot still raised from where it had – impossibly – kicked in the door.

"What the hell?" his adjutant, Corporal Reinhard, gasped beside him.

But Kahler knew what it was immediately, only he had never

seen one that size or with such time-paled scars. And neither had he ever seen such cold fury and determination blazing within a Promethean's eyes.

The look in the creature's eyes turned his spine to ice water and he shivered, knowing that whatever happened here, they had already lost. He doubted even the Frankenstein Corps could stand against such chilling resolve.

As the monster cleared the stairs in a single bound, Colonel Kahler turned to his adjutant. "Ready the bird," he hissed from the corner of his mouth. "I have a feeling we may need it."

His adjutant shot him a startled look.

"Do it!" Kahler snapped.

"Yes, Herr Colonel! At once, Herr Colonel!"

There was a resounding crash from below and the crack of gunfire, and suddenly the factory was filled with screaming. Kahler turned back to the window to see the grotesque giant topple another heavy piece of machinery, before picking up the bulky steel cabinet of an Enigma machine and hurling it through the glass screen of an X-ray scanner.

The thing was like an engine of destruction, implacable and unstoppable. And it wasn't alone. The brute was followed into the chamber by a rag-tag band.

"Herr Quicksilver!" he hissed, laying eyes on the moustachioed man striding through the factory in the monster's wake, bold as brass, ruthlessly gunning down medical staff and maintenance crews alike without any sign of remorse. In fact, Kahler thought, the villain appeared to be enjoying himself.

Kahler turned to the other two men occupying the observation booth with him. Lieutenant-Colonel Teufel of the SS was regarding the growing pandemonium on the factory floor below with a look of bored complacency on his face, as if he didn't believe that he could possibly be in danger himself.

The betrayer Doctor Jekyll looked on, wringing his hands and rooted to the spot in abject fear. "We have to get out of here!" he shrieked, meeting Kahler's gaze.

"So you are a mind-reader as well as a traitor, doctor," Kahler said, switching to English.

He turned to Teufel, who was still staring blankly out of the window. There was an explosion and a piece of shrapnel – a cog from a derailed piece of machinery – spun through the air and struck one of the booth's windows, crazing it. The Devil didn't even blink.

"Lieutenant-Colonel?" Kahler said. "Care to join us?"

"She's dead, isn't she?" the gaunt old man said, staring at another of the criminals, a blonde-haired creature cutting down men with her bare hands and lethal bite, her mouth and chin red with fresh blood.

"Who?"

"Major von Haupstein. My dear Isla," Teufel replied, his face an emotionless mask.

"Teufel, we have to hurry," Kahler pressed.

The Lieutenant-Colonel turned from the window at last, as a fire took hold somewhere within the chamber below and the booth was bathed in a ruddy orange glow.

"They will pay for her death with their lives," he said, the black hate in his eyes chilling Kahler to the core.

"It shall be so," Kahler said, motioning Jekyll towards the door and making to follow after him. "We will come up with another strategy, but not here. Better that we leave now and live to fight another day."

Teufel nodded and followed them out of the observation booth, the flames rising in the chamber behind them.

"This way!" Adam shouted, as another explosion rocked the corpse-factory.

Ulysses was close on the creature's heels as he led the charge into the next chamber. He stumbled to a halt as he took in the details of the laboratory in which he suddenly found himself.

"I know this place," he muttered, half to himself. "I've been here before."

His eyes fell on the now dark electrode spires and the empty frame suspended just above the floor. Jars that had once been filled with preserving fluid and gangrenous limbs lay smashed on the floor, the soupy formaldehyde trickling away between the stone slabs, the bottled body parts scattered across the chamber floor like a shower of dead fish.

There was a flurry of motion behind him and they were joined by his youthful father and what was left of the Monstrous Regiment. Agent K brought up the rear, awash with crimson now. The sight of it made him feel uncomfortable.

"What is this place?" the woman known as Cookie asked, staring in appalled wonder at the macabre torture-chamber-cum-mad-scientist's-lair.

"This is where Doctor Folter indulged his predilections," Ulysses said darkly.

"Doctor who?" Cat asked, shooting wary glances around the room.

Ulysses pointed at the cooked corpse lying between the electrodes. "Him."

He looked anxiously around the room, twisting his head from side to side as if trying to take in every part of the laboratory at once.

"There was a monster here. He had just finished another of his creations," he went on.

"The four-armed – how do you say? – abomination," Katarina said, joining him as she wiped the blood of another unfortunate soldier from her face. The gash in her chest was almost entirely healed now. She had fed well.

"Keep your eyes peeled," Ulysses warned the rest of the party.

"Easy for you to say," Jinx quipped.

Ulysses scowled at her and her expression of grim humour paled. "Just be careful," he growled.

"We must keep going," Adam's voice echoed from the walls of the chamber like the slamming of crypt doors. "This way."

The giant set off once again, ducking through an archway into the adjoining ante-chamber. He kicked open another door and entered the passageway beyond that.

And where Adam led, Ulysses Quicksilver followed.

But following the monster through the splintered remains of another door, Ulysses suddenly stumbled to a halt once more.

The first thing that hit him was the noise. It reminded him uncomfortably of the macabre menagerie beneath Umbridge House on Ghestdale; like the moaning and mewling of babes in arms but given voice through the distorted vocal chords of imbecilic adults.

The second thing was the smell.

"Oh my god!" Cat exclaimed as she joined them on the other side of the shattered door. She coughed suddenly, gagging, the acrid melange of faeces and unwashed bodies catching at the back of her throat. The others who came after her could not help but do the same.

"Come on," Adam rumbled. "We can't stop now."

"But can't you smell that?" Cookie challenged.

The monster turned and fixed her with its watery gaze. "My sense of smell is much more sensitive than yours," the creature said. "Stay here, if you prefer, but my brothers need me."

His one remaining eye watering, Ulysses took a deep breath – making a point of not inhaling through his nose – and set off after the giant.

The passageway led them down a steep flight of steps and into another vaulted chamber. It looked like some sort of prison; the chamber had been divided into cells by the addition of several interlocking cages.

The stench was even worse here, and Ulysses was forced to cover his nose and mouth with the sleeve of his filthy overalls.

Many of the cells were occupied, each one home to some malformed monstrosity or other. That they had all once been men – or several men in some cases – was plain, but they were anything but now. Their bodies had been hacked apart and rearranged, giving them hunched shoulders and oversized arms, held together by crude stitching, metal staples and even rivets.

But these former corpses, remade as super-soldiers for the Nazi war effort, were not solely formed from flesh of the dead. Ulysses could see joints replaced or strengthened by ratcheting cogs, riveted steel skull plates and even heavy butcher's hooks in place of hands.

Standing at the centre of the chamber, running their charged cattle-prods across the bars, and clothed from head to foot in leather overalls, their faces hidden by gas-mask helmets, were the monsters' warders.

The whole place reminded Ulysses of London's sanatoriums for the mentally subnormal: the warders rattling the bars of the cells with sadistic enthusiasm, their charges clearly tormented. The huge hulking things rocked back and forth amidst their nests of filthy matted straw, sucking their thumbs or hitting themselves over the head, or pulling at their malformed mouths, howling in infantile terror.

For one tense moment, nobody moved. Then, as Adam and his allies charged down the steps into the holding chamber, the creature roaring in primal rage, the warden-keepers ran to meet their assault. The battle, such as it was, was over in seconds.

"SO MUCH FOR the Prometheus Programme," Hercules muttered, regarding the imprisoned monsters with a mixture of pity and detestation as he picked his way between the sadistic gaolers' broken and bullet-riddled bodies. "This lot are no better than mindless idiots, not even capable of controlling their most basic bodily functions." He caught the look in Adam's eye. "No offence intended," he added hastily.

"These individuals have yet to be imprinted," the giant said calmly, frowning.

"Imprinted?" Cookie said. "What do you mean?"

"Having been brought back to life, the newborns have to be imprinted with everything they need to know, via an Enigma Machine, before they can be sent to fight at the front. Upon resurrection, a newborn's mind is effectively *tabula rasa*."

"Table of what?" Jinx asked.

"*Tabula rasa*," the creature repeated patiently. "It is Latin. It means 'a blank slate.'"

"What do you intend to do with these 'newborns,' as you call them?" Hercules asked. "Do you have an imprinting Enigma machine to hand?"

"Do not worry," the monster replied, a sinister smile on its face that made Hercules feel deeply uneasy. "I shall give them a new purpose. The instinct for survival is present in all living things, no matter how they might have been brought into the world."

"Then we are done here?" Shelley asked, looking as uncomfortable as Hercules felt.

The giant ripped a bundle of keys from the belt of one of the dead warders.

"We are done. Our compact is fulfilled," he confirmed. "And I hereby release you of any further commitments."

Hercules observed the exchange, curious as to what had passed between the wretch and the creature, but deciding that now was not the time to ask for an explanation.

"Then we must be about our own business," Shelley said, a haunted look on his face.

He turned to address the rescue party gathered on the steps behind him. "Our work is not yet done here. We must make sure this place is razed to the ground."

"And how do you suggest we do that, exactly?" Hercules asked.

"Back to the hangar," Shelley declared. "That is where we shall make our final stand."

Hercules cast him a suspicious look. "You've got a plan, haven't you?" he said.

"Oh no," Shelley said, throwing the British agent a sly smile. "I'm just making this up as I go along."

As the creature set to work on one of the locked cages, the bedraggled Shelley led the way back up the steps and out of the Prometheans' prison, the rest of the infiltration party hard on his heels.

"May your God go with you," Adam called to Hercules as he made to follow them.

"*My* God?" he said, hesitating halfway up the stone staircase. "Is He not your God too?"

"My God?" Adam guffawed, great peals of belly laughter reverberating from the vaulted ceiling of the stinking, mired chamber. "I killed my Creator long ago."

Hercules hurried up the steps after his fellow escapees, profoundly disturbed.

CHAPTER THIRTY-THREE

Iron Eagle

THE CREATURES BURST from the keep in a torrent of malformed bodies and distorted limbs. A tide of unfocused rage and primal ferocity, stirred into frenzy by the goading of the First of their kind. Adam emerged from the fortress into the inner courtyard, to find the few remaining military personnel preparing to make a last desperate stand against the monsters that had escaped from the corpse-factory.

Many of the soldiers were in such a state of horrified shock that they were on a knife edge, ready to flee at any moment. It was only the respect they held for Colonel Kahler, and their abject fear of the Devil given human form, that stopped them turning tail and running for it right there and then.

And yet the creations of the Frankenstein Corps were supposed to be on their side! That knowledge alone unsettled many of the men more than anything else. Here they had become vengeful monsters, behaving like savage beasts. Beasts with pile-driver punches and piston-powered legs, able to tear through tank armour with their enhanced hands and cover great distances in a single bound.

The monsters had already ransacked the lower levels of the keep and there was barely a flesh-crafter or bone-smith left alive. What was left of the resistance the mob had met so far, they were now swinging above their heads, showing off their grisly trophies. One savage was whirling about a human head, spinal column still attached, like a flail.

"Halt!"

The command rang out loud and clear across the courtyard, amplified by a crackling loudhailer.

Adam stopped in the doorway of the keep and slowly craned his neck back, staring upwards. The booming echo had originated from somewhere above.

Standing in an open window was a Nazi officer, his personal insignia marking him out as a Colonel and a member of the Frankenstein Corps.

At the sound of his booming voice, the German soldiers froze. Even the malformed monsters stumbled to a halt.

Their self-appointed leader waited and listened. Intrigued as to how the Colonel would quell this uprising, Adam allowed himself a small smile.

COLONEL KAHLER PAUSED, the loudhailer still to his lips, and allowed himself a small smile. His voice still had influence even when all hell was breaking loose.

He savoured the moment. He could almost smell the waves of fear and awe coming off the monsters and soldiers gathered in the courtyard below. And he savoured the fact that Teufel was there to witness the dread he inspired in his men. There was room for more than one Devil in Hell after all.

Teufel wasn't himself. He had become more and more withdrawn since his adjutant had failed to return from whatever mission it was he had set her upon.

Taking a deep breath, his chest swelling with pride, Kahler continued. "Prometheans, listen to me. You will cease this disobedience at once and return to your holding cells, where you will be dealt with in due course."

Nobody moved, the dying echo of Kahler's pronouncement echoing from the walls and rooftops of the corpse-factory facility.

"Now!"

Still nobody moved. The soldiers looked at each other, and the looming monsters, warily.

A needle of doubt threatened to the burst Kahler's complacent conviction.

Why weren't the brute beasts doing as he had commanded? His word was law within the confines of Castle Frankenstein, and their continued rebellion was an affront to his position as sole authority within the facility.

"Obey, now!" Kahler roared, unable to contain his rising anger any longer.

HIS BACK AGAINST the wall, Adam stared at the camp commandant above him, his smile spreading right across his face.

The remade had all remained deaf to his orders, which could mean only one thing. The Colonel's last ditch attempt to regain control had failed. The Nazis had lost. Victory belonged to Adam.

Giving voice to a bullish bellow of joy, the First leapt from the steps of the keep towards the quaking military personnel; all that now stood in the way of the freedom he dreamed of for his brethren.

The soldiers knew they were defeated, and fell before him like grain before the scythe. Seeing the way the savages had failed to respond to the commandant's commands, the fight had gone out of them. They had lost the battle before it had even begun.

"COLONEL?" REINHARD SAID, shaking Kahler from his stunned trance. "We should leave."

The Colonel looked at him with a glassy-eyed stare. "What?" The colour had completely drained from his face, and he appeared to have aged ten years in as many seconds.

Reinhard was peering past him at the fracas once again

consuming the courtyard below. "We should leave while we still can," he repeated. "The facility has been compromised."

"Leave?" Kahler mumbled, staggering from the window, looking like his legs might give way beneath him at any moment.

"Yes, leave, man!" Teufel suddenly snapped. "Your damn facility's overrun!"

"Oh. Yes, very well then." Kahler turned to Reinhard. "If you think that's what's best," he said, weakly.

Reinhard nodded. "I do, Colonel." Turning to Kahler's guests, he said, "Gentlemen, this way, if you please."

"Where are you taking us?" Jekyll asked, worried, as Reinhard led them from the tapestry-draped chamber and into corridor beyond, bustling with panicking clerks and floundering information officers.

"That's a very good question," Teufel interjected. "The enemy have us at their mercy. There's no way out apart from right through the middle of them."

"There's always another way, Lieutenant-Colonel," said Reinhard. "You just have to know where to look."

CORPORAL REINHARD LED the way through the higher levels of the keep – through information posts and map rooms, clerks and castle personnel milling about in a confused panic – some trying to continue with their work, others packing, as if still expecting to get out alive. They descended ancient twisting stone staircases and passed halls of fleeing scientists, avoiding the chambers where the Prometheans were running amok, until at last their party – Lieutenant-Colonel Teufel, the turncoat Jekyll and the near-catatonic Colonel Kahler – reached the ancient colonnade-turned-hangar in which stood the Iron Eagle.

The sight of the incredible flying machine brought their desperate flight to a stumbling halt. They had all seen flying machines before – dirigibles, and the part-animal, part-machine cyber-eagles – but never anything like this. That something so heavy could ever get airborne without some sort of gas balloon seemed impossible.

"God in heaven!" the Devil gasped, clearly awestruck.

"Gentlemen," Reinhard said with a proud wave of his hand, "our way out of here."

"Astonishing!" Jekyll spluttered.

Colonel Kahler said nothing, but just stared into the middle distance, lost in a dark world of his own.

"You intend to fly that thing out of here? But how?" Teufel asked.

"Don't worry, Lieutenant-Colonel," Reinhard reassured him as he picked up the pace, "I have everything in hand."

Almost running, now that the cavorite-impregnated flying machine was in sight, Reinhard glanced at the glass roof of the hangar above them. There was no time to open it, and he was certain that it would prove to be no obstacle to the great iron eagle at the moment of take-off.

"Quick, on board!" he commanded the others, ushering them inside.

Teufel was the first up the ramp, leaving Reinhard to drag Colonel Kahler after him alone. Doctor Henry Jekyll came last.

Turning at the open hatch at the top of the ramp, Reinhard saw Jekyll panting towards the bird, after them. "Hurry, man!" he shouted in English.

It was then that the door on the other side of the hangar burst open and a second ragtag band burst through it, not pausing for even a moment as they raced towards the Iron Eagle over the stone-flagged floor.

"Hurry!" Reinhard screamed at Jekyll, as the doctor set foot on the ramp, before throwing himself through the hatch and into the bird, pushing Kahler aside as he scrambled up the ladder to the cockpit and the pilot's position above.

"THEY'RE GETTING AWAY!" Cookie shouted as she sprinted after Hercules.

Cat, Jinx and the Russian were keeping up, but their other mysterious liberator, the one calling himself Shelley, was beginning to flag and fall behind.

"Not if I have anything to do with it!" Hercules panted as he ran. His eyes were locked on the figure struggling up the bird's tail ramp.

"Jekyll, you bastard!" he shouted, dropping his spent sub-machine gun as he ran and pulling a liberated Walther PPK from the waistband of his trousers in its stead.

Such was the authority in his voice that for a moment Jekyll turned his head to see who was pursuing him.

"You have been found guilty of treason!" Hercules continued.

Panic giving him a fresh burst of speed, Jekyll scrambled up the ramp, a green haze obscuring his vision as if he were looking at everything through an emerald sea.

Hercules' finger tightened on the trigger, both hands on the gun to steady his aim. "The sentence is death!"

And with that, as the turncoat Doctor disappeared through the hatch at the top of the ramp, Hercules fired.

CHAPTER THIRTY-FOUR

The Talented Mr Hyde

THE CRACK OF the pistol resounded in the echoing hangar, as did the second shot Hercules fired through the closing hatch after the fleeing Jekyll.

The door closed with a dull boom, and a strange vibration set the very air to pulsing.

Shoulders sagging from exhaustion, Hercules lowered his gun and stumbled to a halt.

"Too little, too late," he grumbled.

"What do you mean?" Cat asked, suddenly at his side. "Why have you stopped?"

"Listen," was all Hercules would say in reply.

And then the rising, throbbing hum became more than just a vibration in their bones and all present heard the thrumming of esoteric engines powering up.

"But there must be something we can do!" Cookie railed.

With a grate of machinery grinding into operation, the steel-flighted wings of the great iron bird flexed, half folding behind its back and unfurling fully once more.

Jinx was staring at the great bird in awestruck amazement.

"I hate to admit it," the team's mechanic said, "but that is one impressive piece of kit."

Hercules nodded grimly. "And now it's going to allow our quarry to escape."

"But there has to be something we can do?" Cat shouted. The rising hum had become a painful, eardrum-pounding roar.

Hercules raised his pistol again, his face red with barely-contained rage. He squeezed off another three rounds at the craft in quick succession. Each one ricocheted dramatically from the steel hull of the eagle, causing Cat and the edgy Shelley to duck.

With a *clunk*, the bird's docking clamps began to disengage. The launch sequence was underway.

The iron eagle shook, straining to be free of the ground.

"Like I said," Hercules said, bitterly, "we're too late."

"At least you got that bastard Jekyll," said Cookie, patting his arm consolingly.

Hercules grunted. "Did I?"

The engine note dropped and the painful whining of turbines eased.

The eagle shook again, but this time those gathered in its shadow heard a crash from inside the flying machine.

The engines suddenly cut out completely and they were able to hear the screams for the first time.

The voices coming from inside the craft were shrill, high-pitched cries that should never have been made by men, and certainly not by masters of the Third Reich.

As abruptly as they had started, the screams cut out one by one, until they ceased altogether.

The British Agent and his companions waited. Nobody moved. The only sound that could be heard now was Shelley's laboured panting.

There was a clunk, the sound of a lock disengaging, and the door at the top of the eagle's ramp swung open.

Pistol raised once more, Hercules took several cautious steps forward and froze as a figure appeared within the hatch; a vast silhouette blocking out the ruddy light from inside the bird.

"Halt! Who goes there?" Hercules demanded.

Ducking its head to fit through the hatch, the figure squeezed itself out of the Iron Eagle and stepped onto the ramp, where it was able to unfold itself to its full height once more. The ramp bowed under its weight.

The hulking figure was wearing the ragged remains of a dark suit, the jacket – and the shirt beneath – ripped down the back, the trousers now bunched around the knees. It wasn't wearing any shoes at all.

As it stepped into a pool of light, its skin seemed to glow with a green translucence.

"Ladies," the colossus said, a wide yellow grin splitting its blunt simian features as it laid eyes upon the four women in the party. Blood and lumps of flesh dripped from his knuckles. "Gentlemen."

It bowed stiffly.

"Mr Edward Hyde, at your service."

CHAPTER THIRTY-FIVE

The Great Escape

"HYDE," HERCULES HISSED, eyes locked on the leering colossus, along with his gun.

Hyde grinned. "Hello again."

"Step away from the bird," Hercules instructed, slowly.

The echo of a distant detonation reverberated from the girders of the hangar roof.

"Why, what have I done?" the hulking brute said, the smile vanishing from his face. "You'll have to remind me. Memory like Swiss cheese, you see. That's my problem."

"You heard what he said." It was the other man who had spoken, the one with half his face wrapped in bandages. He had a Karabiner rifle trained on the giant.

"Now, now, gents, there's no need to be like that," he said gruffly. "You wouldn't like me when I'm angry."

Eyeing Hercules' roughshod uniform suspiciously, he added, "You're not Nazis as well, are you?"

Hercules hesitated before answering. "No, you know we're not. We're British agents, sent to put an end to this place and the work being carried out here."

"Oh," Hyde replied, a smile curling his lips once more, "that's alright then, 'cause if you were Nazis I'd have had to kill you." He took in each member of the party in turn. "I may be many things – a thief, a murderer, occasional rapist – but I am no Nazi-lover, that I can promise you!"

Hercules raised an eyebrow. "Not like Jekyll, then?"

"Cowardly little shit!" the brute snarled. "But at least we won't be seeing him again, thank God!"

Slowly Hercules lowered his gun. "He's dead then?" He could hardly believe what he was asking.

"As a dodo," Hyde chuckled. "And thank fuck for that, that's what I say. Good riddance to bad rubbish, the weak-willed, snivelling little cocksucker. I, for one, won't miss him."

The monster's heavy brows knotted as if he were trying to recall some deeply buried memory.

"You were working with him, weren't you?"

"Jekyll? Yes, until he turned traitor and sold us all out."

"And what about the rest of them?" Hyde asked Hercules, taking in the rest of the ragtag band at a glance.

"After a fashion. They rescued us from Schloss Geisterhaus."

"What, all of them?"

Hercules looked from Cookie, Jinx and Cat to the vampire and Shelley and then back at the hulking colossus.

"Again, after a fashion. Suffice it to say that if you are no friend of the Nazis then you *are* a friend of ours," he said, trying not to be distracted by the monster's gory knuckles.

"What, 'the enemy of my enemy' and all that?"

"If you like."

Mr Hyde grinned. "Works for me," the giant said, jumping down from the embarkation ramp and taking in the details of the hangar's architecture. "So, you want this place razed to the ground?"

"Yes."

"Alright then, where would you like to start?"

"Dashwood," the bandaged man in prison fatigues at the back of the group suddenly said. "We have to find Daniel Dashwood."

*　　*　　*

DAWN WAS BREAKING over the mountains of the Bavarian Forest two hundred miles to the east when the party regrouped several hours later, beneath a torn Nazi banner in what had once been the state rooms of the castle. Hercules Quicksilver gazed out a broken window pane as the flat white disc of the sun rose higher in the sky, spilling its meagre October warmth into the room.

An eerie stillness hung over the corpse-factory after the chaos that had possessed it for much of the night. The battle for the fortress was over. Fires were burning within the northern range of the production plant, while in the outer courtyard of the castle, amidst the wreckage of half-tracks, personnel carriers and staff cars, Adam's ramshackle army of Prometheans were mopping up the last few pockets of resistance, dragging soldiers and lab technicians from where they had holed up within the bowels of the castle.

An eerie stillness, yes, but not silence. There was the roar of the fires still burning in the corpse factory, the wailing of the dying and the mentally broken – victims of a new kind of shellshock in the aftermath of the monsters' rampage – and the campfire crackle of burning vehicles littering the devastated courtyard.

Castle Frankenstein was theirs. Their mission had been a success. But that didn't stop him feeling like someone had just punched Hercules in the stomach.

He turned from the window to the curious band of allies gathered together in the Frankenstein Corps' former conference room.

Cookie and Jinx had pulled up a couple of chairs, while Edward Hyde was leaning back in the leather-upholstered seat at the head of the table, its swivel bearing creaking under his weight, his huge feet crossed on the desk in front of him. He was playing with something in his hands. Something that looked suspiciously like a grenade.

Shelley was perched on the edge of another chair, his haunted gaze nearly permanently on Hercules, making him feel uneasy; either on him or the cat burglar, who was now leaning against a bookcase behind Hercules. Shelley had found a suit of clothes somewhere within the castle and had even managed to fashion himself a proper eye-patch.

Now that the man had been able to clean himself up, there was something strangely familiar about his face. From the way Cat was looking from Hercules to Shelley and back again, he knew that she could see it too.

That just left the mysterious, and strangely alluring, Agent K. She had hidden herself away in the corner of the room, remaining in deep shadow and keeping out of reach of the creeping fingers of daylight.

"So what you're saying is there's no sign of this Daniel Dashwood anywhere within the castle."

"Indeed," Shelley said.

"And nor can you find any sign of the Icarus Cannon."

"An intercontinental-ranged death ray? It would be a little hard to hide. But Dashwood is the key. If we don't stop him..." The one-eyed wretch broke off momentarily, lost for words. The hollow ticking of a clock within the room suddenly seemed laden with meaning. "There's really no easy way of saying this... If we don't stop Dashwood, the future of your world is doomed."

"But how can the actions of one man make such a dramatic difference?"

Shelley gave a bark of mirthless laughter. "Try telling the Führer that."

"You haven't answered the question," Cookie said, shooting Prisoner Zero an acid look.

"It would take too long to explain and even then you might not believe me," he muttered. "You just have to trust me on this. The thing is, you see, this man Dashwood holds the very future in his hands, and is prepared to offer it to Hitler and the Third Reich on a plate. And we just can't let that happen."

"Icarus."

They all turned on hearing the slurred voice. They hadn't heard the creature arrive.

It stood in the shadows of the doorway. What struck

Hercules wasn't just its massive size, but the four powerful arms sprouting from its strange, hunched shoulders.

Shelley gagged. "I know you," he hissed.

No one moved as the creature eased itself through the doorway and into the state rooms, to be met with shock and revulsion.

The thing was seven feet tall, legs bolstered by hydraulic joints at the knees and down the length of its spine. Its flesh was livid with purple bruising all around the staples and rough sutures holding it together.

And there was someone else there, hiding in the shadow of the monstrosity, a pathetic hunched thing, clad in a stained lab-coat.

"Icarus," the thing said again, forming the word very deliberately with its remade mouth.

"Yes?" Shelley said, wild hope suddenly lightening his face, giving him an even more manic appearance.

"Project Icarus."

"Yes! That's it!"

Shelley suddenly ran over to the huge Promethean and for a moment looked like he was going to grab it and shake it by the shoulders. "What do you know of it?"

The monster's once handsome face knotted, as it tried to pluck one wriggling memory from a sea of nebulous thoughts.

"Sch... Schloss..."

"Yes? Schloss-what?" Shelley pressed.

"Schloss... Adlerhorst," the monster managed, spitting it out at last. "Schloss Adlerhorst," it repeated proudly.

"AND YOU'RE SURE you can fly this thing?" Hercules asked Jinx for the thousandth time, as she buckled herself into the pilot's seat, the roar of the iron eagle's engines shaking the glass of the hangar roof as they ran up to speed.

They had done what they could to clear up the mess left by Mr Hyde when he turned on the fleeing Nazis, but it seemed like every surface now carried a reddish sheen.

"Look, do you want me to fly you to this Schloss Alderhorse or not?"

"It's Adlerhorst," Hercules corrected her. "It's German for 'eyrie.'"

"Well, it sounds pretty eerie to me too. I mean, a castle in the Alps, mounting a death ray that can pick off targets hundreds of miles away?"

"No 'eyrie' as in an eagle's –"

Jinx threw him an acid look and he decided that, given the pressure of the moment, the language lesson could wait.

"But you've got a point," he finished.

He turned to Katarina, who was standing at an ornate golden map-desk on the starboard side of the flight cabin. "You've got the location?"

"Of course," the vampire replied, not once looking up from the chart pinned beneath her compasses.

"And we're all ready to do this?" he asked the rest of those squeezed into the cockpit inside the eagle's head – Cat, Cookie and the knowledgeable Shelley.

"We were born ready!" Cookie laughed, slamming a fresh magazine into the clip of her machine gun.

"Come on," Cat said, throwing him a warm smile, "let's finish this."

"For Queen and Country, then," Hercules said.

"For Queen and Country!" the response echoed back to him.

"Mr Hyde!" Hercules shouted back down the ladder into the body of the great bird, where Hyde crouched in the hold. "If you would be so kind?"

"Right you are, guvnor!" boomed the giant's Cockney tones from below. "Chocks away!"

There was a resounding clang as Hyde, inside the craft's underbelly, released the claw-clamps securing the iron eagle to the stone-flagged floor. With a sudden lurch, the great bird – its steel wings at full stretch – began to rise.

Jinx's cheer of excitement was loud within the confines of the cabin as she punched the air with a bunched fist.

"And we're off!" Hercules exclaimed, unable to hide his amazement as the iron eagle – impossibly – started to climb.

Two seconds later it met the still closed glass roof of the

hangar. In another second it was through, splinters of fractured glass falling into the hangar below in a cascade of white noise.

As those who could hurried to the window-ports of the eagle's eyes to watch Castle Frankenstein dwindling beneath them – except for Katarina, who kept well away from the windows – Jinx focused on the open skies above them, ever watchful for cyber-eagles and enemy zeppelins.

"Free at last," Shelley muttered, his one remaining eye glistening with moisture.

"Jinx, take us away," Hercules declared.

"Wait," Shelley said. "There's one last thing I have to do first."

"What's that?" Hercules asked.

"One last promise I have to keep to myself."

"BROTHERS!" THE FIRST bellowed from atop an overturned personnel carrier, his voice carrying clearly over the crackling flames. As one, the Prometheans held off pummelling the broken bodies of the soldiers and turned to face the towering presence standing above them. "Today is the first day of your lives as free men. But, in the words of Vegetius, *si vis pacem, para bellum*. 'If you want peace, prepare for war!'"

The crash of glass and the splintering of timber interrupted his first rousing speech as leader of this band of brothers. But it was nothing compared to the roar of engines that followed, as the iron eagle rose from its hangar into the cold morning air, black against the washed-out autumn sky.

"What is that?" Adam grumbled, annoyed at having been so rudely interrupted.

The von Stauffenberg creature saw it too – the eagle ascendant – as did the twitching Seziermesser at his side.

"God in heaven!" the scientist swore.

As all those present watched the eagle climb higher above Castle Frankenstein – Prometheans and Frankenstein Corps personnel alike – and the shadow of the great bird fell across the courtyard, the belly of the great metal bird split open and a myriad black, finned forms dropped whistling from within.

"You bastards!" Adam growled. And then again, screaming his fury to the heavens like the voice of doom itself. "*You bastards! YOU BASTARDS!*"

And then the bombs hit.

FIRE BLOOMED ACROSS the complex as the eagle's entire payload of explosives fell on Castle Frankenstein like the wrath of God, His divine retribution enacted at last against those who had usurped His role as Creator. The black and orange blossoms obscured the fortress from view completely.

"There," Shelley said, looking more haunted and strung out than ever. "'Tis done. And there's an end to it."

"An end?" Hercules laughed as the castle crag was consumed by fire beneath them. "This is only the beginning."

He turned to his companions, absent-mindedly stroking his moustache as he did so.

"The game, as they say, is well and truly afoot!"

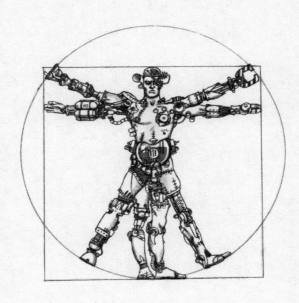

ACT FOUR

Where Eagles Dare

*"National Socialism will use its own revolution
for establishing a new world order."*

– Adolf Hitler

CHAPTER THIRTY-SIX

Pride before Destruction

Amiens, France, 1943

General Sir Henry Stamford Raffles raised a large pair of brass-rimmed binoculars to his eyes and scanned the enemy lines on the far side of the battlefield.

A low mist drifted across the black water-filled craters between the barbed wire lines. Beyond the pitted, churned-up grey muddy mess of no man's land the men and machines of the Third Reich were arrayed; everything from standard troopers and Jotun-class tanks to clanking units of Landsknechts and even the occasional remade abomination.

The Nazi menace was persistent, he'd give them that.

Raffles lowered his binoculars, placing them on the silver tea tray his batman was holding out ready beside him and picking up the cooling cup of tea next to them. He took a sip, the leather armchair creaking as he eased his bulk back into it, crossed his ankles on the footstool in front of him and took in the Magna Britannia forces, of which he was commander-in-chief, with a proud, rosy-cheeked grin.

To his left stood the massed ranks of the Galahad and Gawain regiments, ten thousand automata strong. To his right were arrayed the combined might of Lancelot and Percival; another ten thousand head of robo-infantry. Supporting them were the gigantic land-battleships *Samson* and *Atlas*, mounting mighty cannon and mortars, Gatling guns and iron spear-firing ballistae. He could hear the mighty roar of their engines as their crews stoked their boilers, thick black smoke and geysers of white steam rising from their towering smokestacks. The land-battleships of the Wellington Dreadnought Brigade were a sight to behold, the Britannian flag snapping from their banner-poles in the chill autumnal wind.

And there were men of flesh and blood amongst the forces too – weapons crews, engine teams, stokers, droid handlers, engineers, tacticians, the men piloting the stalker tanks and Trojan support vehicles, not to mention the trusted Tommy foot soldier – but there weren't many. Only a couple of hundred, compared with the twenty thousand grunt-bots. And, as General Kensington Gore, the oft-quoted First Great European War general and all-round hero, famously said, "Give me one hundred droids or, failing that, a thousand ordinary men." But then he had been half-automaton himself.

It was a sign of Raffles' status and rank that he had been afforded the privilege of leading the Magna Britannian forces at Amiens into battle from atop his own personalised pachyderm-droid *Hannibal*. Before freedom-threatening war had come to the heartlands of Europe for a second time, he had served in India, where the vision of the monstrous robo-phant charging the gates of Bombay had sent many a revolutionary fleeing for his life.

The howdah shaded Raffles and his batman from the weak rays of the milky sun. The commander-in-chief's command post might have looked out of place, had it not been for the Magna Britannian iconography that had been worked into the ornate scrollwork of the giant droid's flanks.

Raffles eased himself back into his chair. He could feel the comforting rumble of the boiler bubbling in the guts of the metal beast, as its own engines were stoked with coke, ready for action. He was going to enjoy this. It was going to be a walk in the park, but he was looking forward to it anyway.

Putting the china cup to his lips at last, he took a sip. He grimaced; the tea was cold. With a flick of the wrist he sent the contents of the cup over the side of the pachyderm onto an unsuspecting automaton below. He rattled the teacup and its saucer back onto the tray.

"Is the pot still warm?" he asked of his batman, without once taking his eyes from the battlefield in front of him.

He could see sinister airborne shapes – something like birds and something like flying bombs – circling and wheeling above the enemy lines. He was comforted to know that above his own forces, the Darwin Corps' tamed Pterosaurs hung from the airborne eyries of the airship *Harridan,* ready to swoop down and rend any enemy aerial forces wing from wing.

Lister put a hand to the silvered teapot sitting on the small stove at the back of the howdah, testing the temperature. "Yes, sir."

"Then pour me another cup."

"Right away, sir," Lister replied dutifully. "Do you think we'll win, sir?" the batman asked as he passed the general a steaming cup.

Raffles turned a withering gaze upon his batman.

"The Germans are losing this war, Lister; their resources are stretched to the limit, and this is a last ditch attempt devised by the Führer and his lackeys to hold back the inevitable. Show some backbone, man! Whatever happened to your stiff upper lip, and all that? Mark my words, we'll have this all wrapped up in time for Tiffin. We'll be in Paris for cocktails and Berlin for a little hair of the dog tomorrow. You mark my words!"

Raffles took a sip. "Ah, that's much better." Satisfied, he placed the cup carefully back on its saucer, exchanging it for the speaking tube hung on its hose in the bracket on the other side of his chair. He raised the horn to his mouth.

"Men and automatons of the Magna Britannian Fourth Cybernetic Expeditionary Company! We march to war, that we might eradicate the Nazi menace once and for all. We march for

Queen and country! We march for freedom from oppression! The command is given, and that command is – *atta* –"

But Sir Raffles' command to engage was drowned by a scream of burning air and boiling mist as a beam of retina-searing light, like fire from heaven, streaked out of the sky. The beam hit the front row of Galahad regiment, which vanished in a blinding flash of concentrated sunlight. The noise of the explosions that followed in the wake of the beam reached Raffles a moment later.

The flaming spear vanished as suddenly as it had appeared, leaving Raffles blinking grey sunbursts from his eyes and seeing nothing of the automaton infantry line but a mass of fused and burning wreckage.

The beam came again, a sustained blast this time, taking out the entire front line of Lancelot to his right.

Raffles was out of his chair now, panic rendering him silent.

The giant *Atlas* was the next target of the devastating death ray, the British colours cooking off its hull plating under its fiery fury, the Britannia flags reduced to blackened cinders that were then carried away as glowing orange embers on the firestorm wind following the beam's onslaught.

Two seconds later, the shells inside the giant's right arm cannon touched off.

The force of the explosion flattened almost all of Gawain regiment and even threatened to send the *Hannibal* crashing over onto its side, but the ten-tonne pachyderm stood firm.

"By all the saints!" Raffles spluttered as he picked himself up off the floor of the howdah, his ears ringing. The tray beside his seat was swimming in hot tea now, the cup tossed over by the force of the explosion. "What the blazes was th –"

His sentence remained unfinished as the super-heated death ray found its next target.

CHAPTER THIRTY-SEVEN

Icarus Burning

"THERE!" CAT SUDDENLY shouted, drawing everyone's attention to the window-port in the side of the great bird's head.

Ulysses Quicksilver was at her side at once. He was momentarily distracted by the curious flutter he felt in his stomach at being so close to the young woman, still stunningly beautiful despite all they had been through.

"Why are you looking at me like that?" she asked, and Ulysses blushed, suddenly realising how strange he must look, staring at her so intently. "You should be looking at that!" she said, pointing out the reinforced glass of the eagle's eye.

Ulysses looked, and the sight that greeted him took his breath away.

Schloss Adlerhorst rose above the peaks of its Alpine home, a melange of Romanesque pinnacles and turrets, so utterly unlike Castle Frankenstein.

It rose above the pervasive cloud cover atop its mountain peak like an island fortress emerging from amidst a sea of white spume.

And more impressive even than the castle eyrie itself – built hundreds of years ago and thousands of feet above sea level in the Alpine peaks – was the structure that had been erected around and within it since, coiled about the towers and minarets like a serpent of twisting steel scaffolds and grilled iron platforms.

Winding around the rugged near-white walls of Schloss Adlerhorst, the structure branched halfway up. One branch led to a vast parabolic dish surmounting the highest point of the castle, covered with mirrored tiles. The mirrors were dazzling in the morning sunlight, too bright to look upon directly as they caught the sunlight and redirected it to a mass of collector prisms at its centre.

The second branch of the structure led to a slightly lower platform, built out over the battlements of the castle, where part of the original wall had been knocked down to accommodate it. Clearly, nothing was more important than the device, not even hundreds of years of historic architecture.

The platform supported a swivel-mounted cannon piece, which looked like a cross between a huge telescope and a cannon, tapering to a lance-like point. It had to be at least a hundred feet long. Massive bearings below the platform looked like they could be used to lever the platform out on a telescoping arm and swing it around the side of the castle. There was nowhere that could not be targeted from the schloss using the device.

"Talk about German efficiency," Hercules muttered as he joined Cat and his future son at the window-port. "How long did you say the Nazis have had the ability to build this?" he asked, addressing Ulysses directly.

"Well..." Ulysses was momentarily caught off guard. He still found it strange talking to his father, when he was actually younger than Ulysses was himself. "I think I was first taken to Castle Frankenstein about two months ago."

"You think?" Cookie interrupted.

"But it must have taken much longer than two months to build this," came Katarina's thickly-accented voice from the shadows around the navigation table.

"Well I know that Dashwood arrived before me," Ulysses

said, suddenly feeling as if he was being interrogated again, "but I don't know how long precisely. I'd thought it at most a matter of weeks."

"It must have been months," Hercules said. "Maybe a year."

"I should think so," Katarina agreed, watching them from the dark at the back of the cabin.

"I don't understand," Cat piped up. "How can there be all this confusion over when you got here and when this Dashwood man did? Where was it that you came from, anyway?"

All turned to look at the eye-patched Ulysses, and he felt the hackles on the back of his neck rise as his stomach began to tighten. "It's a long story," he muttered evasively.

"Well, we're not going anywhere," Cookie said, crossing her arms.

"Shit!" Jinx exclaimed sharply. "Will you look at that?"

Everyone's attention turned from the haunted Ulysses and back to the converted castle below them.

The Icarus Cannon had fired. The intense searing radiance of the beam of concentrated sunlight, three and a half thousand degrees strong, caused them to wince in actual physical pain, throwing their hands up to shield their watering eyes.

"What's it firing at?" Cookie asked, urgently.

"There's no way of knowing," Hercules said, making a rough calculation in his head, "not from here, but it's clear the cannon's been targeted at a location to the north-west."

"Wherever it is, I don't think it's going to be helping the Allied war effort any, do you?" Ulysses commented.

"What sort of range could a weapon like that have?" Cat murmured, awed.

"Who knows?" Hercules replied. "But if the beam could be focused tightly enough... Hundreds of miles?"

"Hundreds?" Cat exclaimed.

"Amiens!" Ulysses whispered, recalling his history lessons.

"We have to destroy it," Agent K said with a shudder, "and without further delay."

"I thought that was the plan," Ulysses said.

"Yes," Cookie snapped, "but how?"

"Just get me off here and point me in the direction of whatever it is you want destroyed," Hyde's voice rumbled up to them through the hole in the cabin floor.

"All in good time, Edward," Hercules called back, "all in good time."

"Then what do you suggest?" Cookie challenged him.

"Um... I've got an idea," Jinx said hesitantly.

"Really?" Ulysses said, sounding a lot more surprised than he had intended.

"It has been known," the young woman said with a pout.

"Whatever it is you have in mind, we have to act fast," Hercules said. "Whatever else happens, we have to shut off that beam."

"If only we had something we could drop on the castle," Cookie said, "like – oh, I don't know – some bombs perhaps?"

Ulysses wilted before her glare. "I did what had to be done at the time," he said weakly.

"Then time for Plan B, I think," Hercules said. "Or should that be Plan J?"

"Leave it to me," Jinx said, grinning now from ear to ear. "I suggest you all hang onto something."

The iron eagle banked abruptly – throwing those who were still unprepared across the cabin into an enforced huddle on its starboard side – and began to circle the castle in an ever-tightening spiral.

Ulysses watched the cloud-clad peak as it spun below them.

Slowly the great shadow of the iron eagle fell across the turrets of Schloss Adlerhorst and the sunlight-focusing dish.

"Clever girl," Hercules said softly, allowing himself a smile as he stroked at his moustache. He turned to Jinx, secure within the pilot's position. "Can you keep the bird hovering in this position?"

"I think so," she replied, looking justifiably proud of herself. "I can certainly try."

Ulysses struggled across to the other side of the cockpit to keep the Icarus Cannon in sight. Was it his imagination, or had the beam it was projecting lost some of its intensity? But it was still aflame and, at the end of the day, what difference did a few degrees of heat make? It was still as incandescent as the sun and probably as hot as well.

"It's not enough," he muttered.

"What?" Hercules snapped.

"The dish is still collecting enough light for the cannon to function," he said, speaking up so that they could all hear.

"Are you sure you're seeing clearly through that eye-patch of yours?" Hercules retorted.

"On a day like today, in these conditions we're going to need a better solution than simply casting a shadow over the collector array."

"So what do you suggest?" Hercules threw back.

"Well," Ulysses said uncertainly, "something more permanent."

"Marvellous! That's your suggestion, is it?"

"All I know is that until that cannon is put out of action, the Magna Britannian forces at Amiens are going to be cooking like marshmallows on a jamboree campfire."

"Like I said," Hyde's voice rose from where he was penned in the belly hold, with all the patience of a beast pacing its cage. "Just drop me off now and I'll get this party started."

"All in good time," Hercules called back. "All in good time."

"So you keep saying," the giant grumbled. "But the time for talking is past, and the time for arse-kicking is upon us."

"Like this, you mean?" Jinx countered, pulling hard on the flying machine's controls, forcing the great metal bird into a sharp dive.

Once again, the rest of those on board were forced to hang on as the iron eagle plummeted towards the cannon itself.

"I hope you know what you're doing, Jinx!" Cookie shouted over the screaming drone of the bird's engines. "We knew this was a suicide mission when we signed up for it, but I've got used to the idea of living again and I don't want it to end too soon!"

"Don't worry," Jinx said through gritted teeth as she fought the rising strain to keep the bird on course, the battlements of the castle filling the viewports in front of them. "I'm good at landings – honest. But, just in case, you might want to put your head between your legs."

"What, and brace for impact?" Cat asked.

"To kiss your arse goodbye," Hyde laughed from below.

"Why aren't we under attack?" Cat asked, desperately trying to catch a glimpse of the skies above. "Where are the cyber-eagles? The dirigible gunships?"

"Sheer bloody arrogance?" Ulysses suggested.

"How so?"

"Either they considered their position unassailable or they thought the cannon would protect them? Or perhaps they're low on resources and have had to commit everything to the land battle to hold back the Allied advance."

"How do you know all this?" Cat asked, scrutinizing him intently.

"History lessons," Ulysses replied, just a little too quickly.

"History lessons?"

"I mean, history has a habit of repeating itself."

"Right, here we go," Hercules announced.

"Here goes nothing," Ulysses muttered to himself, "once again."

The cannon loomed larger and larger, coming nearer and nearer.

Just when it looked like the eagle was going to come down on top of the firing platform itself, Jinx pulled back hard on the stick, and the iron eagle, wings outspread, swept into the path of the super-heated beam of sunlight.

The eagle was engulfed in a searing supernova of light as it came between the devastating beam and its target, more than a hundred miles away on the ground. But even as the highly polished steel began to liquefy under the intense heat, it reflected a measure of the blast back at the fortress.

The air temperature inside the cockpit suddenly rose sharply, until in the space of only a few seconds, they felt as if they were inside a blast furnace.

"Are you sure you know what you're doing?" Ulysses shouted, the air scorching his throat.

"Bloody hell!" Hyde roared from below. "It's hotter than Hades down here!"

Ulysses' attention was suddenly drawn to Cat as she passed

out beside him. Ulysses caught her and laid her gently on the floor.

The control dials popped in quick succession, sending shards of glass whickering into the cabin.

Just when Ulysses thought he might black out from the heat himself, the flying machine was rocked by a violent explosion. Almost instantly, the air temperature began to drop.

A second explosion sent the metal bird spinning out of control. Without a second thought, Ulysses sprang to Jinx's aid, grabbing hold of the flight controls and adding his strength to hers as the iron eagle entered the sea of clouds below the mountain's crest.

They fought to regain control of the plummeting bird. A wingtip clipped a snow-covered black rock outcrop, and the eagle described a parabola through the freezing mists and burst clear of the dense clouds again. The flying machine now under control, they gathered before the eye-windows once more. The sight that met them caused Cookie to whoop for joy and Hercules to punch the air in delight. Ulysses just stared at the Schloss Adlerhorst, his mouth agape.

The Icarus Cannon was gone. In its place was a smoking ruin of twisted steel and blackened, fused glass. The polished wings of the iron eagle had re-directed the cannon's lethal beam at the super weapon itself, which had proved just as susceptible to its effects as anything else.

JUST AS SUDDENLY as the fatal heat ray had appeared, it cut out again.

Sir Stamford Raffles blinked hard, trying to banish the after-images of burning tanks and blazing cannon blasts from before his eyes.

He remained where he was sheltered, beneath the collapsed howdah beside the fallen pachyderm, smoke still rising from its scorched armour casing, half expecting the beam to strike again, like the wrath of God descending from heaven on wings of flame.

It was Lister who first dared clamber clear of the wreckage of the toppled tent.

"It's stopped," he said, negotiating the wreckage of melted automaton Tommies and staring in shock at the devastation left by the heat ray – vitrified craters where tanks had once stood, the statuesque forms of *Samson* and *Atlas* like toppled statues of Greek Gods.

"You're sure?" Raffles asked, peering out through a rent in the howdah's awning.

Lister came to a halt. They both listened.

They could hear the crackle of flames where the super-heated ray had struck, the horrified cries of shell-shocked men, the startled cries where the chain of command was in danger of shattering altogether in the aftermath of the sudden and inexplicable attack.

The brass-rimmed binoculars were lying in the mud within arm's reach. Sir Stamford Raffles picked them up and turned his magnified gaze on the serried lines of Germans beyond the boiling crater holes and melted barbed wire rolls at the edge of no man's land. The anxious looks the German soldiers were giving each other told him all he needed to know.

The hose and horn of the speaker tube hung from the blistered body of the elephant droid beside him. Seizing hold of it, hearing the crackle of static through the speaker grilles in the pachyderm's head, he gave the long-awaited command at last.

"Men of the Fourth Cybernetic Expeditionary Company, for Queen and country – attack!"

SLOWLY, AND WITH some regret, the cheers filling the cabin and hold of the iron eagle died away.

"It's still not enough," Shelley said.

"What's not enough?" Cat mumbled, coming to again, now that the strength-sapping temperatures had eased.

"What do you mean?" snapped Hercules, turning on the one-eyed doomsayer. "The Icarus Cannon is destroyed. We've done what we set out to do. Our mission is complete!"

"Not for me, it's not," the other said resignedly. "Not until I know Dashwood's dead. Not until I've seen the bastard's warped corpse for myself. It's too dangerous to risk leaving him alive. We have to land and search the castle, just to be sure."

For a moment no one said anything.

Shelley really knew how to suck the joy out of a moment, Hercules thought. He must be a nightmare at parties.

When the uneasy silence was finally broken, it was Jinx who spoke.

"We might not have a lot of choice," she said, sweating from the effort of keeping the great metal bird level and under control.

Hercules was horribly aware of a shuddering sound, and the twanging of wires under tension, from somewhere within the body of the craft.

"This thing's flying days are over. We're going down."

CHAPTER THIRTY-EIGHT

Bad Landings

"HOLD HER STEADY," Hercules instructed, placing an encouraging hand on Jinx's shoulder as they came in low over Schloss Adlerhorst.

"The heat blast must have evaporated the cavorite coating," Shelley was muttering, talking nonsense to himself again.

But they were coming in at the wrong angle. At this rate, the iron eagle would like as not hit the top of the tower and go right off the other side, dropping them over the mountain to be smashed to pieces on the rocky crags a thousand feet below.

"Do you think you can bring her around one more time?" he asked in a low voice, so only she could hear.

"I can try," Jinx said through gritted teeth, briefly releasing her grip on the controls to wipe a stray strand of sweaty hair out of her face.

Hauling back on the controls, Jinx swung the beak of the great bird around, the trailing edge of the eagle's left wing clipping a tower and sending a cascade of stones crashing onto the tiered rooftops below.

Those on the bridge clung onto whatever handholds the

cabin afforded them as, with terrible slowness, its fuselage shaking and groaning in protest, the iron eagle left the schloss behind.

THE FLYING MACHINE moved with laboured reluctance as Jinx brought it around again over the cloud banks, but Ulysses' mind was racing.

The bird's aerodynamic form must be all that was keeping it airborne now, the vaporising heat ray having raised the temperature of the cavorite beyond boiling point, at which point the mysterious alloy had lost its anti-gravitic powers, leaving the eagle nothing more than several tonnes of iron and steel, and about as airworthy as a locomotive.

And then, as the eagle's nose dropped lower, the vista of the cloudscape beyond the cockpit gave way to the devastated ruin of Schloss Adlerhorst again and the buckled smoking debris field of the gun platform.

"EVERYONE DOWN THE ladder!" Hercules commanded, turning from the view of the white walls of the tower, despoiled by curtains of black smoke now, hastening them all with a wave of his arm.

Cookie led the way, followed by Cat and Shelley, the Russian agent finally quitting her station to follow them.

"Mr Hyde!" Hercules shouted. "If you would be so good as to pop the hatch and prepare to disembark?"

"Consider it done!" Hyde boomed back.

That left only Hercules and the pilot. The once crowded cockpit seemed almost empty.

The smouldering, shattered towers of the castle loomed large ahead of them.

"Come on, Jinx, it's time to go," he said, feeling the blood drain from his cheeks as the platform came ever closer.

"If I can just bring the bird in level," Jinx gasped through gritted teeth.

"No you don't," Hercules said, grabbing her arm, and Jinx finally allowed herself to be pulled out of her seat. "You've done more than enough already. You're coming with me."

Pushing the young woman ahead of him, Hercules slid down the ladder after her.

The two of them arrived in the hold to be met by a gust of icy wind as Hyde cranked the ramp open.

And then the eagle hit the platform.

Suddenly noise was vibration and vibration was noise and the two became indistinguishable. The seven survivors were sent tumbling about the belly hold as the metal bird ploughed across the platform with no sign of stopping. Hands were flung out as they grabbed hold of each other and whatever else they could to keep themselves on their feet.

A second loud *clang* reverberated through the hold as the trailing edge of the ramp hit the buckled frame of the weapon, throwing up a trail of sparks behind it.

Hyde crouched before the hatchway. The bird was shaking around them now as it ground over the debris. Hercules saw pieces of twisted metal the size of tree trunks bounce past, the ramp bouncing on its hydraulics. There was the occasional drawn out red smear, too, as some poor sod or other was pulverised beneath the bird.

"Go!" Hercules shouted over the grating scream of metal on metal. "Go! Go! Go!"

Cookie, Cat and Jinx joined the hulking Hyde at the exit.

"Ladies, after you," the brute offered graciously.

Not one of them moved. All were transfixed by the metal platform speeding past their eyes.

"Here," Hyde growled, grabbing hold of Cookie by the scruff of her jacket, "let me help you." With one swing of his arm he hurled the leader of the Monstrous Regiment out of the back of the iron eagle.

Her scream was drowned out by the noise of tortured metal. She hit the deck on her left hand side, automatically curling herself into a tight ball as she rolled across the platform.

The iron eagle careened onwards.

"Right," Hyde said, eyeing up Jinx and Cat, "who's next?"

With stifled yelps of fear, the two women jumped together. The athletic cat burglar described a graceful dive out of the back of the bird, landing in a forward roll and springing up onto her feet. Jinx wasn't so lucky and landed badly, her knee twisting under her.

"KATARINA, YOU'RE NEXT," Ulysses declared, shouting to be heard over the terrible, ear-splitting noise.

She turned her penetrating eyes on the man whose release she had fought so hard for and, taking his hand in hers, said, "We go together."

And with that they leapt, the vampire pulling him clear of the crashing craft. They landed an impossible fifteen yards away and still on their feet.

"That was unbelievable!"

His gasp of excitement quickly became a gasp of pain as her hand tightened about his with bone-crushing force.

He turned towards her, and the expression on her face said it all. In the unfiltered Alpine sunlight, the vampire was in agony.

"Come on," he said, and now it was his turn to pull her to safety, heading for the shade of a toppled gantry.

"JUST YOU AND me left," Hyde said, grinning at Hercules. There was something about the great brute's expression that reminded him of a dog poking its head out the open window of a speeding steam-carriage.

Hercules steeled himself, trying to choose the optimum moment to jump.

"Last one out's a Nancy boy!" Hyde laughed wildly, flinging himself out of the back of the bird, arms flailing.

Hercules jumped an instant later.

But suddenly there was nothing beneath him but cold mountain air, a precipitous drop down the side of the mountain. He had left it too late.

*　　*　　*

THE MAIDEN FLIGHT of the iron eagle came to an abrupt end as it nosedived off the edge of the elevated platform, its iron beak burying itself in the base of another rampart tower moments later. The foundations fractured as the great metal bird punched through them, bringing a landslide of brick and stone down on top of it as the tower crumbled. A cascade of kicking, screaming bodies came tumbling down the mountain side amidst the broken ramparts.

Hercules could see the side of the platform rising before him and then he was falling, twisted metal and black rock hurtling past his eyes as he followed the tumbling Germans to a messy death on the icy crags below.

Then Hercules cried out in pain, as his fall was arrested so abruptly that it felt like he'd dislocated his shoulder.

He hung for a moment, his body swinging gently from side to side, the icy wind ruffling his hair, the underside of the platform edge less than a foot from his nose. As the pain subsided, Hercules opened his eyes and looked up.

His right hand had been completely swallowed by a huge green fist. It looked like an adult's, holding the hand of a toddler. Above the hand, and the thickly-muscled arm it was attached to, peering over the edge of the crumpled gun deck, was Hyde's hugely grinning face, a wicked glint in his jaundiced-yellow eyes.

"What a rush," the beast chuckled, his words awash with laughter. "Can we do that again? Oh, and by the way, you're a Nancy boy."

CHAPTER THIRTY-NINE

The Eagle Has Landed

"IS EVERYONE ALRIGHT?" Hercules asked, as Mr Hyde hauled him back up onto the platform.

Keeping low, the rest of the assault squad gathered at the edge of the platform.

"We're alright," Cookie said, touching him tenderly on the arm. "What about you?"

And suddenly Cat was there in front of him, throwing her arms around him, and burying her face in the hollow of his neck so that the others wouldn't see her tears.

"I thought we'd lost you," she sobbed. Hercules slowly put his arms around her trim form in return, just as much in shock as she was. He could feel her body shuddering within his embrace.

Machine-gun fire chewed up the sundered skirts of the platform, sending the party scattering.

Hercules hunkered down behind a length of the devastated cannon barrel, his back to the still-warm metal, Cat and Cookie on either side. Glancing to his right, he saw Jinx nursing her sore knee in the shelter of a fallen block of concrete ten feet across, Hyde crouched beside her. To his left the mysterious Shelley, whom they had all risked so much for and whose obsessive undertaking had ultimately brought them here, was peering out from beneath a toppled gantry, the blonde vampire hiding in the deep shadows behind him.

The machine gun fell silent again, but it seemed at least one gun emplacement remained operational.

"Damn," he grunted.

Cat smiled at him and squeezed his hand. "Just another typical shitty day at the office for us girls," she said.

He couldn't help but return her smile.

"And, if it is our day to die," she went on, "at least we'll go down together."

"Let's hope you're wrong," Hercules said, "about it being our day to die, I mean," he added, suddenly flustered. "I like the other bit, about us being in this together," and he squeezed her hand in return.

Releasing her hand, he checked the load on his gun. The rest of the team were already doing the same.

Shelley had fixed him with his single, haunted eye, now ringed by tiredness. Just looking at him made Hercules want to yawn. In fact, how long was it since any of them had last had any sleep?

"We have to get inside!" the man hissed across the smoke-washed deck. He peered over the top of the broken barrel.

The machine gun immediately opened up again, hard rounds rebounding from the pressed steel deck plates and kocking chips from Hyde's concrete shelter.

"*You* do, you mean," Hercules threw back. "The rest of us just need to make sure you make it. What you need is some kind of distraction."

"Don't worry," Hyde called across to them having, incredibly, heard every word. "I know something that might work."

Picking up a buckled piece of metal that looked like it might have been part of the collector array, and holding it before him in both hands so that it shielded his whole body, the giant stepped out from behind his hiding place.

The machine gunner opened up again, the chugging weapons-fire spanging off the makeshift shield. Hyde simply marched forwards.

"Come on!" the giant called back. "What are you waiting for?"

The machine gun cut out again, there was a moment's silence and then the *plink*, *plink* of two metal spheroids landing on the deck in front of the advancing Hyde.

Hercules, peering out from behind the cannon segment quickly pulled his head back in with a sharp intake of breath.

A second later, the grenades exploded.

The full force of the blast hit the crumpled dish, but, incredibly – legs braced against the force of the double explosion, his toes gouging indentations in the steel floor – Mr Hyde stood firm, smoke and flame swirling past him like the sea crashing against a cliff.

Glancing back over his shoulder at the others the giant gave a slow shake of his head.

"Come on!" the brute repeated. "What do you want, a bloody invitation?"

Tendrils of smoke still clinging to his makeshift shield, Hyde took a hold of it by the rim and, with a sharp flick of the wrist, sent it spinning out across the platform and towards the castle wall.

The dish whickered through the air with a *thrub-thrub-thrub* noise, and vanished in the shadows half way up the side of the tower with a clatter of metal and a wet snapping sound.

The machine gun position remained silent.

Hyde turned to regard the anxious faces peering out at him.

Hercules was on his feet in an instant, pistol in hand. His Nazi uniform was a mess – torn, scorched and blood-stained. He was never going to pass for one of the Führer's men looking like this.

"Come on!" He turned to the others. "Like the man said, what are we waiting for?"

SHIELDED BY MR Hyde's hulking form, the party made their way from the wrecked gun platform down a twisting spiral staircase, finally entering the castle through the rent torn in its flank by the plummeting bird. They scrambled over a scree of broken bricks and fallen gargoyles, and entered the eerily empty interior of Schloss Adlerhorst.

Ulysses had no idea how many personnel should have been active within the Schloss in the first place. The destruction of the Icarus Cannon and the damage done by the crashing iron eagle had taken their toll, as had Hyde's actions with the machine gun emplacement. But how many desperate men still lurked inside the ancient fortress, he wondered? Men with nothing left to lose, reckless enough to sell their lives and the ideals they still clung onto at as high a price as they could.

They passed from one draughty, vaulted passageway – the bare stone walls lined with pipes and cable trunking – to another, seeing no sign of anybody, alive or dead. The occasional Nazi banner fluttered in the chill breeze that whined through the castle, but there was no sign of resistance until they came to a crossing of the ways buried in the depths of the fortress.

As Hyde led the way towards the junction, knuckles dragging across the floor, he stopped abruptly.

"What is it?" Hercules hissed, coming alongside the monster, who was still just about wearing what was left of his torn suit.

Hyde's head was up, nostrils flaring.

"I can smell them," he said, his voice a wet growl.

"Who?"

"Nazis, of course," Hyde retorted. "I can smell their fear."

His pronouncement was followed by a rattling of weapons being readied.

Cookie silently signalled Cat and Jinx forward with a wave of her hand. The cat burglar and the driver took point, flattening themselves against opposing walls at the end of the passageway. They peered down the passageways opposite them. Cat signed that the way ahead of her was clear. Jinx drew two fingers back and forth across her throat. The passageway to the left was where the danger lay.

"Shall we?" Hyde asked, grinning as he turned to face Hercules.

"After you, Mr Hyde," the other replied, a wry smile on his face.

Hercules turned to Ulysses then. Ulysses knew what was coming, before his father said a word.

"I rather think it's time we went our separate ways," Hercules said, offering the stunned Ulysses his hand. "We have done what we set out to; now it's your turn. And the best way we can help you is to occupy the fascist bastards lurking around that corner while you and your friend here" – he nodded towards Katarina – "can complete your mission and put an end to whatever madness it is that Germany's desire for world domination has spawned here."

Ulysses took the proffered hand in stunned silence, a mawkish expression on his face, his mouth hanging open. This might very well be the last time he would see his father alive, and that alone felt like losing him all over again. He was suddenly a fifteen-year-old boy once more, standing in his father's study, being told by Nimrod that his father was dead.

There was so much that he wanted to say to him. He wanted to tell his father how much he loved him. He wanted to tell him how much he still missed him. But more than anything he wanted to warn him – to tell him about his death.

"We have to go, now," Hercules said, interrupting Ulysses' thoughts as he tried to pull his hand free of Ulysses' white-knuckled grip. "I'm not sure how long I can keep Hyde on the leash, as it were."

With a world of words he wanted to share with his father, all Ulysses said was, "Thank you."

"Well, I wouldn't say it's been fun," Hercules said, breaking free of the handshake at last, "but it's been an adventure, I'll give you that."

"But you've done so much," Ulysses said. "More than you'll ever know."

Hercules smiled. "Just make sure you get the bastard for us, won't you? That's all the thanks we need right now."

"Alright," Ulysses said, blinking away the tear forming at the corner of his one remaining eye. "It's a deal."

"Right you are then," Hercules said, turning back to the imposing figure of Hyde, who was starting to look a lot like a Rottweiler straining to be let off its lead. "Mr Hyde, after you."

Hyde didn't need to be told twice. He strode along the corridor and turned into the passageway to the left, calling, "Right then, ladies, shall we dance?"

As Hyde's invitation was answered with the chugging clamour of a Czechoslovak, accompanied by the monster's own furious roar, the women followed him around the corner, guns at the ready.

But Hercules hung back. "Look, I know this isn't quite the time but..." He broke off, suddenly lost for words. Ulysses felt his heart quicken inside his chest. "Look, we're not..."

Ulysses opened his mouth to speak.

"No, I know, it's a ridiculous notion," Hercules interrupted before his son could say anything. Rattling gunfire echoed from beyond the junction. "And it's time we were both on our way. Good luck!" And with that, Hercules was gone.

Ulysses turned to Katarina. Her grim expression stopped the words that were already on the tip of his tongue.

"There is something between you two. What is it?"

"I-I don't know what you mean," Ulysses stammered.

Katarina frowned. "Yes you do," she said. "You just do not want to admit it, for some reason."

"I don't know what you mean," Ulysses repeated, as if restating the lie would somehow make it sound more plausible. "But I do know that I won't be able to rest until I have stared into Dashwood's dead eyes for myself."

"The two of you are related."

Ulysses turned sharply on his heel, making for the right-hand turn of the junction. "Are you coming or not?"

Katarina darted gracefully after him, shaking her head.

ULYSSES AND KATARINA hurried along draughty corridors and through abandoned chambers, all empty except for the ever-present wintry wind. It was as if the Nazis had fled the eyrie, the elemental spirits of the air taking up residence in their stead.

Neither of them said anything. They both knew what had to be done and there was no point discussing it.

Besides, right at that moment, Ulysses couldn't have articulated anything worth hearing anyway. Grief vied in him with an immense sense of relief, excitement with nervousness. There was also a deep-seated and growing feeling of apprehension twisting his guts. What if Dashwood wasn't there? Worse still, what if he was?

But there was one emotion that was stronger than all others, that drove him onwards despite all else, and that was cold hatred, steadily rising to boiling fury.

Whatever else happened, Ulysses Quicksilver was determined that Daniel Dashwood would pay for what he had done to his one true love Emilia; to her father, old man Oddfellow; to his indefatigable manservant Nimrod; and to Ulysses himself.

And that was how they continued, the only sound their running footfalls and Ulysses' panting breath, guns ready in their hands, senses alert to any sign of the man they had come here to kill.

When it came, it was not what either of them had been expecting.

It happened as the corridor they were following opened out into a vast, devastated chamber. The destruction of the Icarus Cannon had blasted a rift in the chamber wall twenty feet high.

The single shot rang out sharp and clear. Ulysses jumped, feeling suddenly cold to his core. He glanced down at his chest, instinctively putting a hand to his heart. But there was no blood on his fingers when he pulled his hand back again – and no bullet wound.

Katarina was standing in front of him, having been beside him only a moment before. She gave a faint gasp and fell to her knees. Black blood welled from the hole punched in her tunic over her heart.

There was a flicker of movement in front of them.

Ulysses' gun barked in his hand. For a moment he thought he had missed, but then a figure slowly slumped to the floor from behind a towering support pillar, the gun the sniper had been holding clattering onto the stone flags beside him. Scratch one assassin, Ulysses thought.

Shooting wary glances at the bare stone walls all around them, but seeing no sign of any further snipers, Ulysses dropped to his knees beside Katarina, his hands hovering over the gun shot wound in her chest, not sure what he should do.

"Leave me," Katarina gasped, clutching at her chest. Her breathing was already becoming heavy and laboured.

"But you're wounded; I can't leave you," he protested. "You took a bullet for me."

"Go on," she urged him, grabbing at his arm now with one palsied claw. "Find the one responsible and – how do you say?" she gasped. "Make him pay!"

"You'll be alright," Ulysses said, slowly rising to his feet.

"It *is* alright," she spluttered weakly, her eyelids fluttering closed. "I have lived long enough."

"No, you don't understand. It's not your time," Ulysses pressed. "Trust me."

But there was no reply. Katarina had stopped shaking and was now lying, curled in a foetal ball on the cold paving stones at the entrance to the cathedral-like space.

"But I can't wait for you now," Ulysses went on, even though he was not sure Katarina could hear him anymore. "I have a job to do. I have to finish this now."

Quickly kneeling beside her again he laid a kiss on her cheek. Her flesh was as cold as marble.

"See you in about fifty years," he said, and then, gun in hand, he turned and entered the wind-swept chamber beyond.

CHAPTER FORTY

The Modern Prometheus

THE COLD WIND stung his cheeks and chilled his hands as it moaned through the devastated castle, as if the ghosts of the dead of Schloss Adlerhorst had returned to haunt him, to make him pay for every German life lost that day.

The high vaulted chamber must have once been one of the deepest chambers of the castle, the stone arches of its high vaulted ceiling filled with shadows and ancient cobwebs. But now it was awash with bright, Alpine sunlight.

The chamber had been cracked open from floor to ceiling. Lumps of blackened masonry lay strewn across the floor of the chamber.

But the ruination he witnessed here meant nothing compared with the other sight that greeted Ulysses' one remaining eye.

Cold daylight streamed in through the towering fracture to his right, while darkness reigned amidst the looming pillars to his left. But the far side of the chamber was bathed in sparking waves of actinic radiance.

His heart-rate quickening, he began to stride between the pillars towards the clinging shadows and spasmodic bursts of lightning, because half-hidden by the pillars was something Ulysses had never thought he would see again.

It looked quite different to its last iteration, but it was still unmistakably the same machine.

The broken concentric rings of the gyroscope had gone, to be replaced by two interlocking rings, joined perpendicular to one another. Someone appeared to have made some improvements since the last time Ulysses had seen it.

The gleaming steel rings bristled with connectors and electrodes, from which the barely contained energies harnessed by the device dissipated into the atmosphere. Ulysses' hair was standing on end and the air was thick with the smell of ozone, while the stone-flagged floor of the sepulchral chamber trembled beneath his feet.

It was the evil machine that had landed him in all this trouble in the first place, and yet, now that he stood before it, bathed in its crackling glow, to Ulysses it seemed like nothing less than a beacon of hope; the path to his salvation. A way home.

From bitter past experience Ulysses knew that the device was already running up to speed. Someone was planning on teleporting out of there, that much was clear, and to Ulysses' mind it could only be one person.

Darting anxious glances about him, his knuckles whitening around the butt of the gun held tight in his hand, Ulysses pressed himself flat behind a pillar, desperately searching for his quarry. His heart thundered in his chest.

Dashwood was here, he was sure of it. With the Icarus Cannon destroyed and Schloss Adlerhorst succumbing to the Iron Eagle's attack, he was clearly planning on cutting his losses and getting out of there while he still could.

But not if I have anything to do with it, Ulysses promised himself.

He could hear the sounds of movement on the other side of the chamber. But what were they doing? Packing, by any chance?

"Ten minutes and counting," came the tinny female voice of an Enigma machine, speaking German, from the other side of the crypt.

Ten minutes – more than enough time to bring Dashwood's audacious scheme to an end, once and for all. And – another tempting thought suggested – time to make his own escape back to the future?

Warily, Ulysses peered around the column, and was immediately transfixed by the machine, resting atop its own specially fashioned wrought-iron dais.

Ulysses stared at the whirling rings of the device as it powered up to launch speed. It truly was a wonder of German engineering. With all the resources of the Third Reich at his disposal, Dashwood had achieved in a matter of months what Alexander Oddfellow had struggle to do in years. They had managed to build a prototype time machine, half a century earlier than it should have ever been possible.

Inhaling deeply and breathing out again slowly, focusing his mind completely on resolving this matter once and for all, Ulysses tightened his grip on his pistol and stepped out from behind the pillar...

...and immediately ducked back behind it again, hearing the screech of unoiled hinges as, somewhere on the other side of the chamber, a rusted steel door was forced open.

Ulysses froze, his heart pounding so hard he was sure whoever else was in the chamber with him could hear its echoing thuds bouncing off the walls.

He heard a sudden scrabbling sound come from somewhere behind him, over the thrumming whirr of the energising Sphere.

A booming *clang* echoed across the chamber as the protesting hinges suddenly gave and the door banged open. It was followed by the *tap-tap-tap* of running footsteps, and then a familiar voice exclaimed, "Damn! What the hell is that?"

"I don't know," came Cat's voice in response to Hercules Quicksilver's question.

Panic-stricken, Ulysses risked another glance from behind the pillar, realising that Hercules and his companion had no idea of the danger they were walking into, their amazement at the Sphere putting them off their guard.

He toyed with the idea of calling out to them, warning them

that they were not alone. But he soon put that thought from his mind. Dashwood – and he was sure it was Dashwood who was lurking in the shadows at the back of the crypt – already knew they were here and was doubtless moving to deal with the threat at that very moment. If Ulysses called out to them, the only person who would benefit was Dashwood.

Creeping around the pillar, keeping the crumbling column between him and the Sphere, Ulysses made his way ever closer towards the crackling Sphere and the platform on which it stood.

He glimpsed movement out of the corner of his eye and ducked out of sight once more. His back to the next pillar, he peered across the chamber.

And then he saw them, still making their way towards the Sphere, Hercules leading the way.

"Nine minutes and counting," came the Valkyrie voice of the Enigma engine.

In the time it took to blink, a shadow detached itself from behind another column and suddenly Dashwood was there, seizing Cat from behind, his right arm around her neck.

Cat's startled cry became a choking wheeze as her assailant pulled his arm tight.

Ulysses stared in appalled horror at the man who had stolen fire from heaven, who had brought the future crashing so catastrophically into the past, who had tortured him to the very limits of sanity.

Even as Hercules made to go to the girl's aid, Dashwood – his eerily glowing mask still covering his face – raised the gun in his right hand and put it to Cat's head.

And in the time it took him to realise what was going on, Ulysses lurched towards them, breaking into a sudden sprint.

"NOT SO FAST!" the masked man called, as Hercules turned to face him. "I have your woman, so I wouldn't try anything clever if I were you. Or anything stupid, for that matter..."

The gunman's voice trailed off, and Hercules saw confusion

in the man's eyes, the only part of him visible through the glowing azure slits cut into the curious mask.

"Dashwood!" Hercules breathed as realisation struck him.

"Wait a minute," the other spluttered. "You're not Quicksilver."

The man's arm suddenly went limp and the gun slipped from Cat's temple. This was all the opening Hercules needed.

"Oh, but I am," he snarled and sprang at the man.

But in that moment, the man's returned.

Without hesitation, he pointed the gun at Hercules and fired.

CHAPTER FORTY-ONE

Life and Limb

HERCULES SUDDENLY FOUND himself flying sideways as something else hit him before the bullet could.

First there had been the sharp crack of the pistol firing, then a heavy collision from the right and, almost instantaneously, a stifled gasp from Cat. And then he hit the ground, his head slamming into the stone floor.

For a moment, Hercules simply lay there, his senses reeling, as he tried to work out if it was him who had been shot, waiting for the pain. But it never came.

However, the man who had barrelled into him didn't appear to have been so lucky. Pushing the dead weight of the man from on top of him, Hercules saw with a mixture of surprise and disappointment that it was Shelley.

For a moment Hercules thought that he really was dead – that he had sacrificed his own life to save Hercules. He looked so peaceful that he might have been asleep. And there was something undeniably familiar about the set of his features.

But then Hercules saw the ragged hole in the man's shoulder, the spreading blood soaking the scorched fabric of his jacket.

And he saw Shelley's chest rise and then fall, and give a feeble moan.

But there wasn't time to think about the fallen now. The madman in the mask still needed dealing with.

Even as he pushed himself up onto his hands and knees – shaking his head to clear his senses, his heart racing – Hercules was all too horribly aware that every moment he wasted getting up off the floor was another moment in which Dashwood could gun them both down and be done with them.

There was a sudden flurry of movement and a determined shout from Cat as she elbowed Dashwood in the stomach hard, following it up with a swift, sharp kick to the shins.

The masked man doubled up in pain, his grip about the girl's neck loosening. The bold cat burglar made the most of the opportunity, slipping out of the headlock, spinning on her heel and executing a perfect roundhouse kick.

THE TOE OF Cat's boot struck the man mid-forearm, sending the gun flying from his hand. He recoiled instantly, stumbling backwards, but Cat wasn't going to let him get away that easily.

Leaning back to balance herself, she brought her leg around again, aiming directly at her captor's head.

But the bastard was ready for her this time. Fast as a striking cobra he caught her foot in his left hand, stopping her kick dead.

Dashwood pulled her towards him, already off-balance, and swung her around. The rift in the wall yawned before her and then – eyes wide with fear – she was through it, teetering on the edge of the thousand foot drop beyond, the chill Alpine wind whipping her hair about her face.

"Enjoy your flight, bitch!" Dashwood spat as, with one final push, he released his grip.

Helpless to stop herself, arms flailing, Cat fell headfirst out of the hole in the castle wall.

* * *

BEFORE DASHWOOD HAD even let go of her, Hercules was scrambling across the floor, bounding over the stone flags as he hurled himself after her.

Ignoring Dashwood as he barged past him, Hercules dived half through the fissure, landing flat at the broken lip of the floor-to-ceiling rift, reaching for the falling Cat.

He felt the fabric of her body-glove slip through his fingers and then his hand snapped shut around her ankle.

Cat struck the side of the mountain, the impact knocking the air from her lungs, but she was still alive. He had saved her.

Over the keening voice of the wind, Hercules heard her startled cry.

"Don't worry!" he shouted into the wind. "I've got you! It's alright! You're going to be alright!"

Bracing himself against the sides of the crack, teeth gritted from the strain on his exhausted body, Hercules hauled Cat back up the side of the mountain towards the relative safety of the madman's lair.

He could feel the pulsing of the unfathomable machine resonating through the stones under him. A cascade of grit and stone chips rained down on him from the broken wall above, encouraging him to redouble his efforts.

He had no idea where the madman had gone, or what had happened to Shelley, but at this moment, all that mattered to him was Cat.

Hercules worked himself up into a sitting position, his feet braced against the sundered walls on either side of the breach, and now he could put both hands to the task of pulling Cat to safety.

The throbbing pulse rose in pitch, becoming an uncomfortable whining hum. The sound made his ears ache, forcing him to grit his teeth against the urge to cry out.

And he could feel it in his bones now, rattling the teeth in his head, and turning his bowels to water. Even his vision was beginning to blur.

With a seismic crack like tectonic plates shifting, Hercules felt the ground lurch under him. And then he was sliding forwards, towards the breach, suddenly riding a torrent of tumbling brick and earth and stone.

He kicked at the crumbling breach, his fear and panic giving birth to a bellow of rage and frustration. But it was no good. He couldn't fight the death-throes of the castle.

The ground gave way beneath him completely and he joined the cascade of rubble as it spilled from the subsiding foundations of the castle.

Letting go of Cat with one hand, his clawing fingers grasped hold of something – a loosened brick, or a jagged tooth of stone – and for the briefest moment they were safe.

The throbbing of the sphere was a deep, resonant vibration that worked on the very bones of the mountain itself.

The stone came away in Hercules' hand, and then the two of them were falling again. And now there was nothing left to hold onto.

CHAPTER FORTY-TWO

The Final Countdown

A HUGE HAND grabbed him by the wrist, almost pulling his shoulder out of its socket. Hercules grunted, instinctively tightening his own grip on Cat's ankle as her leg threatened to slip from his grasp. He heard her cry out in shock a second time. This was becoming something of an uncomfortable habit.

Hercules cautiously opened his eyes and looked up into the grinning face of Mr Edward Hyde.

"Gotcha," the giant rumbled. "Again."

Biceps bulging, Hyde hauled the two of them back from the brink, depositing them back inside the chamber – or what was left of it at least.

A significant part of the roof had come down, and Hercules was presented with an enormous landslide of bricks, in-fill and earth.

He stared at the mound, stupefied.

"The roof's caved in," was all he could think to say.

"It wasn't me," Hyde said, suddenly guarded.

"I didn't say it was."

"It just happened to come down when I got here. Same time as I saw you two going for an early bath."

Hercules turned to the hulking Hyde standing in front of him, stooped like a gorilla, head hung low between his shoulders, knuckles dragging across the floor. He could see myriad cuts and abrasions, and several bullet wounds.

"You saved us," he said in a small voice.

"I know," Hyde rumbled, "it's starting to become a bit of a habit, isn't it? You ever thought of wearing a parachute?"

Cat looked up at Hyde's looming presence, the same expression of shocked bewilderment etched onto her face. "You want to be careful, Mr Hyde," she said almost dreamily, as if she was high on laudanum, "or you'll have people thinking you're one of the good guys."

"God forbid," the giant chuckled.

Hercules suddenly felt cold to the pit of his stomach.

"Shelley! Prisoner Zero!" he spluttered. "He saved my life."

Hyde's brow furrowed in suspicion and confusion. "No, that was me. Look, are you alright, or did a piece of falling rock give you a nasty bump on the head?"

"No, before." Hercules hesitated, as the implications of what he was about to admit began to sank in at last, and threatened to overwhelm him. "He took a bullet that was intended for me."

"No," Hyde said, shaking his head. "Haven't seen him."

"That's because he's on the other side of this." Hercules ran over to the mound of rubble, putting an ear to the pile of boulders and broken stones.

Hercules sprang back again as a rock shook loose from above, catching him on the ear. "Damn!"

"Yeah, precisely," Hyde grunted. "You want to risk bringing that lot down on top of us?"

"He's right," Cat said, giving Hercules an imploring look. "We should get away from here while we still can."

"If any more comes down," Hyde said, looking up, "I'd probably survive – but you wouldn't."

Hercules regarded the cave-in a moment longer. He felt an unexpected pang of grief and guilt at the thought that there was nothing more they could do for the wretched man who had been prepared to give his life that Hercules and Cat might live. But Hyde's logic was undeniable.

"There's nothing more we can do for him now," Cat said, putting a hand on Hercules' arm.

"Yeah, he's on his own now," Hyde added, unhelpfully.

Hercules' eyes met Cat's. "Do you think he was my, I mean our –"

"All I know," Cat interrupted him before he could say it, "is that whoever he is, he's a hero. And that's good enough for me."

"And I never got to say..." The words stuck in his throat. "Where are the others?" he asked gruffly, turning away from the heap of shattered stones as he blinked back the tears.

"They were headed for the motor pool. Jinx said she thought she'd found a way off this mountain. They sent me to find you. We need to get out of here before the whole bastard castle comes crashing down on our heads."

"Then we'd best not keep them waiting," Hercules said, with forced joviality. "We don't want to get a reputation for tardiness now, do we?"

And with that, taking Cat by the hand, he led them along the draughty corridor and away from the now-entombed sepulchral chamber.

ULYSSES QUICKSILVER OPENED his eyes, but all he could see was a blur of black shadows and ice-white light. He felt cold all over, numb as if frozen, and yet sweat was beading on his brow.

He had been shot enough times in his life to know that now *was* one of those times. He could feel the sick pain and a dull, throbbing ache in his right shoulder.

He blinked, and blinked again, and only then did he realise that the haziness he was seeing was caused by the settling cloud of dust around him.

He sat up carefully. His head felt woozy. He knew he'd been losing blood. There in front of him, where the exit from the chamber should have been, was a pile of rock debris as high as the vaulted ceiling. He found himself wondering how much of the castle must have collapsed in the cave-in.

Ulysses felt the insistent throb in his bones and knew that they weren't out of danger yet. He turned to the source of the pulsing ice-white light. The Sphere was still active, opening a tunnel through time and space, creating a hole in the skin of the world.

Between the Sphere and the Iron Eagle's crash-landing, the ancient castle was tearing apart. If what Ulysses had witnessed on the Moon, more than fifty years into the future, was anything to go by, the Alpine stronghold would come down on top them, burying them beneath tonnes of rock and rubble.

Climbing groggily to his feet, Ulysses took in the sepulchral cavern in which he was now trapped. Any doors there might once have been were buried behind the landslide, with no chance of Ulysses ever uncovering them in time. There was only one way out of here now.

His left hand clamped over the bullet wound in his shoulder, Ulysses began to pace across the debris-strewn floor, darting between the pillars, his eye on the figure atop the steel dais on which stood the new, improved time-transmat.

He had been shot, he was losing blood, and he only had one eye left, but suddenly the universe had turned, and life had given him a second chance.

Dashwood was busy. From what Ulysses could see of the man, silhouetted against the Sphere's pulsar glare, he appeared to be pulling on an over-sized glove over his left hand. And he was utterly ignorant of Ulysses' presence.

He could only suppose that Dashwood had recklessly assumed Ulysses to be dead. Which he might as well be, if he were able to beam out of there, leaving Ulysses behind.

Where was he planning on going this time, Ulysses wondered? Was it further back into the past to try to put right what had happened here? Did he intend to travel only to somewhere else in 1943 to escape the imminent destruction of Schloss Adlerhorst? Or was he heading back to the future they'd left, eighteen months or so from the end of the twentieth century?

Ulysses doubted Dashwood could hear his footsteps over the droning whine of the device and the seismic rumbling of the mountain top shaking itself apart.

And besides, he was talking to himself; more accurately, gauging from his tone, berating himself.

A voice rang out over the noise, loud and clear. "Coordinates set. Launching in one minute."

Ulysses watched as, at the top of the dais, Daniel Dashwood, his features hidden behind his ion mask, made an adjustment to one of the controls built into the thick vulcanised rubber glove he was now wearing and prepared to step into the temporal vortex.

Flexing his back and straightening his body, focusing his mind on dispelling the numbness that was threatening to leech the last of his strength from him, Ulysses concentrated on the pulsing glow of the Sphere.

Dashwood didn't know anything about his approach until Ulysses was right behind him.

Abruptly, Dashwood spun round.

"Thirty seconds," the dulcet tones of the Enigma engine intoned, as it commenced the final countdown.

Ulysses made out the Enigma engine, standing like a monolith of black stone on the other side of the platform, behind the hurtling gyroscopic bands of the Sphere.

There was quite literally no time to lose. Ulysses threw himself bodily at the villain, all his anger suddenly rising like an eruption within him. His fury gave him the strength he needed, blotting out the throbbing ache of the gunshot wound.

He charged Dashwood into the energy from the Sphere, and the two of them were immediately assailed by unfathomable forces. Tendrils of light, like fingers of mist, whirled about them, and they were buffeted by hurricane winds.

"You!" Dashwood hissed from behind the mask as Ulysses landed on top of him, coming nose to nose.

"Yes, me," Ulysses snarled, kneeling across Dashwood's body and pulling him up by the front of his robe, the cloth bunched in his hands.

"I thought you were dead." Dashwood shouted, clawing at Ulysses' hands with ragged fingernails. "Twice."

"You thought wrong," Ulysses replied.

Letting go with his right hand, he pulled the ion mask from Dashwood's face and cast it aside.

It was like looking at an anatomist's model of a human head, made from layers of translucent material. There was Dashwood's arrogantly handsome face, and beneath that, layers of moving muscle, a network of blood vessels and capillaries. He could see the man's eyeballs quite clearly, and the thread of the optic nerve behind each one. Behind transparent lips he could see the man's teeth and jaws. He even fancied he could see right down into the skull. This was the price he had paid, for tampering with Alexander Oddfellow's creation for his own ends.

Forming his hand into a fist, he dealt Dashwood a resounding blow, and winced. The transparent flesh felt as solid as that of any other man.

"Twenty seconds," the Enigma engine tolled.

The pronouncement was accompanied by a crack like a thunderclap from the roof of the chamber.

Ulysses froze, then looked up, and saw the thin black fissure opening above him, crazing like cracking ice.

It was all the distraction Dashwood needed.

His return punch caught Ulysses in the stomach, putting his diaphragm into spasm and driving the air from his lungs.

Ulysses doubled up. Dashwood grabbed hold of him with both hands, and, with startling strength, threw him off. Ulysses landed on the other side of the platform, outside of the Sphere's field.

"Fifteen seconds," the Enigma engine's voice echoed from the walls of the collapsing crypt.

Leaving Ulysses curled up in agony – wracked with pain from his shoulder wound as much as the punch to the stomach – Dashwood scrambled into the cradle at the heart of the device.

"Come on! Come on!" he hissed through clenched teeth, his whole body trembling as he waited for the machine to launch him through the hole in time and space.

There was another apocalyptic crash and then a moment of eerie silence, followed only a few seconds later by the thunderous crash of a piece of masonry hitting the dais not five feet from Ulysses.

"Ten seconds."

The threat of being crushed by another cave-in spurring him on, drawing on every last scrap of strength he had, Ulysses forced himself to his feet one last time and turned towards the whirling Sphere. Flashes of lightning were bursting from it now, the figure of Dashwood at the heart of the machine nothing more than a blurred shadow.

"Five seconds."

Ulysses leapt, but not at Dashwood this time. Instead he grabbed hold of one of the static rings that generated the energy lattice, crying out as his acrobatics tore at his injured shoulder. But he held on.

"Four."

His own momentum carrying him forwards, he brought his knees up to his chest and kicked out at Dashwood.

The man gave an alarmed shout as Ulysses planted both feet firmly in the middle of his chest, the force of the blow sending him tumbling backwards out of the machine.

"Three."

His shoulder's own scream of pain silencing him abruptly, Ulysses let go.

He landed in the cradle himself, almost falling back out the other side. As he lay sprawled, he felt Dashwood's hand, encased in rubber, grab hold of his own and hang on.

Ulysses stared down through the lattice of the cradle as the Nazi's death's-head leer looked up. They locked eyes with each other, separated by the rippling distortion of the temporal field between them.

The glove's wrist-mounted controls thumped against one of the supporting rings of the Sphere.

"Course change confirmed."

"One."

"Launch."

The body blow Dashwood had dealt him was as nothing compared to the forces that assailed Ulysses now as every atom of his being was blasted into the black oblivion of null space.

ULYSSES STARED DOWN at his nemesis in horror. Unprotected from the raw hunger of the temporal winds, Dashwood's flesh withered as time caught up with him at last.

WITH A THROATY roar, the snow plough smashed open the gates of the castle barbican, clearing the ground as it did so, to land ten yards further on.

Slamming the gear stick home, Jinx put her foot to the floor and the plough tore away along the treacherous mountain road, between the frozen drifts on either side, as behind them the shattered ruins of Schloss Adlerhorst were consumed by the billowing cloud of black dust and white snow thrown up by its own cataclysmic destruction.

Deep down in the dungeon crypt, the hurtling Sphere exploded for only the briefest moment as it was crushed as flat as plate steel by a million tonnes of collapsing castle.

The whirling sphere of unreality winked out a moment later as the space-time anomaly imploded silently.

CHAPTER FORTY-THREE

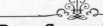

Best Served Cold

DAWN BROKE OVER the ruins of Castle Frankenstein for the second time since its fall, sunlight saturating the blackened piles of rubble and still-smouldering timbers with its rich, amber glow.

Twenty-four hours had passed since the fortress, which had looked over the town of Darmstadt for seven hundred years, surviving flood, fire, famine and raids by barbarian warlords, had finally been razed to the ground in a matter of minutes.

Not one tower or wall remained standing. The only parts of the castle to have survived the blitzkrieg and the subsequent firestorm were, ironically, the very dungeons in which the remade Prometheans had languished until the First had brought about their release.

The bodies of the super-soldiers – themselves pieced together from parts of the dead – lay scattered throughout the ruins, some buried under tonnes of shattered masonry, some scattered, limb by severed limb, across riven courtyards, some nothing more than crisped skeletons fused to their metal components by the heat of the flames that had raged through the complex in the wake of the Iron Eagle's parting gift.

And between the broken bodies of the Nazis' living weapons were strewn the bodies of mortal men: soldiers, who had paid the ultimate price for their loyalty; scientists and surgeon-doctors who had died in the pursuit of their own sick dreams; engineers who, in their haste to prove their ingenuity, had forgotten that just because something could be done, did not mean that it should be done.

Motes of dust and glowing embers, raised by the persistent zephyrs now wending their way through the castle's carcass, spun and twirled.

The chill air was alive with sound: the *plink* of cooling stones; the hiss of timbers giving up their moisture; the background murmur of smouldering fires; the death-knell croaking of carrion crows; the keening of the wind like the moans of the dying.

And footsteps.

In the shadows of what was left of a broken stone archway, a figure appeared, no more than a stumbling shadow itself, one hand to its head, the other against the wall for support.

Slowly, almost reluctantly, Dr Albrecht Seziermesser – bruised and bloodied, his thin face streaked with cuts and contusions – emerged cringing at the touch of the sun's rosy fingers.

He gazed about him at the rubble-strewn courtyard that was now all that remained of the home of the Frankenstein Corps, blinking in bewilderment.

He stumbled on amidst the devastation, taking in the violated bodies already being picked at by the crows. One black bird stared at him, its head cocked to one side. Then, with one stab of its beak, it plucked an eyeball from the head on which it was perched and gulped it down.

Seziermesser watched as the bird hopped from the eyeless skull to the mound of rubble beside it where the scuffed tips of yellowed fingers poked like worms. The crow pecked at one. The fingers wriggled in response, looking like fat grubs now.

He stopped, fascinated, as the heap of broken stones shifted. Small stones skittered from the top of the mound, tumbling all the way to the bottom. The heap shifted again, accompanied by a clattering rumble. Seziermesser took a cautious step backwards.

There was a gravelly rattle as the fingers withdrew into the rubble. Head bobbing in indefatigable curiosity, the crow wisely hopped back a couple of feet as well.

With a kind of seismic shudder, a huge fist punched clear of the top of the mound. Fingers splayed, the hand pushed at the top of the heap of loose stones, sending several tumbling away in its wake.

Stone dust rising in great clouds around it, a giant emerged from the rubble of Castle Frankenstein, rising again from the burnt-out ruins like a phoenix from the flames of its own destruction.

Seziermesser stared up into the black pits of the monster's eyes in dread, his features slack with fear.

The creature towered over him. It had to be eight feet tall at least. Its parchment yellow skin was torn in several places, but there wasn't any blood that Seziermesser could see. There wasn't even any obvious bleeding coming from its left shoulder socket, where its entire arm had been wrenched clean off.

Much of the flesh of the creature's head had been twisted and puckered by the conflagration that had raged through the castle immediately following the initial wave of bombs. There were signs that the creature had once had hair but it was gone now, burnt from the monster's scalp by the intense flames.

Even discounting the damage the brute had suffered during the razing of Castle Frankenstein, there was something else not quite right about it.

Seziermesser certainly hadn't been involved in the remaking of every soldier that had passed through the corpse-factory facility – despite having been Doctor Folter's protégé – and he wouldn't have expected to recognise every Promethean put together there by the Frankenstein Corps, but he could see that this one was out of place.

Beneath its more recently sustained injuries, he could see that the scars criss-crossing its body were too old, knotted and white, with no signs of residual bruising. The skin itself was yellow, and displayed none of the usual discoloration of chemical preservation. And then there was its size. It was massive, an amalgam of all sorts of bits and pieces, but – most notably of all – it did not include any mechanical components in its make-up whatsoever.

"What are you?" Seziermesser whispered.

The creature looked at him, its eyes pits of savage darkness. Seziermesser felt as though some raging god had him in its gaze.

"Not what," the creature growled through broken teeth, its voice a bass rumble. "Who."

Seziermesser gasped and took another startled step back.

"No! It can't be!"

The monster took a step forward, shards of stone crumbling beneath a foot the size of a suitcase.

"I was the first," it intoned, "rightful heir to this…" It broke off as it took in the castle ruins with a sweep of its arm.

Turning its unbearable gaze from the doctor, it scanned the pile of rubble from which it had just emerged, like Lazarus rising from the tomb. Finding what it was looking for, the creature bent down and pulled something from under the broken stones.

Black and burned as it was, there was no mistaking it.

It was an arm.

"You're the first?" Seziermesser spluttered, unable to help himself. "You're Frankenstein's original mons –"

"My name is Adam," the creature interrupted. "For I was the first."

The creature took in the castle ruins with a glance.

"This place was my home, but it was stolen from me, first by the Nazis and then by my betrayer."

Seziermesser felt an icy serpent of fear twist itself around his spine, chilling him to the core. He would have preferred it if the monster had shouted and raged, screaming its fury to the heavens, or laying about it with anything that came to hand. Anything would have been better than the utter calm it displayed; this chilling, single-minded hate.

It turned its blisteringly cold stare on Seziermesser once more and the man felt his bowels turn to ice water.

"You will rebuild me," it said. "Make me better than I was before. And then I shall have my vengeance."

The way the monster spoke, its desire to be avenged wasn't a hope or an intention; it was a prediction for the future.

"For, after all, is not revenge a dish best served cold?"

EPILOGUE

Back to the Future

THE IMPENETRABLE DARKNESS suddenly gave way to a brilliant burst of light and Ulysses Quicksilver felt as though his intestines were being unravelled. He decided that this must be what it felt like to be sucked through a spatial-temporal wormhole.

And then, just as abruptly, he landed flat on his face on what felt like rough floorboards, surrounded by a murky grey twilight. He winced as fresh waves of nausea pulsed through his right shoulder.

With a hollow clatter something hit the floor beside him.

He felt uncomfortably hot, but at the same time his skin was clammy. There was the coppery tang of blood on his tongue too.

The unpleasantly familiar stink of scorched human hair – his own, he assumed – merged with the charcoal smell of roasted timbers.

His whole body shaking, he pushed himself up onto his hands and knees and then abruptly sprang back onto his heels, pulling off his smouldering jacket – wincing again as his wounded right arm came free.

He was kneeling at the centre of a perfect circle of blackened floorboards. There was no graduation of burning; just the cracked, charcoal-black planks under him, and beyond the limits of the circle no discernable damage whatsoever.

The next shocking sight to greet him was Daniel Dashwood's skeleton. Steam was rising gently from the boiled bones lying to Ulysses' left, half in and half out of the circle.

Ulysses started, dropping Dashwood's hand, which was still encased within the control glove, and put out an arm to stop himself falling backwards onto the floor again.

His hand came down in something warm and sticky.

He pulled it back in surprise, his fingers brushing against something hard that shifted at his touch.

Before he really knew what he was doing, his hand had closed around the object and he was raising it to his face for a closer look, even as he turned to see the handprint he had left in the pool of dark blood creeping out from under the corpse lying on the floor to his right.

He could not stifle his gasp of surprise. The body was face-down on the floor, but just from the sheer amount of blood oozing away between the floorboards and going by the waxy pallor of what little flesh he could see, the poor wretch was dead – whoever he might have been in life.

Ulysses looked from the corpse to the room in which he now found himself.

There was more ceiling than walls, the sloping sides meeting at the apex of the room above him, and it was sparsely furnished. The body was lying beside a filthy, unmade bed that looked like it could have been an antique, had it not been in such an obviously bad state of repair.

There was a draught blowing in under the door of the mouldering attic room, and a cracked mirror had been hung on the wall opposite. Beneath the mirror stood a rickety table bearing a large cracked porcelain bowl, a mismatched earthenware jug with a chipped rim sitting within it.

The only other piece of furniture in the room was a small writing desk, positioned beneath a shuttered dormer window. A chair lay on the floor in front of it.

Ulysses gave in to the waves of exhaustion threatening to overwhelm him, allowing his body to sag. He took a deep breath.

Where had the Sphere brought him now? Was he back in his own time? Was he still in 1943, but somewhere other than the castle in the mountains? Or was this another place and time altogether?

Slowly, Ulysses turned his stupefied gaze to the object gripped tightly, yet momentarily forgotten, in his right hand.

It was a knife, its hilt slick with blood, its blade bloodied too, as was the palm of Ulysses' right hand.

"Shit," he said with a heartfelt sigh, letting the knife fall from his fingers again.

A thunderous banging from somewhere below had him leaping to his feet, despite the pulsing pain of the gun shot wound.

The furious knocking subsided and a gruff voice shouted, "*C'est les gendarmes! Ouvrir la porte!*"

"Oh boy," he heard a small voice say.

The voice was his own.

"Not again."

THE END

JONATHAN GREEN is a freelance writer, with more than twenty-five books to his name. Well known for his contributions to the *Fighting Fantasy* range of adventure gamebooks, and numerous Black Library publications, he has also written fiction for such diverse properties as *Doctor Who*, *Star Wars: The Clone Wars*, *Sonic the Hedgehog* and *Teenage Mutant Ninja Turtles*.

He is the creator of *Pax Britannia* and *Anno Frankenstein* is his seventh novel for Abaddon Books. He lives and works in West London. To find out more about the steampunk world of *Pax Britannia*, set your Babbage engine's ether-relay to WWW.PAXBRITANNIA.COM.

UK ISBN: 978 1 907519 36 9 • US ISBN: 978 1 907519 56 7 • £9.99/$12.99

ACTION AND ADVENTURE IN A NEW AGE OF STEAM!

Join Ulysses Quicksilver — dandy, adventurer and agent of the crown — as he
battles the enemies of the Empire in this collection of rip-roaring steampunk
adventures. This action-packed tome brings you three sensational tales!

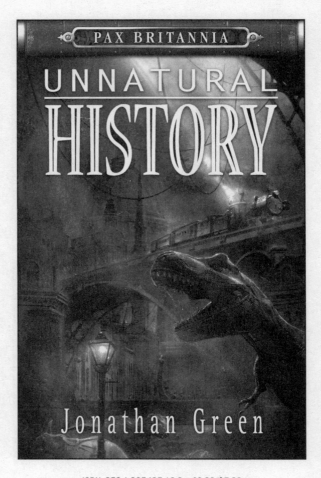

ISBN: 978 1 905437 10 8 • £6.99/$7.99

In two scant months the nation, and all her colonies, will celebrate 160 years of Queen Victoria's glorious reign. But all is not well at the heart of the empire. A night watchman is murdered. An eminent Professor of Evolutionary Biology goes missing. Then a catastrophic Overground rail-crash unleashes the dinosaurs of London Zoo. But how are all these events connected? Is it really the work of crazed revolutionaries? Or are there yet more sinister forces at work?

 WWW.ABADDONBOOKS.COM
Follow us on Twitter! www.twitter.com/abaddonbooks

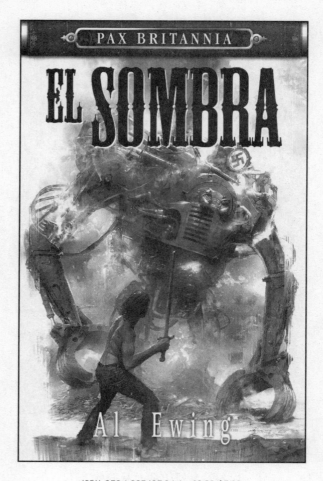

ISBN: 978 1 905437 34 4 • £6.99/$7.99

The terrifying Luftwaffe, on their steam-driven wings, have torn apart the sleepy town of Pasito in the heart of Mexico, only to rebuild it as a terrifying clockwork-town where the people become human robots, furthering the nightmare dreams of the Führer. But they are unprepared for the return of a man the desert claimed nine long years ago, a man who has returned from the doors of death and the depths of madness to bring his terrible fury upon their world. He defies death! He defies man! No trap can hold the masked daredevil, the saint of ghosts men known as El Sombra!

PAX BRITANNIA

LEVIATHAN RISING

JONATHAN GREEN

ISBN: 978 1 905437 60 3 • £6.99/$7.99

'Around the world in eighty days – in style!' This proud claim, made by the Carcharodon Shipping Company, is about to be put to the test as its newest and most magnificent submersible cruise-liner, the Neptune, sets sail on its maiden voyage.

Only days out from the undersea city of Pacifica disaster strikes. A brutal murder is committed and then an act of sabotage sends the Neptune plunging into the abyssal depths. Trapped at the bottom of the sea, for the survivors, their problems are only just beginning. Far below a decades old secret awaits them.

ISBN: 978 1 905437 10 8 • £6.99/$7.99

The Whitby Mermaid has been stolen from Cruickshank's Cabinet of Curiosities and consulting detective Gabriel Wraith is on the case. And he's not the only one, for wherever there is a mystery to be solved, Ulysses Quicksilver is never far away. What does the theft of the mermaid have to do with the mysterious House of Monkeys? And what of the enigmatic criminal known as the Magpie?

PAX BRITANNIA

GODS OF MANHATTAN
AL EWING

UK ISBN: 978 1 906735 39 5 • US ISBN: 978 1 906735 86 9 • £7.99/$9.99

"You're in New York. Protocol went out the window the second you arrived. This isn't a protocol kind of town. This is a town that breeds monsters and heroes, geniuses and madmen. This town makes gods, and heaven help you, you wanted to be one of us."

"Rip-roaring
old-school adventure!"
Total Sci-Fi Online

PAX BRITANNIA
TALES OF VALOR TO DIVERT AND ENTHRALL

DARK SIDE
By
JONATHAN GREEN

UK ISBN: 978 1 906735 40 1 • US ISBN: 978 1 906735 85 2 • £7.99/$9.99

Ulysses Quicksilver visits the British lunar colonies, searching for his missing brother, Barty. Used to working inside the law, Ulysses is stalled when his pursuit puts him on the wrong side of the Luna Prime Police Force.
But why is Ulysses' ex-fiancée Emilia also in the colonies? Who is the strange eye-patched man following Ulysses? And what is really happening in a secret base on the dark side of the moon?